W9-ABI-377

TECHNICAL COLLEGE OF THE LOWCOUNTRY
LEARNING RESOURCES CENTER
POST OFFICE BOX 1288
BEAUFORT, SOUTH CAROLINA 29901-1288

# MISTAKEN IDENTITY

*Also by Nayantara Sahgal*

TECHNICAL COLLEGE OF THE LOWCOUNTRY
LEARNING RESOURCES CENTER
POST OFFICE BOX 1288
BEAUFORT, SOUTH CAROLINA 29901-1288

# MISTAKEN IDENTITY

*Nayantara Sahgal*

A NEW DIRECTIONS BOOK

TECHNICAL COLLEGE OF THE LOWCOUNTRY
LEARNING RESOURCES CENTER
POST OFFICE BOX 1288
BEAUFORT, SOUTH CAROLINA 29901-1288

Copyright © 1988 by Nayantara Sahgal

All rights reserved. Except for brief passages quoted in a newspaper, magazine, radio, or television review, no part of this book may be reproduced in any form or by any means, electronic or mechanical, including photocopying and recording, or by any information storage or retrieval system, without permission in writing from the Publisher.

Manufactured in the United States of America.

New Directions Books are printed on acid-free paper.

This U.S. edition is published by arrangement with William Heinemann Ltd., London, who first issued *Mistaken Identity* in 1988.

Library of Congress Cataloging-in-Publication Data

Sahgal, Nayantara, 1927–
  Mistaken identity.
  I. Title.
PR9499.3.S154M5     1988      823      88-29143
ISBN 0-8112-1093-6 (alk. paper)

New Directions Books are published for James Laughlin
by New Directions Publishing Corporation
80 Eighth Avenue, New York 10011

For Edward and Dorothy Thompson
in friendship

# Acknowledgements

The author would like to thank the National Archives of India, New Delhi, for permission to draw on their records of the Meerut Conspiracy Case, from which the words of Comrade Iyer's defence on page 162 are taken, and for the quotes on page 71 from Motilal Nehru and Amar Nath Dutt taken from the debate in the Legislative Assembly, Simla, on September 14, 1929.

On page 76, the verse is from 'A Persian Lute Song' by Sarojini Naidu.

On page 129, the poem 'Whose Land?' is by Mohammed Iqbal, translated from the Urdu by Kuldip Akhtar.

# MISTAKEN IDENTITY

*SEE PAGE 195 FOR GLOSSARY*

# Chapter One

As soon as the *Conte Rosso* docked at Bombay's Ballard Pier, the usual bunch of port officials in white drill came on board. I was sitting in the first-class saloon fanning myself with last night's gala menu when three of them strode in, stiff and starched as only men with a purpose can be on a sweltering June day. They sat down under the picture of Mussolini and started to examine passports before stamping them with 'Permission to land'. I got up to join the queue but I needn't have hurried. It wasn't moving. The other two times I had been abroad it hadn't taken nearly so long to get off the ship. This time they were vetting British subjects as strictly as other passengers. The seedy-looking Englishman who had mooned around by himself for most of the voyage was held up with a string of questions. Why had he come to India? A job? What job? Here in Bombay? Which newspaper? Never heard of that one. And so on. The high-hatted Parsee after him kept telling all three expressionless officials in a hurt voice that he doubted if the port authorities were aware they were looking at a relative by marriage of the late great industrial magnate, Sir Jamshedji Tata. He was finally allowed to move on to customs, but the Englishman already on his way was summoned back fuming and told he would have to wait while they checked on his unheard-of newspaper. Conversation in the queue had petered out but I heard the man behind me murmur it must be something to do with the Public Safety Act. The fellow looked suspicious. He probably had a Russian or Polish visa.

A stationary ocean liner one has already taken mental leave of is the last place one wants to linger. The saloon, luxuriously furnished and carpeted, with a piano at one end and bridge tables and a bar at the other, had shrunk to a stifling doll size. No sea breeze blew through its portholes and the queue filing funereally past Il Duce filled it to bursting. I spent the time contemplating Mussolini's jutting jaw, and wondering why I had never noticed his striking resemblance to Munna, the club-wielding tough on Father's estate who does a whirlwind job at rent collection time. The Italian dictator was certainly not the most elegant of the postwar crop of men of action. For style I preferred the austere Riza Khan, who had marched on Tehran, mounted the throne and got himself elected Shah with the royal title of Pahlevi, and for matchless flair, the Ottoman soldier turned civilian president who now ruled Turkey and liked to be photographed in a top hat and evening dress.

My turn came. The official opened my passport, put his elbows on the table and his fingertips to his temples, and studied my picture as if it was an archaeological find. Then he compared me with it. If he didn't see an Indian of wealth and status standing before him, and not an underground Bolshevik agent, he was obviously trying to make more work for himself. After a boring delay he returned my passport to me and allowed me to go down the gangway to customs where another lot of officials were diving into luggage with more energy than I would have believed possible on a day hot and humid enough to melt concrete. Here the queue had gone haywire. Cabin trunks lay open with their contents thrown out. One empty suitcase had had its lining ripped. I watched a customs man dig through an old English lady's luggage and come up with a revolver. It couldn't have been fired since the First Afghan War, and everyone heard her say it was her most treasured memento of her dead husband's military career, but they paid no attention to the poor lady's indignant protests and escorted her through a doorway opening into a large office behind the customs shed.

I had a lot of luggage. I had been abroad for several months and naturally I'd done a fair amount of shopping. Apart from clothes for myself, I had bought a set of gold-monogrammed wine glasses with matching goblet in Venice for Father, creams and lotions for Mother, and a crate of new books – some romantic poetry besides other non-subversive subjects. *Wine and Wine Lands of the World* was right on top next to *Famous Trials of History*. This one, which a friend had asked me to get her, the customs officer picked up. He opened it to the table of contents and after a glance at Mary Queen of Scots, Warren Hastings and other textbook favourites, he must have noticed it was compiled by an earl and snapped it shut. The book under it took him longer. It was an edition I had bought for its red and gold leather binding but he didn't seem to know what to make of the title, *The Revolt of the Angels*. He admired the binding, thumbed through it, turned it upside down and reluctantly put it down. After this he hunted through the entire crate and made me take off my shoes and socks for his inspection before he let me go.

As this was not Vijaygarh, I was not expecting a reception committee with garlands at the exit. It would be there in full strength taking up the whole platform at our own little station, and if Mother had her way, there would be an elephant ride home at the head of a procession, with Munna as drumbeater marching ahead. Instead I took the only taxi in sight the short hop to the Taj Mahal Hotel, where the receptionist greeted me respectfully and gave me a suite on the fourth floor. I liked the hotel's solid quadrangular magnificence and its location overlooking the harbour and the Gateway of India. It was unique for its French chef, too, and the latest gadgets and mechanical marvels including its own ice-making plant. An Indian didn't feel out of place in its public rooms, in spite of its European management. There were fresh flowers in my suite. One bed lay invitingly open. I lunched and went to sleep under a fast fan.

I had asked the hotel to make a train booking for Vijaygarh the next day, but Sylla, who had asked me to bring her *Famous Trials of History*, came over in the evening to collect the book and said she wanted me to stay a couple of weeks. She had dramatized *The Scarlet Letter* and there were going to be three performances to collect money for Lady Daruvala's combined charities, but one of the minor players had come down with typhoid. Now that I was here I could play the part. It was only a ten-line appearance. I'd easily be able to manage it.

'Besides, you don't have to be anywhere at any particular time. Give me more room, Jumbo.' Sylla manoeuvred more space than she needed for herself on the chair we were sharing, took a script out of her handbag and gave it to me. 'Here it is. I've marked your lines in red. They're on page five.'

Though in every other way Sylla resembles a Persian rose, her automatic rearrangement of my programme without consulting me made me feel I was snuggling up to a chastely slender, green-eyed army commander in high heels. At one time a change of programme hadn't needed a prop. If we had stayed simple and trusting we could have dispensed with *The Scarlet Letter*. But we had got used to more disguises than diplomats, and when we met after a few months' separation we were diplomats in the dark. It was some time since either of us had asked, What's happening to us? Staying or going didn't seem worth making a fuss about. And she was disconcertingly right. I did not – ever – have to be anywhere else.

Sylla had not merely dramatized Hawthorne. She had re-written him and put their joint effort into a contemporary Bombay setting. With her brainy capacity to snarl up simple language and her advanced views on adultery, she had given the heroine some fiery speeches that Hawthorne's persecuted Hester would have had to be chloroformed (and transported to the twenty-first century) to utter. When the dialogue wasn't menacing, it made the characters sound like amnesia victims wandering through a fog.

'This is ridiculous,' I told her. 'No one is going to understand a word of it.'

'No one,' she agreed happily. 'It'll be a triumph. Don't bother about what I've done to the play, Jumbo. Just cancel your train booking and learn your ten lines. So that's settled then.'

I held her firmly in place. 'In the book, Hester's disappeared husband returns. That's why her pastor lover has to confess to his adultery with her.'

'That wouldn't be contemporary, Jumbo. Hawthorne is far too melodramatic. I've left it vaguer. The husband is supposed to be returning, but it's up to the audience to decide whether he does or not. It's more fun for them to make up their own minds.'

She got up to leave, stopping to powder her nose in front of the mirror near the door and efficiently unclasping my hands from her waist. She turned around to rumple my hair.

'I'm truly grateful, Jumbo.'

I followed her to the door and wrenched her hand off the knob.

'Stay,' I said quietly. 'I'm about to order an enormous dinner.'

'All right,' she conceded, strolling back into the room, 'but no afters. I've really got to rush.'

I was angrier than I had been for years. She needed slapping and savaging. Instead, when I had her in the bedroom, and we lay windmilled across the unused bed, she shifted herself comfortably into position and took charge of operations with her commander's skill, while I did the weary mechanical thing without a hope of recapturing my cleansing anger. The only evidence of it were her spiked crystal beads poking my sweaty cheek. I hadn't given her time to take them off. At the very murmuring end I heard my incoherent voice plead, 'Don't go. I'm nothing but a tadpole without you.'

'Meaning?'

'Meaning I've left the egg but I'm stuck with my gills and tail. How am I to get rid of them? You know I'll never grow to maturity without you.'

Sylla lifted her face from mine and traced my hairline with her finger.

'You look pretty mature to me, Jumbo. It's 1929, and you are twenty-nine years old, you know.'

Yes, I knew. She kept me reminded of my age, partly because it was her age too.

'You're already starting to lose your hair and you're a weensy bit fatter round the middle than when you left, and,' she added, patting my face and sliding off me, 'we've had about eight years to make up our minds, so why haven't we?'

Many women pay you the compliment of looking languorous while they sit at a dressing table, comb their hair and do other feminine things before going into the next room for dinner. I lay on my side watching Sylla.

5

'I hope you ordered pomfret,' she said.

We were more relaxed, on our way to getting normal, over dinner, and would have parted with some affectionate after-glow if she hadn't got brisk again, saying she'd see me at rehearsal tomorrow, and scribbled the address. On the way to the door she was captivated by her mirror image all over again. I came up behind her. There in the mirror I conferred old age and decay on Sylla. I clothed her in folds of flesh and monstrous fat, then abruptly stripped her of it. On her bent and bony frame I hung the rags of her dilapidated breasts. While she smiled unwarily into my eyes I broke her in two and threw her away.

'Lovely dinner, Jumbo. See you tomorrow.' And she was gone.

We met several times apart from rehearsals, but never alone, though we made no special effort to avoid each other either. It was the first time I had felt rudderless in Bombay, which may have been why I seldom went far from the hotel. Most of the time I wandered aimlessly through it. I took seven-storey walks up and down the grand staircase from the floor to the roof. I went past the business establishments on the ground floor so many times that the men in the post and telegraph, and railway-booking offices no longer looked up enquiringly when they saw me. I haunted the bar, the billiard rooms, the shops. There is a wide veranda running the length of the first floor with a fine view of the harbour. I was standing there when the monsoon broke spectacularly over the Arabian Sea two days after my arrival, a spontaneous outburst of a kind that Sylla and I seemed at pains to prevent. An Arab family sat in a row of chairs admiring the downpour. I greeted the sheikh in his flowing robes on the staircase that evening. He lifted his arms, cast reverent eyes up to the lofty ceiling and exulted, 'It rains!'

The sheikh and his family had a suite close to mine. I think my other near neighbour must have been a Turk. He had the ease of a cosmopolite, a handsome, light-skinned man who wore European clothes of excellent cut. Two well-mannered, bright-eyed small boys, unmistakably his, stood solemnly near one of the electric lifts and took a ride in it every time it had a passenger. I bought them sweets and obliged them by being a passenger once or twice. It took my mind off Sylla and me. Their father and I found ourselves at adjoining tables at lunch one day, both of us alone. He said his wife had taken the children to be measured for shoes. After shoe-shopping they were lunching with an old friend of hers. The dining room with its high Moorish arches and far-apart tables was sparsely occupied. I was tired of my own company. I invited him to join me, he accepted with pleasure, and we ate our way through the long menu of French specialities. As I thought, he was Turkish. I asked him tactfully if there were still signs of the veil in Turkey, and was relieved to find there was no need for tact. He was refreshingly frank and forthcoming. It was worn in some regions, he said. The peasant women of Anatolia still muffled up their faces with a towel or anything to hand, and shrank against a wall to let a man pass by, but otherwise no. There had been tremendous changes. He ticked them off jubilantly on his fingers. In '24 they had got rid of the Caliph, in '25 they had dissolved the religious orders, in '26 they had replaced the Sharia with a western civil code. Now they had a new constitution, and European in place of Arab numerals. The Republic of Turkey was by far not a land of sheikhs, sultans and dervishes. Incredible, when just the other day no woman could be seen walking in the street or driving in a carriage with a man, even her own husband.

'I know,' I said, 'I've followed your progress with great admiration. But I've often wondered about the veil.'

'Such things are the last to go,' he admitted. 'Remarkable though my leader is, even he has not legislated against the veil. It would be a very tricky business that.'

'Veil or no veil, the changes are nothing short of miraculous,' I said.

He knew I meant it, and warmly urged me to visit Turkey as his guest. He was a government official who had had the honour to be involved with some of the reforms. I gathered he was about ten years older than myself, one of the enthusiastic young men around Kemal Pasha who had risen rapidly to his present position from humble origins. I couldn't have had a better informed or more entertaining companion. He gave me a hilarious account of how Vahid-ed-Din Mohammed VI, the last

Sultan-Caliph of the House of Osman, had slunk out of his palace on a November morning in 1922 to escape to Malta on a British battleship, with only seven retainers and two eunuchs carrying jewels, gold coffee cups and a gold table. His five wives and children had had to be left behind in the rush, but the British were asked to send them on to his medium-sized villa in Malta. And that was the end of the Sultanate. Vahid-ed-Din's cousin had succeeded him only as Caliph – spiritual head of Islam and representative of the Prophet on earth – but not for long. He was packed off at daybreak a couple of years later – too fast to take his seraglio along – driven to a little railway station outside the city, and there put on an evening train to Switzerland, where he was held up at the frontier because the Swiss didn't admit polygamists. But they made an exception while they looked into his case. And that was the end of the whole caboodle. On the strength of that my Turkish friend ordered another bottle of wine and became lyrical about his leader.

'He is everything to us, a military saviour! a teacher! a dance instructor! You should see him at parties. He makes everybody dance, the ministers, the deputies, everyone. It is the duty of Turks to be good dancers, he says. Believe me, we have the latest western music, Negro jazz, foxtrots, in addition to Viennese waltzes. Why do you go to London and Paris, my friend? Come to Turkey.'

His leader had tried to modernize the fierce national dance called the Zabek. This has Turkish tribesmen jumping around a camp-fire with knives in their mouths, but it hadn't worked out so well in a drawing room after cocktails.

'You may laugh, but we tried it! You do not believe any of this could happen in an Islamic country?'

'But you are not any Islamic country,' I said spiritedly. 'You are Turks!'

I listed their marvels. An eleventh-century Turk had brought Islam to India. Five hundred years later a Turk – great-grand-child of the dreaded Tamerlane – had founded the Mogul dynasty. A Turk had thrown back the Crusaders. A Turk had halted the Mongols. A Turk had finished off the Byzantine empire. I had no trouble believing the Turks could remake themselves if they wanted to. Already they were remaking Islam.

My companion was delighted and renewed his invitation to visit Turkey.

'But don't get the wrong impression,' he warned. 'We are not pagan. We have freed Islam, not renounced it. We say, if English Christianity can be Anglican, why can't Islam be Turkish?'

I told him as far as I was concerned all Islam should henceforward be Turkish, and that I had no more use than he did for the theologians and seminarians of any religion. We drank to that.

'Have widows got a new deal in the new regime?' I asked. 'Your religion and mine don't allow them much of a life.'

His eyes twinkled. 'You are perhaps interested in a Turkish widow?'

We got on famously. He had charm, naturalness, authority. I hoped I would meet him again before he left, and invited him to Sylla's play, but he regretfully refused. They had another engagement that evening.

Sylla is usually right and she was right about her play. It bowled them over from the first incomprehensible line. I could tell by the way the diamonds in their Cartier settings heaved-ho on dowager *décolletée* bosoms, and the bright bewildered way Lady Daruvala and her cronies led the applause. The next day's *Times of India* carried a rave review I didn't see till many days later, calling the performance an outstanding success. The stage setting I had found so cold and spare, with a contraption resembling a guillotine as the main prop, came in for paeans of praise. So did the sheets of metal that shook, flashed and thundered through the play. The critic congratulated Sylla for daringly dispensing with footlights and using a searchlight instead. Sylla appeared in front of the blue velvet curtain to take bows, with Bombay, or the sliver of it that Lady Daruvala's private theatre held, at her feet. From the end of the third row where I had taken a seat when my ten lines were over, I heard her deliver a graceful little speech of gratitude to Lady Daruvala. Through an old deep torment I had never dreamed could be so searingly revived, I waited for the cheers and applause to die, and for someone to put a record of 'God Save the King' on the gramophone. As soon as the audience stood to attention, I got up and left.

There was time to catch the night train if I could get a berth on it. I packed feverishly. I had only to go down, pay my bill and leave, but, valise in hand, I sank into the chair nearest me to succumb at last to a pain more brilliantly intense than any pain before. It had waited hours to make its grand entrance and it was in no hurry to depart. It flowered into writhing sheaves of blossom, a nightburst of gigantic bouquets that dwarfed the room and left me whimpering. I passed no one on my way down to the reception desk. I left no note for Sylla. She might never forgive me for disappearing like Hester's husband, but she was resourceful and I knew she would find someone to speak my ten-line part for the remaining two performances. Mine was over. There is nothing for the dead but burial. I was going back to Vijaygarh for good.

# Chapter Two

The hotel sent a servant with me to the Victoria Railway Terminal to settle me into my compartment. I was lucky to have one to myself. The platform was so crowded it had been a job getting all my luggage on board. Above the vendors' din I heard the station master bellowing at a passenger to get out of the Englishman's compartment next to mine, and the passenger's rattling replies. I locked my door to make sure he wasn't pushed into mine. A mob had collected. The hotel bearer stood gawking with the rest, as this class of person will. I had to shout for his attention. He ploughed his way to a fruit barrow, bought me half a dozen ripe mangoes and handed them to me through the window. He had already laid out my bedding and got me a tub of ice for my supply of soda-water bottles. I gave him a tip and dismissed him. The train started, leaving my luckless neighbour gesticulating on the platform.

I woke during the night, covered with soot and cinders, to find it had stopped. It was pitch dark and someone was pounding on the door demanding to be let in. I opened it to an Anglo-Indian police sergeant who told me he had a warrant for my arrest. Without asking my permission he ordered his men to lift out my luggage. I was flabbergasted. I forbade them to touch it and our quarrelling voices fell away into the vast dark void about us. The train moved on with a clank and grind. The sergeant and I sat in a strip of moonlight at the wayside station waiting for another one, as far from each other as possible on the only bench. I soon stopped bombarding him with my futile protests. He might have been a deaf mute. During my trip abroad an unseen hurricane had blasted the expressions off official faces and left blanks where familiar landmarks like noses, eyes and mouths had been. We must have sat smoking in stony silence for the better part of an hour. An express train raced past. A peasant in a waistcloth tucked around his scrawny loins, his huge shoes crackling like dry branches, crossed the moonlit tracks, looking like a piece of ancient driftwood himself. There was not a breath of air nor a drop of rain. Here in the north the monsoon was still a month away. Another train came. I stretched out beddingless on a leather berth under the sergeant's eye and fell asleep covered with flying soot, realizing I was powerless to prevent myself being hurtled through the night in the wrong direction. Early in the morning the sergeant roused me, took me to a police lock-up in a tonga, and went away.

A day and a night later I had had my fill of this farce. They had had plenty of time to rectify their atrocious mistake. I had had no sleep on a bed that sagged worse than a hammock. Mosquitoes gorged with my blood hung from its sides. I shouted, 'Koi hai?' just as a servant boy came to my cell with a mug of tea and a lump of stale bread on a dirty tray, put down the tray and unlocked the cell door. I kicked the tea into the mud where it fell with a dusty splash and hurled the bread after it. A heavily pregnant pariah bitch pulled herself upright on stiff shuddering legs, then thought better of it as a kite swooped to snatch the bread lump. The boy shrugged, picked up the mug and took himself off, and I went back to sit on the sagging bed and curse the rathole I was in. The fierce dry heat was an infuriating reminder that I was in my own province, not far from home. I had a crashing headache. I couldn't stop scratching my inflamed, mosquito-bitten arms. I could see the kite on a branch overhanging the yard, tearing at the crust in its talons with a ferocious precision. As much as I'd had of my only love, that crust. Dry bread, a starvation ration, snatched before I could swallow it.

The sergeant was back in the afternoon to take me to the district jail where a jailer with a fat face, long eyelashes and eyes thick with kajal, apologized profusely for having to welcome me to his jail. He didn't know how it could possibly be the case, but I had been charged with 'conspiracy to deprive the King Emperor of his sovereignty over India'. This was such utter rubbish, I told him he must be off his head. He smiled like a hospitable host, under no strain at having to fit the courtesies into his outrageous task, and made out a receipt for my gold cigarette case, money, and the few other items I was carrying. An affable informal host in a baggy shalwar and a fez too small for his head. He sat down opposite me at the rickety table, gave me a limpid look and grabbed my hands, shoving them into filthy black ink to take my palm and fingerprints, then gave me a filthier rag to wipe them on. He hitched up his shalwar, steadied his wobbling fez, and ushered me through a back door into the jail compound. The barrack on the right, he chatted, was the condemned block where eight murderers were waiting to be hanged. I said I thought the entire compound looked so God-forsaken that those who escaped hanging probably died of depression. The jailer smiled and nodded, straightening his fez. We went past the condemned block to a barrack coated, like the others, with mud and cowdung plaster, at the end of the compound. This was it, he informed me. It had nine men, all charged with conspiracy. 'You will be the tenth,' he said, making me wonder if they had arrested me to make a nice round number. He said a pleasant goodbye and locked me in. My fellow conspirators surrounded me and cheered.

I had hardly got used to the company I was keeping when Father's doddering lawyer showed up with a bottle of citronella two days later. He had come in response to the telegraphic message I had asked the jail superintendent to send. He had taken a tonga from the station and it was waiting with food, clothes and a medical kit Mother had sent. He was full of wheezy greetings on my safe return from overseas, and the preparations Mother was making to welcome me home. I would be home before I knew it.

'We have nothing to worry about,' he assured me, loud enough for the jail superintendent to hear.

Adjusting his spectacle wire around his ear he glanced across the office and inclined his head graciously in the general direction of the superintendent at his desk.

'You will be out as soon as they know who you are. The government is understandably jittery with so many strikes on their hands. Don't you recall how five men were arrested in Cawnpore in '24 for conspiracy against the King, on no evidence whatsoever?'

But then he remembered that on no evidence whatsoever they had also been sentenced to four years with hard labour, and relapsed into a brief puzzled silence.

'Ah yes!' His frown cleared. 'They had been to Russia.'

Glad as I was to see him, I felt like shaking him till he crumbled. With him defending me, I'd be here for life. He had made his name and fortune conducting costly court battles over succession certificates to titles and property. He knew every *talukdar* in the north and had successfully represented the most powerful of them. Family feuds and land cases were his soul's delight. Suits where senior and junior ranees fought each other like demented rams with locked horns for equal shares in property, or for an adopted son to supersede a natural-born son, had a special place in his affections. He was a tottering encyclopaedia on litigation among the landed gentry. His prize case had been a succession contest to one of our neighbouring estates, whose raja had left no heir. It had taken seventeen years, during which the fossil had gone from youth to early middle age, and his victorious client was just beginning to lose his teeth when the final verdict came. His favourite episode from this odyssey was how in the fourteenth year of the case, when the Privy Council decision came, the losing nephew had charged at the winning uncle with a sword and inflicted a flesh wound on him right in the middle of the uncle's Dussehra durbar, and had had to be bodily removed, screaming vile abuse, by four wrestling champions who happened to be on the scene for a celebration wrestling match. Only the wrestler's bodies were so well oiled for the match that the nephew kept slipping from their grasp. The winning uncle had visited twelve holy places in thanksgiving, fed pilgrims at the Magh Mela in Allahabad, and donated a clock to the town hall, while the loser had appealed to the Privy Council once again, and lost yet again. Which was all very well if it had anything to do with why I was here.

'Why the devil am *I* here?' I snapped. 'I've never set foot in Russia.'

'No, of course you haven't,' he soothed, 'and in any case, what can you possibly have in common with this bunch of provincial troublemakers? They don't own a stick of furniture between them, you can be sure. Remember who you are. All will be well so long as we don't upset the sovereign power.'

The sovereign power turned out to be a ginger-haired magistrate new to the district. He looked young enough to be brand new to his rank as well. We had been told he would hold an enquiry to decide if there was a case for trial. It was held in a big square room in his bungalow. Chintz-covered sofas and chairs had been pushed to the walls to clear space for a courtroom effect and a kewpie doll's squashed celluloid head stuck out from under one of them. There was no dais for the magistrate's desk but a 'dock' had been improvised for us conspirators and straight-backed chairs had been set in the middle of the room for the prosecution and defence. Father's lawyer found these makeshift arrangements reassuring. He sat with the defence, but managed by a subtle trick of posture to disassociate himself from his counterparts. Both hands wrapped around a knee in place of his cane, he screwed up his eyes and peered at the laundry line hung with nappies and rompers at the far end of the garden, saving his spectacles for court business. In a Paris nightclub on this trip a cabaret dancer had planted herself on a man's lap at the table next to mine, and the man had lived through his acute embarrassment by pretending she wasn't there. Father's lawyer must have been pretending the magistrate's court, like the cabaret dancer's buttocks, wasn't there. Or this may have been his tactful way of not upsetting the sovereign power. He had asked to be allowed to speak first as mine was obviously a special case. When he was called he peeled his squint from the laundry line with some difficulty, returned it to his surroundings, and said in his deferential wheeze that his client's arrest was an unfortunate case of mistaken identity. His client, far from being an 'accused', was the son of the Raja of Vijaygarh.

'The raja of what?' demanded the magistrate.

There was a titter from my nine fellow conspirators as the

lawyer repeated the name of Father's *taluk*, adding its geographical position due slightly north-east from where we sat. He explained the raja owned the hundred villages it covered.

'Oh, estate,' said the magistrate, registering its smallness. 'Not one of the princely states. But you say he's a raja just the same.'

The fossil loves explaining. In the *taluks*, he said, rajahood was a title conferred by the British government in return for outstanding loyalty, upon the wealthiest and most deserving among the great landlords. But *talukdars* were not highnesses and had no gun salutes. Only ruling princes had those. This time the nine set up a howl, making the magistrate rap sharply for order.

'Would this man have had access to any weapons?' he asked.

The lawyer raised his hand in modest denial.

'Impossible, your honour. Rest assured. Nothing to speak of. It is true that since 1879 all titled Indian gentlemen have been exempted from having to hold licences, and my client's father is, as I said, a raja. But the government in its wisdom sanctions only reasonable quantities of arms and ammunition, and these must positively be out of date.'

The magistrate rapped above the mirth. He said he would take stern steps unless the conspirators showed respect for the court. He ordered the lawyer to explain himself, and the fossil was in heaven.

'In 1899, your honour, the present Raja Sahib's uncle wanted to arm his five hundred retainers with Enfield rifles, but the authorities insisted he purchase old-fashioned muskets. Apart from this muzzle-loading antique brand of weaponry,' – he spread his arms appealingly – 'they carry arms only for pageantry, lances, lathis, primitive spears. Now I ask you, your honour! In fact, my client's poor showing in blood sport is a grave disappointment to his father, the Raja Sahib. I would go so far as to say, your honour, that where weapons are concerned, my client is a hopeless failure, besides being temperamentally incapable of violence.'

'Can you explain why he lied to the port official, saying he was leaving for Vijaygarh the day after his ship docked? Yet he stayed in Bombay for ten days and took part in a play with a doubtful title,' – he consulted a paper on his desk – '*The Scarlet*

*Letter*. He was reported to leave the hall immediately the national anthem began instead of standing to attention, and a book about revolution was found in his luggage.'

Asked why I was carrying seditious literature it took a minute or so to grasp what they meant. I had bought it for its binding, I said, and *The Revolt of the Angels* was about Lucifer's revolt against God. But instead of disposing of the wild charge against me, this gave it a sinister new dimension. When I sat down the senior counsel for the prosecution led off with, 'It is the case for the prosecution that these accused are Bolsheviks.' This extraordinary opening, together with the speech he launched, was so full of menacing innuendoes and grimaces that Sylla could have used him in her strange version of *The Scarlet Letter*. He ended by accusing us all of plotting to overthrow His Majesty's Government and replace it with Mr Stalin's, and challenged each one of us to deny it. This was so outlandish that Father's fossil chose to ignore the charge and watched the laundry line disdainfully. But the nine, far from denying it, said they agreed with every word, except for putting Mr Stalin in His Majesty's place, since they had no plans to replace His Majesty with anybody. When the others had spoken, the mild old conspirator known as Bhaiji jumped up stammering with emotion and demanded one good reason why anyone should be loyal to a government that had captured the country by wickedness and hung on to it by force. He sat down shaking like an excited leaf.

Two months later the enquiry still dragged on. The kewpie had been rescued. A skipping rope lay around for a few days. Other scraps of the magistrate's life came and went along with the hair oils and body odours of a couple of hundred witnesses. A motley crew, some in tatters who mumbled, others slightly better dressed who recited in the singsong of sentences committed to memory. Not a gentleman among them. The magistrate developed prickly heat. My mosquito bites had risen in red welts and subsided, and Mother's citronella kept away the newborn mosquitoes hatched in the open drain outside our barrack. Father's fossil's one achievement had been to arrange meals for me from a run-down local eatery. The others cooked their own meals on coal stoves out of gritty rations bought in the local bazaar. The jailer made regular tender enquiries after our, especially my, comfort.

I had sorted out my barrack mates. Bhaiji belonged to the Indian National Congress. He had two hangers-on who might as well have been nameless. They did as they were told and sat around looking up to him. They must have got themselves arrested because they wouldn't have known when to sneeze without him. I thought of them as the twins though they were different shapes, sizes and ages. One was tall and hairy, the other small and dumpy. Of the rest, one turned out to be a government agent spying on four of the others. He had been arrested with them and hadn't known when to stop pretending he was a conspirator. He was spirited away one night to continue his incognito activities. The four he had been spying on were grey-haired trade unionists who called each other comrade and had never met before. The remaining prisoner was a boy of nineteen, too young to be anything in particular.

When another parade of witnesses began to appear on the stand the fossil confessed this was more than he had bargained for. This lot told hair-raising stories of plots in the making. They had infiltrated discussion groups and listened to strategies of revolt being planned. The textile workers' strike in Bombay was proof positive. They had heard 'Workers of the world, unite'. They had seen the Red Flag. All this with their own eyes and ears. They had photographs and statistics of processions as well. Lively as they were, and a definite improvement on the first shifty lot, I could not make head or tail of it. As they went on the witness stand in rapid succession, a vision of crisis and cataclysm rose and hovered in the magistrate's court. But I couldn't understand if it had already happened, or was about to. Maybe we had been arrested just in case. I was none the wiser when the comrades took the witness stand, and they were more nonplussed than I was. Pillai denied attending the meeting they were pinning on him because he had been in the south, not in Bombay that day, and not being a yogi he couldn't be in two places at the same time.

'That is not my handwriting,' declared Comrade Yusuf, 'and the other piece of paper is blank. No, I've never conducted a correspondence in invisible ink, or led a procession wearing a cap to make me invisible.'

Comrade Dey was accused of opening a bureau to inform the public about the orient.

'Someone has to do it,' he said testily. 'We only get the news you give us, and you stuff us with news about Europe. We know nothing at all about Persia, Afghanistan, China, and what you're up to there.'

Comrade Iyer denied having set foot on Russian soil though this was one of the items on his agenda before he expired. It must have been another Iyer who was spotted in the queue at Lenin's tomb. He had no brothers either, which was why he had never been able to leave India. But he admired Russia. He had wanted to leave for Russia as soon as news of the Revolution broke through the British censors, but he had been foiled by his paternal uncles. One uncle could have been disobeyed but five banded together were too much.

The room grew scaldingly hot between torrential downpours. The rain got so loud I didn't hear a witness say he had seen a poem by me in a magazine published in Moscow. Father's fossil got up to remonstrate. A person may write poems, where is the harm? And poems will be published here and there, how is a person responsible? Furthermore, his client's poetry was of no consequence whatsoever. Had anybody ever heard of him? His poor showing in poetry as in blood sport was a grave disappointment to his father, the Raja Sahib, who was a crack shot and a lover and patron of poetry. This exasperated me so much I felt like yanking the fossil off the court floor, packing him into a tonga and sending him clattering home. 'The Bridge' might have been the worst poem I had ever written, but at least it achieved some kind of fame. I had been told Lenin had hailed it as a significant example of social realism shortly before he died. But the magistrate, who became less and less like a family man as the enquiry proceeded, made no comment.

Three months after our first appearance the enquiry wound up with the defence lawyer's fervent plea to the magistrate to release us all immediately for lack of a particle of evidence, lest the jewel of British justice be tarnished. At this my eight barrack mates became hysterical. Bhaiji laughed so much he got a stitch in his side he was complaining about for the rest of the week. The magistrate put a cold stop to the party mood with his announcement that all nine of us were to be put on trial in three weeks' time under Section 121-a of the Indian Penal Code for offences involving treason. The last thing I saw as we were led away was the fossil's dropped jaw. Later he came to tell me he had urgently requested separate quarters for me. Put him among common criminals, he had impressed upon the jail authorities, a solitary cell if need be, but not among these men whose first act, if they had the chance, would be to dispossess him of his rightful inheritance. The jail superintendent had been understanding, but the jail was full and he couldn't oblige.

'Never bloody mind,' I said wearily. 'Go home.'

It was bad enough being in this ludicrous, humiliating situation. I saw no advantage in rooming with murderers I didn't know rather than my eight new acquaintances. And only the fossil could have thought up a solitary cell as a cunning way to protect my patrimony from a future Bolshevist takeover.

Back in the barrack the eight called a conference. I was too upset to take much notice but I heard the comrades grumbling about being jailed so far from their various home states simply because they had happened to be attending a meeting of different revolutionary groups in this area. By rights they should have been lodged in Calcutta or Madras or a jail noted for conspiracy prisoners like Lahore or Cawnpore, both of which were receiving attention in the press. But they had been deliberately dumped in this *mofussil* jail no newspaper would ever cover, far away from friends and advisers. The conference became a shouting match when Bhaiji declared being in jail was an honour.

'Every Indian must get used to going to jail. Let it become our national profession,' he said loftily.

The comrades said he could stay as long as he liked, they were getting out as fast as they could arrange it. But this was the problem. They didn't belong to a party. They were communists the way health freaks are nature lovers and nudists. They had no connections, no organization that could come to their aid, and except for their trade unionism, no links. They decided to conduct their own defence. Comrade Dey beckoned the youngster, Sen, from his corner. He put a hand on the dejected boy's head and said his defence would be their responsibility. Sen was taken into their combined protective custody and began to look less lost and scared. Bhaiji was forgotten. He announced to whomever might be listening that he would contact a local political-minded advocate he knew to conduct his case and the twins'. He wanted to make it quite clear he and the twins had no wish to be unjustly detained, but it was necessary to have the right attitude to suffering. No one was listening but me on my string cot. Bhaiji invited me to join his group and be defended by his advocate. The comrades had started squabbling about their line of defence, but Dey motioned for quiet so that they could hear my reply.

'Yes, what position are you taking?' Comrade Iyer asked curiously.

I said I had no position because I had no politics. I hadn't a clue why I was here. I had led the sort of life where things happen to you because someone knows your father. I must have been overwrought. I rambled on about myself and my family. I told them Mother believed Grigori Efimovich Rasputin had been a tantric sadhu. After all, I said, salvation through sexual rapture was as old as the hills. Priests and queens had had ceremonial sexual unions, and in our own chief ritual of antiquity, hadn't the queen united with a freshly killed horse? There was a moment's silence, then Comrade Iyer asked if the comrades could form a study circle with me as their topic. Would I mind? I didn't mind. The drumming rain shut us in as securely as the iron-barred doors at either end of the barrack. It was obvious there would be plenty of time for study.

# Chapter Three

Anything that defies explanation makes perfect sense to Mother. The traditional five senses have never been enough for her. She has to have something more. If Father had sent her here instead of his fossil lawyer, she would have extracted some crazy meaning out of this. The fossil had said she was thinking of me night and day. Apparently Father isn't. A son who whiled away a college year doing the turkey trot and, according to him, never did much else, is not Father's idea of a son. He gave up petitioning and badgering to have his title made hereditary years ago.

When they are not working on their defence, my background helps to pass the time for the comrades. Bhaiji is not interested. He says one *talukdar* family is much like another and he has come up against a good few during his party work in the countryside. I've begun at the beginning as Comrade Iyer asked me to, remarking that it took me nine years instead of months to be born, if one counted the time my parents spent bribing and bargaining with every major deity in the pantheon for a son. Before I learned better I was convinced I had spent nine years in Mother's womb.

'We would like you to stick to facts,' interrupts Comrade Iyer.

Bhaiji, who is not supposed to be listening, gives a knowing chuckle and tells the twins some people should stick to statistics about urban labourers. What do they know about family, religion, tradition? But I do my best to oblige.

My parents spent a year travelling on pilgrimage to the southern shrines with four hundred of their tenants, and the following year they toured the northern shrines with two hundred. There wasn't a sacred inch they hadn't covered before Mother conceived, sudden and miraculous though they called it. I had heard it told and retold so often I felt I had actually seen Mother prostrate herself into a state of nervous exhaustion across the subcontinent, uprighting herself after one shrine only to lay herself flat in front of another. But not, mind you, like a humble suppliant for divine or human favour. She was more like a warrior queen falling on her sword in defiance of defeat and disgrace. It wouldn't have surprised me if between her two official pilgrimages with Father she had run off to join a caravan of muleteers, or trekked on foot with nomads over cliff-shadowed mountain tracks to Persia, to hang an amulet on the tomb of Cyrus the Great, called the Mosque of Solomon's Mother by women praying for fertility.

Father had been head of the two expeditions but I don't recall him figuring much in accounts of actual exertion. The toil had been Mother's single-handed triumph, maybe because Father was short-winded and inclined to be podgy, and didn't have her light-footed agility or her rubbery spine. As a child I imagined her journeying more or less horizontal across limitless legendary expanses, garlanding every deity, anointing every sacred rock with vermilion from the snowline down to tropical jungle, from sea to sea. It was the first evidence I had of a country outside Vijaygarh, not that this sort of evidence carried much weight. My parents' country was Vijaygarh, an ancient corner of the level oblong close to Ayodhya, birthplace of Vishnu's divine incarnations, Rama and Krishna. Devotees could take their pick. Mother chose Krishna. No ordinary tract this, made up of birds, flowers, tigers, rainfall and square miles. This was holy land, flatland of the Ganges, Hinduism's heartland. The soil defiled and desecrated by Muslim invasions was where Rama once virtuously ruled, where Krishna had slain demons and danced with his milkmaids to the Divine Orchestra. The air we breathed was sanctified by miracles. Hereabouts the yogi Goraknath had used his yogic powers to feed thousands on a grain of rice. Mother's favourite was Krishna's birth. No wonder mine was such a let-down. Krishna's parents' guards fell asleep. Light flooded their prison. Its gates flew open and the babe's father carried him to safety to a cowherd's home across the Jumna. So Krishna, his parents' eighth-born, escaped being dashed against rock at birth by his Uncle Kans who had killed the first six while he waited for his future destroyer. The seventh foetus dodged Kans by getting himself miraculously transferred to another womb.

I fully expect the comrades to clamour for facts, but Comrade Pillai is busy taking it all down in a notebook. The other three are digesting it. While I take a breather they agree all superstition hangs from the same tree, whether it's grains of rice, loaves and fishes, or Kans and Herod.

But back to geography. One of our two rivers has vanished, or was always a myth. In these parts one never knows for sure. But the other, the Jumna, is real enough and does eventually join the mighty Ganges at Allahabad. But so does the vanished river, because it's the junction of all three – the Triveni – that millions throng to every year for a redeeming bath, and there's nothing imaginary about those colossal columns of sweating, footsore pilgrims. Iyer cautions me about facts again, and Bhaiji delivers another piece of chuckling sarcasm to the twins.

'First of all they don't believe in anything sacred,' he says. 'On top of that they are trying to educate the people.'

But Sylla would have sympathized with the comrades. I can hear her saying, 'Can you see me up-country, Jumbo, living beside a river that isn't there, and peeping out at the world through latticework? I'd go stark staring mad.' Up-country for Sylla starts one step north of Bombay, but nor can I see her anywhere in India but her Malabar Hill house, and definitely not walled up in a zenana a short tonga ride from a Shiva temple, and only a little further from the decaying tile-domed mosque where the muezzin raises his call to prayer.

Mother and her senior maidservant, Bittan, gossiped about the nine-year saga in the afternoons. Somnolent talk, while Mother lay on her bed after lunch and Bittan kneaded her back and legs. Her strong old hands picked up each dainty foot, cranked the ankle, pulled and cracked its toes, and closed, all

drowsily pious, with, 'Your prayers were answered, that's w
counts. What does it matter how long it took. You had a so
'And smoke-and-ashes good it did me,' growled Mother, fa
down in her green pillow, pale green being her astrologer
prescription for peace of mind. Bittan's murmur of 'As the Potter
wills' arched Mother's head back from her pillow and Bittan
switched to the less controversial subject of Mother's labour from
its first welcome wince to my jagged delivery the wrong way
round, with my head and shoulders causing lasting havoc. Some
afternoons this was the wrong subject too. I'm told Mother and
the women around her bed registered the whole repertoire of
human sound. For years afterward Bittan, stroking the soles and
tops of Mother's feet, consoled her with the litany, 'At least you
have a son, no matter what else has happened.' And whatever
had happened, she could never help adding, because by this time
in the retold saga Mother gently snored, was the Potter's frolic.
'The Potter makes and breaks us women on his wheel.' But the
saga that had brought me into being had taken so drearily long
that Mother was twenty-two years old by the time I was born
and had been lamenting lost time since my head and shoulders
burst free and I heard her first tormented cry.

Until I was seven I lived in Mother's apartment in the zenana.
High walls blocked it off from the rest of the sprawling mansion,
and every house all over the estate, Hindu or Muslim, mud or
marble, was subdivided like it into male and female. There were
two sexes, no doubt about it. In the afternoon heat the green
paint of Mother's shuttered windows gave her bedroom a twilit
glimmer. Lying moulded against her narrow hollowed back until
she turned over to clasp me close, I used to think she would
melt goldenly as wax if sunlight ever touched her skin.

When all her maidservants were in the room together their
voices had the suffocated squawk of captive geese who have
been fed and tranquillized into docility. One of them slept at the
foot of Mother's bed, the others unrolled their beddings in the
passage outside, but in the daytime they were all over the place,
human swings and seesaws and sandpits for me to tumble and be
tumbled on. I was lifted struggling from my belly crawl, passed
from the crook of one arm to another, tossed far into the air,

caught midway before my gurgles of terrified joy became wails, cradled and cushioned and suckled by a soft, vast, collective mattress of a breast. I can't remember when I realized they were separate women, each with a face and tongue of her own, who fondled and dandled me with entirely separate pairs of hands. Bittan commanded this gaggle. Her age gave her the freedom of our cluster of buildings. She went in and out of the public rooms, kitchens and courtyards, losing her greenish tinge away from the bedroom shutters. As soon as I could walk I trailed her from the zenana to a back veranda to see her change colour.

Mother saw the world through the slit between her carriage curtains when she went out, more rarely through tinted glass after Father bought cars, because she preferred her carriage. And otherwise she saw it through barred windows whose pointed Mogul arches were inlaid with flower sprays of semi-precious stones delicately powdered with decades of dust, too high for a thorough cleaning. Now *there* was an empire that had known how to treat an ally, Mother said of the dusty glitter. They had taken brides from Rajput clans, produced half-Hindu emperors, shared glory. Not like now.

'Now we're nothing but rent receivers for the British and spend our lives pocketing their insults.'

The fly-blown jewels up there were all we had left of the true empire, to remind us of the brilliant centuries between the barbarous hordes of Ghazni and Ghori, and the barbarous British. Mother was no historian, but all time is story time on the Ganges plain.

Mother's geese were giggling fools. My impression was she spoke to the walls and the walls to her, responding with a fitting, resonating silence to the cruel joke of a martial caste deprived of arms and ammunition, of substitute battles for rank, seating at table, titles that should have been granted without all this boot-licking, and an insufferable Commissioner, arrogant bastard who kept our biggest, richest landlords waiting on his veranda. The biggest and richest didn't help by making donkeys of themselves. Like the great actress she was, she imitated the Raja of Ramgunj bowing low before the Commissioner and backing away bent over double until he bumped his backside against a wall and

jarred to a compulsory halt. For the Viceroy he'd have gone through the wall. It was one of her repeated dozen stories, the signal for her maidservants to giggle dutifully, and for Mother to laugh as she did everything else, throwing caution and control to the winds, her head flung back, that mass of hair unwinding in coils over her shoulders as she reached under it to hold her skull like some precious breakable object whose fate she hadn't quite decided yet. The signal, too, for Bittan to wait shrewd and impassive, hands on hips, for Mother to stop. Whatever had come over the shy thirteen-year-old rosebud bride she had brought to Vijaygarh? What in the world could have happened in something so ordinary as marriage to wound her dove, her timid little love? Every custom-ritual had been observed, every detail perfectly planned and beautifully carried out. The child had been pledged at five, delivered at menstruation to this house. A late bloomer, it was true, piteously reluctant to bleed, unfold, be a woman. She had run to hide whenever there was talk of marriage. Her fingers had had to be pried loose from her mother's neck when it was time to say goodbye, but all brides sob heartbrokenly. So do their parents. All that was to be expected, but look at her now! Mistress of the three universes to hear her! Frightening when she danced herself into a frenzy with friends and maidservants at the Shiva *puja* a visiting sadhu presided over every year. Danced like a drunk, a woman pos-sessed, hair flying, sari slipping, a woman in flames. Was this a story Bittan told me, or do I remember myself at two, up from my seat on the warm dark winter layers of a widowed goose's lap, to copy her, holding the corners of my embroidered muslin *kurta*, and tripping about to a deafening chant till I am snatched up from the path of Mother's frenzied feet? I have a clear re-collection of lying pinned against her ribs for years of afternoon naps, tracing the joins down her spine while she slept. Bittan hovered above us to gather me into her arms, and always changed her mind in case I yelled and woke her love, her troubled dove.

I went with Bittan to the bazaar on Mother's errands where she beat down prices and out-argued tradesmen with the end of her sari pulled right down over her face. A man servant walked ahead keeping the sturdy beggar horde at bay and Bittan had me reined in tighter than a pup on a leash. She had my questions reined in too. What does that beggar want? Nothing. Why does he look like that? Don't look. Who is he? Nobody. If we lagged behind, their noseless faces, gouged eyes and withered arms encircled us. A handful of coins scattered them but I was sure soon after sunset when shopkeepers put their shutters down and went home, the nobodies heard the music of the Divine Orchestra to which Krishna and his lovesick milkmaids had danced, and beggar life swarmed out. The bazaar crawled with it, as it did with termites after the first hard monsoon shower, and with bats and scorpions after dark. The royally maimed and mutilated among them led the dance. The rank and file capered after them. They went into misshapen ecstasies, fell on each other in random copulation as bazaar dogs did, and before daybreak when the revelry ended, poured back like larvae into the cracks from which they'd come, leaving a sample sprinkling behind. All part of the Potter's frolic, I supposed, or a different Potter maybe from the one who'd broken Mother on his wheel.

Mother's toe-pulling talk became earnest when Father heard it rumoured the Commissioner was drawing up a list of candidates who might be eligible for rajahood if they passed all the tests, and he was on it. District officers were checking up on candidates. If so, the sooner the local one heard about Father's wealth and hand-outs the better. His outspoken loyalty hadn't got him very far all by itself. She prodded Father to get organized about his campaign and start building a temple to Shiva before the Commissioner examined the evidence. He himself thought of putting a grain market around it for profitable measure, and gave away cash, cows and elephants the day the foundations were laid. Soon after, he decided he might as well build an Anglo-Vernacular Female College for Domestic Arts by way of another public service, and ordered Munna to go slow about extorting fodder from the tenants for his stable of elephants.

'All those elephants!' Sylla said early in our acquaintance, and gave me my ghastly nickname after one of my Vijaygarh stories. 'You're a lot like an elephant yourself with your horribly old memory.'

'If I can call you Sylla, why can't you call me Bhushan?'

Peals of Sylla merriment. Because she couldn't twang the *n*. And the *Bh* was impossible. A swift flowing relationship could not be impeded by consonants, so she named me Jumbo.

Mother, who had given Father's campaign a flying start, hated it herself. Unthinkable this, in the day of the true empire. This raj treated everyone like a servant. She lumped the district officers and their presiding Commissioner together as miserable sons of pigs. It had taken Father's closest friend and neighbour, Raja Wali Khan's family, a quarter-century to get their title made hereditary. The Commissioner had made Wali Khan's father hang around like a cook's mate and then he only got it extended for his son's lifetime. It wasn't till ten years after *that* that he finally made it. And his only slightly less rich cousin's family had waited six insulted generations for theirs. Examine the evidence indeed! And in a fit of energy no one mistook for temper she ordered the geese to stop their squawking and get out of her room.

Mother's energy was famous. Her face was tense as a bow-string when she sat at her dressing table hunting ruthlessly for a crease in her flawless skin, or grey in the shining purple-black that a rinse of boiled hibiscus flowers gave her hair. Her wrist pivoted her silver hairbrush like a javelin. Bittan's advice to ignore Father's absences – 'a man goes from flower to flower' – triggered a fabulous display. A chorus of superstitious horror bubbled out of the geese's throats when Mother tore the tapestry of a prancing Hanuman from the wall and sent her water pitcher crashing. They moved away to give Mother room. Their combined gaze swept after the damage. If Mother threw herself on her bed with the passion that had taken her over mountains and rivers when she was petitioning the pantheon for a son, they matched her mood with eye movements and gestures settled long ago for the occasion.

But Mother had a careful side. She personally instructed the goldsmith on the other side of the curtain what to do with the gold chunks his assistant had weighed in jeweller's scales, how much of it to melt down for a new armlet or pendant. She gave her ornaments the minute attention to microscopic detail that great masters' apprentices devote to corners of crowded canvases. Jewellery was constantly being made and unmade, cleaned and polished. Yet she wasn't avid about jewellery. She was avid by nature, the life and soul of purdah parties. When I clambered on and off slippery silk laps and raced around among the begums' and ranees' thighs, knocking their teacups over, I was charged with Mother's vitality, not my own. But love and respect jewellery she did, naming me Jewel. She could be sure of jewellery. Naturally she sympathized with that other great jewel fancier, the Tsarina, who made up for being English by ruling a country as remote from England in every possible way as Vijaygarh.

For a person whose knowledge of the world depended on the slit between her carriage curtains, Mother was remarkably well informed. She had once known her alphabet and written a round baby hand, but had left these skills behind with her toys when she came to Vijaygarh. As soon as I learned to read I became her informant. We went from nursery tales to history lessons together, supplemented by books I found in a mouldering library collected by a forebear who after a disgraceful defeat in battle had fallen upon books instead of his sword and was not mentioned in family chronicles. Travels and adventure fascinated Mother and we read several moth-eaten accounts. But her contemporary favourite was the Tsarina. She loved the Tsarina's simplicity. An example to us all, she would tell the geese. The Russian royal family did not live in Catherine the Great's sumptuous palace at Tsarskoe Selo. It was too showy for them with its marble floors inlaid with lapis lazuli and mother-of-pearl, its Chinese and Japanese decorations. They lived in a simple little palace. The bedroom had pink-flowered wallpaper and curtains. The beds had plain brass rails and knobs. The royal bedroom was full of photographs and icons. Very likely every evening incense and oil lamps were lit before the Tsarina's main icons as they were here, making miniature pyramids of flames in the Russian as in the Vijaygarh dusk. And what wonders the sadhu Rasputin had performed for her son. Why shouldn't she receive Rasputin in her room? What did his low birth matter? The famous tantrics were all low born – leather workers, woodcutters, stable cleaners. Meat, drink and carousing were all in the tradition. Who could doubt that the huge strapping peasant with the hypnotic eyes had the authentic healing power? Any mother would have been out of her mind with anxiety for her only beloved son.

Bittan, bored to death with the Russian maharanee, and alert to the dreamy, Rasputin-induced look in Mother's eyes, steered the talk nearer home with another of the dozen stories in the pack. This was the one about Viceroy Curzon's durbar in Lucknow in 1899, when I was minus one year old, but so strenuously prayed for, I was as good as expected. Father had broken down and wept in the *talukdar* enclosure. He was picturing me at his side, a cuddlesome version of himself in a replica of his gold-brocaded robe, a toy diadem on my head, and a tiny gem-encrusted sword in my fist. Mother's dreamy look faded. She stroked the solid knowable gold bangle on her wrist and rallied. The Tsar should have listened to the holy men, she said, above all to the deaf and dumb peasant who had written warning him against the atheists around his throne. Either he hadn't got that letter, or hadn't believed the prophecy it contained, that the Romanovs were going to be blown to bits and their throne smashed for ever. Where the Tsarina would have crossed herself, Mother breathed '*Hari Om*'.

'Please carry on,' prompts Comrade Pillai, while the others sit mesmerized. 'What did your mother say when it happened?'

I couldn't remember. The year the Tsar was dethroned had had other concerns for me, but her grief had certainly been disastrous, a landmark in my life. She was never herself again. I don't have to say anything. They are comparing Vijaygarh with other feudal backwaters, but Comrade Yusuf is quiet.

'She must have found it psychologically disturbing,' he says. 'My father, a devout Muslim wept as if the world was coming to an end when Soviet republics came up in Russian Turkistan.'

I try to explain Mother. She could weep with the best of them but at heart she wasn't a weeper, nor what I call devout, nor run-of-the-mill religious. She had a good bargaining relationship with the Potter. She couldn't be bothered fasting and praying and venerating cows except when strictly necessary as part of a bargain. What she enjoyed was the fantastic range of feats. After all, it's the greatest show on earth. She could spend hours listening to stories of special powers. She entertained an amazing assortment of sadhus on the other side of her curtain, from an exhibitionist who could wind his penis round a rod, to a yogi who could become a giant or slip himself through a crevice, and one I recall who had conquered hunger and thirst by concentrating on the hollow of his throat. As for the art of being in two places at the same time, any number had mastered that. Whether they were broad-chested virile specimens, or skin and bone, smeared with the ashes of funeral pyres, they all had the trademark: eyes that bored holes through you. Mother made use of gifts where she found them, including a clairvoyant tailor in the bazaar who constantly found things her geese had misplaced, without taking his hand off his sewing machine handle.

'But exploits don't dazzle her any more,' I tell Yusuf. 'About the time the Tsar's family were shot in the cellar, she lost interest, I think in everything.'

'The shock,' observes Yusuf.

I cycled around the cartloads of bricks piling up outside the west wing, the other end from Mother's apartment, and never wondered why. She must have known at once bricks meant a wall. It would have been the first inkling she had of yet another wedding in the family.

'You were saying?' Yusuf prompts sympathetically.

'She's never been the same since. She has another ambition. She wants to turn into stone.'

The comrades shift restlessly. Pillai puts his notebook away and Iyer tries to rescue my factual lapse with his historical analogy of Mirabai, the medieval princess turned saint who, legend had it, danced herself into stone in the temple to Krishna at Dwarka. They pass cigarettes around. The session is over.

Comrade Yusuf stays when the others disperse. He is the friendliest of them.

'You made it seem the wall informed your mother of your father's coming marriage,' he says.

I could not have put it better myself, and suddenly it is an effort to speak.

'He did tell her about it when the wall was halfway up. He

said his elder brother had insisted on it, to extend his influence in the district and make him more eligible for rajahood, and he was bound to obey his elder brother. But Mother never forgave him. She'd already forgiven him once, when he married for the second time in 1908 because his best friend, Raja Wali Khan, had recommended it.'

Yusuf is a perceptive man. 'It's the publicity that sometimes hurts more than the event,' he says.

This third time round Father took a thousand people with him in the bridegroom's train and brought his bride home to a week's music and banqueting. Our public buildings were electrically illuminated by special generators – Vijaygarh didn't get electricity until a few years ago – and there were more singers, dancers, wrestlers, acrobats, food, drink and poetry than the first or second time. Yes, it was very public, and a very popular wedding. People said he had waited nine years for his only son so far, and neither boy nor girl to follow, from Mother or the 1908 wife.

'Tell me,' says Yusuf, 'are you tempted to believe in those exploits you were talking about?'

'It depends. The tailor did find lost things. I can vouch for the penis. I saw it myself. A sadhu who held his breath for a hundred and eight minutes was actually timed with a stop-watch. And there are plenty of men with strange assorted gifts roaming the bazaar. But of course one doesn't believe everything one sees.'

Yusuf thoughtfully agrees.

The fat jailer visits us on his rounds and greets me with an air of complicity, my companions less cordially. He isn't sure of the conventions where they are concerned. He has discreetly let me know he can arrange whatever I want, girl, boy, bhang. I've told him I desperately need a toilet I can sit on English-style. I find it impossible to squat over the hole in the ground they provide in the yard, and the one behind a soiled curtain in a corner of the barrack for night use.

# Chapter Four

August has ended but not the rains. Clouds of heat steam up from the sodden ground. Hot wet blankets of it stifle us between downpours. The white-robed sheikh must be getting his money's worth if he's still vacationing at the Taj.

The comrades have sent for legal volumes and are busy writing rough drafts of a defence they are going to put together as one document, if they can manage to agree for five consecutive minutes. They have the beacon light of revolution in common but they belong to different revolutionary groups. I don't know if Comrade Pillai's introduction is just plain stupid or supposed to be funny, but I doubt if any judge will laugh. I lie on my cot with nothing to do but hear him read it. It says they are amused at being charged with conspiracy against the King Emperor because nothing is further from their minds than conspiracy. They've never made any secret of wanting to be rid of him and his set-up so that they can get on with creating a new industrial order . . . I turn on my side, taking care not to fall off the cot, and try dozing, but Comrade Pillai's voice is as unsecret as his plans. It rolls over the barrack, ridiculing 'the fuss about violence, considering the grotesque violence of imperialism across the centuries'. Good grief, he is declaring in stentorian tones that they don't rule out violence. 'Nothing will be allowed to sabotage the economic struggle of the workers.' And more of this. Now they're arguing. How these greyheads harangue, about every sentence and part of a sentence. Pillai wants to condemn

Gandhi's trade union. He's pleased with his short sharp insertion, 'Workers don't need advice from Gandhi and his mill-owning capitalist friends.' Dey and Iyer want it out. They quibble. In, out, I don't know who wins but a nap becomes impossible. I prop myself on an elbow towards Bhaiji, who has the cot between the twins and mine, and say I don't think this line of defence will go down very well with the judge, and conspiracy trials don't have juries. Bhaiji is sitting on the ground. His cot, never used till lights out, is neat as a pin.

'All these ringing open declarations aren't going to get them out of jail,' I point out.

Bhaiji says primly, 'It is more important to be honest and sincere.'

I have landed among lunatics who've never met a judge.

Bhaiji never lounges. He takes his little *takli* out of the tin trunk the authorities have let him keep after going through its pathetic contents, and begins busily to spin. On alternate days he spins on his spinning wheel which folds up small and lies in his trunk. The tiresome twins take turns at it too. When they're not spinning they hunt roaches. It is so hot and sweaty I haven't the energy to swat a fly.

'For once these fellows are not saying one thing and doing another,' he elaborates. 'I got fed up with the local communists during our no-tax campaign. They kept pretending it was their campaign. As if! And the way they go on about Wages Front, this Front, that Front! Is there some war on?'

Father's *taluk* is notorious for a sly sort of rack-renting, he tells me. Extra dues are demanded when he buys another car or wants feed for his elephants. This isn't news to me but the picture of Bhaiji and the twins cleverly outfoxing Munna as they tramp through the *taluk* persuading peasants not to pay hiked-up rent sounds smarter than anything the comrades have said so far.

'What are you doing about your defence?' he asks. 'Why don't you join my group? Naturally you can't join these communists.'

I hate to hurt his feelings but my case would be ruined if I got mixed up with either group. Actually I have less in common with Bhaiji's party than with the comrades who at least aren't humbugs. Gandhi makes no sense to me at all. Goes on bleating about Hindu–Muslim love but a Hindu–Muslim marriage would send him on a fifty-day fast. He's all for public brotherly embraces, for Hindu rajas building mosques for their Muslim tenants, Muslim rajas building cow shelters for their Hindu ones, and processions hollering 'Be one!' in the streets, but the day you take them at their word there's hell to pay. The unifiers take care not to let us blood-mingle. They don't know, poor sods, we're in each other's blood already. By unity they mean their trumped-up unities, public emotions gushed on like taps, then each to his lair until it's time to tear each other to pieces again. I've never been able to interest myself in their treacherous politics.

Unlike me my companions buzz with politics. I don't think they know what a personal life is, and they refuse to believe I have no public one. Comrade Yusuf remembers reading my poem, 'The Bridge' by Bhushan Singh, in a Soviet magazine. Why had I let my lawyer disparage such a fine poem? I had rightly called it the iron of sorrow, he praised, it had machinery in every line. Truly a worker's-eye view. A description so faithful, he could see the engineering and would recognize the bridge if he came to it. He couldn't accept I had no politics. And where by the way was the bridge?

'Nowhere. I was trying to build one that would flow. A lovers' connecting link. But the poem got interrupted by some- thing I had to do, and when I got back to it, the machinery was all I had left.'

Comrade Yusuf is so pleasant, a man of such impeccable Muslim manners, that I attempt the absurd task of explaining a poem.

'Lovers everywhere have to get away. Love, for one reason or another, isn't allowed. So one needs a bridge.'

'I understand,' he nods.

But I doubt it. He comes from further north. He has no Ganges in his path. Every other river you can get 'beyond'. This one rules the plain. It's always in your path. Its writ runs for a thousand miles.

Sen is having the time of his life. He is an ardent disciple and the comrades mollycoddle him. In these past weeks he has become as cocky as a child basking in the affection of four doting grandfathers. I hear them talking of themselves as having 'grown old in the struggle', and of Sen as if he's a garden they are growing. Comrade Dey is a quoter. Sen's face lights up when he quotes, 'To the altar of revolution we have brought our youth as incense . . .' In the other group it's the other way around. The old one rules the roost.

All eight are talkers. In these pre-trial weeks release seems just around the corner, and the hangman's noose a laughing matter. As for why we're here under a treason charge, or at all, Bhaiji scorns the comrades' theory of a scientific historical pattern working itself out.

'I say we are here by chance,' he insists. 'It is all utterly meaningless.'

Some British bureaucrat went berserk and slammed people into various jails after a *chota peg*. Drink is the cause. Drink is responsible for evil on earth, from wife-beating to imperialism. Bhaiji knows. Once he saw a man drunk. I don't know why he imagines a tipsy bureaucrat would act on whim when all else in Bhaiji's universe is governed by the stars.

'Take it from me,' he expounds, 'this is no deep-laid plot of the government. Likewise there is no deep-laid Bolshevist plot to make everybody Bolshevist. Have you seen Russia? It is full of potholes and beggars. How is it different from here?'

'Have *you* seen Russia?' Comrade Iyer challenges tersely.

Bhaiji's *takli* thread snaps. He looks up, pained and perplexed.

'What for should I see Russia?' he demands. 'What is there for me to see in Russia? But let met tell you I have read a book. They have meddled with agriculture. There is no harvest. They are starving. Have they got time to spread Bolshevism?'

The comrades flounder, but they no more believe in chance happenings than Mother does. They have the past, present and future mapped out like Mother's astrologer. A historical pattern is working itself out and sitting here in jail for no rhyme or reason is apparently part of it.

Speaking for himself and the twins Bhaiji announces, '*We* don't mind being here. In January our party gave the British government one year of grace. If we don't get Home Rule by

the end of the year, we are going to declare for outright independence.'

'What a bargain,' mocks Comrade Iyer. 'The government gets
a year of grace and you get to rot in jail. And I hope your party
knows you're alive, and in this dump.'

But Bhaiji has the last word.

'At least I have a party,' he says.

He urges me to be defended by the local advocate he has
engaged who's also a party member.

'We should stick together,' he says. 'We shouldn't appear to
be divided before the country.'

But a man whose country is Vijaygarh is not the same as a
revolutionary or a nationalist. To me they are Dutchmen; in a
word, distant. And we're divided in any case. It beats me why
these men spend their lives planning strategies to get rid of the
sovereign power. With half a mind and a scrap of real resolve
we'd be rid of it. If we all spat together the sovereign power
would drown. But then what? The pandits and ulemas would
throw each other lifebelts and come bouncing out of the spit to
boss the show. I think I prefer the sovereign power.

The lawyer Father has hired to represent me is here. Nauzer
Vacha is a Parsee from Bombay, said to be a rising star in his
profession. If I didn't know he was a lawyer I would take him
for a homeopath. He asks me if I sleep well, whether I'm slow
or quick to anger, and if I eat more sweet or salt. I don't know
if these irrelevant questions are meant to put me at my ease. He
goes irritatingly on instead of confining himself to the issue that
my arrest is a frame-up or a farce. I should never have been
arrested. I have no politics.

'It's not what you or I know that counts,' he cautions. 'It's
what the other side will get the judge to believe.'

My biography is brief and undistinguished. He already has it.
He knows I was born and brought up in Vijaygarh, spend most
of each year in Bombay, and had just got back from my third
trip abroad when I was arrested.

'What about your first trip abroad?'

'I went to college in America for a year. I didn't like it so I
came away.'

'What didn't you like, the studies?'

'It was too adolescent for me. You know how it is with us. One is a child and then one is a man. There's nothing in between. It's not a stage one can go back to if one's never been through it.'

I see no point in telling him I had done badly in the five or six totally unrelated subjects (including English composition!) they had saddled me with, and the college had been cool about my continuing. Good taste forbids me to tell Mr Vacha that sex rites under professional guidance made what the students called necking and petting a foolproof recipe for a nervous breakdown. I cannot recall ever having been young enough for this deluded and nerve-wracking pastime.

'Any special reason for your other two trips?'

'The usual reasons. A change of scene and air. I ordered new clothes etc., learned the charleston.'

'We have a mutual friend – Sylla,' he says, producing a parcel of books she has sent for me.

'Give her my regards.'

'Sylla has a feel for character, don't you think? She believes you are a man with a secret.'

'Which man isn't?'

'She says restraint has rotted your guts. Those were her very words.'

'Sylla is mad about words.'

It strikes me his homeopathic approach, insidiously becoming psychological, might be Sylla's brainwave. If Sylla has brought this friend of hers to Father's notice in some roundabout way, Sylla is probably masterminding my defence. It is typical of her to assume she can do most things better than other people.

'Well, we mustn't waste time. There's so much I would like to talk about but the trial is upon us. Now then, which well-known figure do you admire most in the world today?'

I can hardly believe the man. Next he'll want to know which six books I would take to a desert island. After that he'll run and hide, call coo-ee and have me dart around looking for him.

'Charles Lindbergh,' he says helpfully, 'or the Mikado, or the Prince of Wales?'

'Mustafa Kemal Pasha.'

He is intrigued. 'A martial hero?'

'With a passion for ballroom dancing and hats.'

Vacha looks astounded. He doesn't seem to have followed it in the press. I give him a brief résumé of Mustafa Kemal's modernizing mania, including his ban on the fez.

'It's not even Turkish in origin,' I explain. 'It's North African. It was foisted on the Turks a hundred years ago by the Sultan and his Grand Vizier.'

Vacha is lost.

'The fez is as archaic as the crinoline or the sari,' I point out. 'Its tassels get knotted in wind and damaged by rain. At one time tassel boys, like shoeshine boys nowadays, used to make a living combing them out. Some military men had their tassels plaited. What kind of headgear is that for modern times?'

'You are a student of the history of costume?'

'Good Lord no. But clothing reform and general reform go together. The fez was an improvement on the skull-caps wrapped with cloth and topped with turbans that the Turks were then wearing. Once that rigmarole was thrown out, so were robes and baggy trousers, and European suits came in. The orthodox didn't mind westernizing their bodies so long as their heads remained Islamic. But hats are going to shake the country. This pasha knows what he's doing. And he puts it simply enough for a village idiot to grasp. You must have read the speech.'

'No, I haven't.'

'It's a classic. "Boots and shoes on our feet, trousers on our legs, shirt and tie, jacket and waistcoat – and of course, to complete these, a cover with a brim on our heads. I want to make this clear. The name of this headgear is *hat*." '

While Vacha thinks of a proper homeopathic rejoinder, I go on to the pasha's use of the foxtrot as a sex equalizer.

'I see.' Vacha relaxes. 'Sylla did tell me you are adamantly opposed to the seclusion of women. Ever been to Turkey?'

'No.'

'Something to look forward to then,' he smiles.

'Mr Vacha, I have no intention of ever going on my travels again.'

'I see. Well! Now then, are you quite certain you have no

trade union connections or sympathies? You know the men with you are trade unionists. I needn't remind you the government has nothing against any genuine trade union.'

'The Congress chaps are khaddar workers,' I correct him. 'The frail old chap is in charge of setting up shops to sell khaddar in this area. The younger two are his assistants.'

'Coarse ugly stuff,' says Vacha. 'Why would anyone choose to wear it? But I was talking to the Superintendent of Police yesterday and he told me they've been involved with peasant agitations.'

I assure him I have nothing to do with trade unions, bogus or genuine. It is probably the literal truth that no worker has ever crossed my path. He is relieved but being a lawyer he double-checks.

'You spend a lot of time in Bombay. Fifty thousand textile workers went on strike in April last year. It went on for six months.'

If they did, I hadn't come across them. Sylla's Bombay is not Bombay.

'There was a regular rash of strikes last year, steel, jute, the East India and South India Railways. The government had to call out troops and armed police. The strike leaders got ten years with hard labour. Didn't you read reports?'

'I seldom read the newspapers. There are more civilized things to read.'

He keeps at it. 'So you've never been near the Bombay tenements, looking into working-class conditions or anything like that for material for a poem? We mustn't be caught on the wrong foot.'

A wasteland in front of a tenement comes to mind. It is littered with rubbish and excrement. Vultures pick a hairless cur clean of flesh, hop off the carcass and waddle a few yards, dragged groundward by their bellies till they can waddle faster, run and take off into the air. Naked children aeroplane over the dog's remains with joyous abandon. Behind them shrouded women move in single file against the tenement wall. They are as indistinguishable as black bundles strung on a pole. I've seen the *chawls*, I tell Vacha, driven past, that's all.

He is satisfied. 'The government is using its new powers only against the communists,' he says, 'and other agitators.'

He shakes my hand firmly with the confidence of a Parsee, on a happier footing with the sovereign power than Father's fossil, and says it won't be long now. Meanwhile I have books to read, when the jail superintendent has checked the parcel.

'You are forgetting this,' he calls after me.

It is Sylla's short letter, left lying open on the table between us. No point in putting it into its envelope now that the superintendent's eyes have raked through it, or taking it with me. It is so untypical, so shorn of her recuperative powers that I have it fixed in my head. But I pick it up and put it in my pocket. Sylla has no repetition in her. She never says hello the same way twice. She's new every day. There's no family pack of a dozen retold stories in her past. Yet this is anguished repetition. 'What made you go off without saying goodbye? I don't understand why you did it, Jumbo. I don't understand why you couldn't have waited a few minutes till I came off the stage. I don't understand why you've been arrested.' And again and again, an expiring echo of 'I don't understand why, why, why you went away.'

'You are permitted to write letters,' says Vacha kindly.

Bhaiji is pleased I have a lawyer, but still puzzled.

'If you have never been in politics, why are you here?'

Who knows? Who knows why any of us is here? I've stopped breaking my head against that wall. The dirty grey barrack exactly matches my frame of mind. Do I really want to be anywhere else? I make a mental list of every place I have ever been to and cross out every one. Bombay. Vijaygarh. My trips abroad, one to the moon or a limbo as remote, the next two to known parts on routine holidays. I never want to see those cities again. Except for my stupefied outrage at being arrested, I had had no feelings worth the name since I left Bombay. I was on my way to Vijaygarh for burial, but this will do.

The toilet seat arrives. The men who bring it into the yard want to know where, at what angle, to set it, as if it's a priceless Hepplewhite chiffonier. I instruct them through the bars. They hang jute sacking on stout bamboo poles around it. The jailer arrives, waves a hand at the finished product, bows. I thank him.

'My pleasure,' he says in his best butter-laden accents.

Anything else I require, boy, girl, bhang, will be arranged. Fruit, sweets, tobacco, anything.

I offer my companions the use of the toilet seat but the comrades decline. They will go on using the hole in the ground all prisoners use. Bhaiji says he uses a hole in the ground at home too. He's not used to these English fads. Nobody bothers about the twins. So it's all mine. Sitting and straining on it I hear the comrades writing off Mussolini as they exercise in the yard. Fascism is a straw in a breeze, here today, gone tomorrow. Who is this Italian anyway but an ex-journalist at a loose end? No ideology, no programme except for bullets and massive doses of castor oil for his opponents. He's so hard up for ideas he's had to fall back on the old imperial Roman salute and symbol. He'll last as long as he has castor oil. Sen, doing sit-ups, guffaws. I yearn for a dose of Mussolini's medicine.

# Chapter Five

After a dry spell what's left of the monsoon comes down furiously on September 28, the opening day of our trial. A warder walks us through muddy puddles to a waiting lorry. We drive to the magistrate's bungalow on a deserted road between rows of black-umbrellaed policemen, proof of how dangerous we are, if there were man or beast to take note.

On our way to the courtroom we come across our belongings spread on soggy straw on a veranda. Mould and damp are eating into my carton of Venetian glass. Our books and clothes have been attacked by white ants. And the courtroom has been re-furnished in keeping with its new status as a sessions court. The pink and purple chintz has gone. In its place there's dull grey so that we will have no excuse to be cheerful. A raised platform has been erected where, instead of the magistrate with his family toys underfoot, sits a rosy-cheeked judge whose cockatoo crest of silver hair peeps out from his abbreviated cap of a wig. There's a picture of the King Emperor above him. The dock has been isolated by cane fencing and now I suppose it looks like a proper dock. Lawyers in black robes fit like birds of ill omen into the décor. In the afternoon we get into the police lorry and are driven through the police corridor back to jail. This is the monotonous sequence day after day. I have to keep reminding myself the entire world is not a barrack, a police corridor and a courtroom, where Nauzer Vacha's presence is the only kind, relieving feature.

Our nights have more variety than our days. A grating, hawking cough across the yard rustles up enough phlegm to float a luxury liner. I hear the grunts, scuffles and roars of angry convicts when the night warder on his quarter-hourly rounds thumps them on the head as he cries out their numbers. Mirthless opium laughter, unnerving as a hyena's, binds us to the criminal jungle we inhabit. Night dissolves differences. All sleepers are part of the same jungle. Sen used to wake us with his recurring nightmare. Now we take it in our stride. He is fleeing from Calcutta across the peninsula on the Howrah–Kalka express. At every station he wraps himself up in the sheet from his bedding roll and crouches in the corner of his wooden berth, vigorously shaking his head when a vendor's hand thrusts in with sweet steaming tea in earthenware or a bunch of ripe bananas. Railway stations, like post offices, teem with British agents and informers. Better starve than be picked up by the police. At Allahabad the police are so busy controlling crowds of pilgrims and naked bushy-haired straggle-bearded sadhus on their way to bathe at the Triveni, that he can slip out for a bite without being nabbed. But a policeman grabs his shoulder and his terrified cries jar us all awake, or used to, when one or another of his grandfathers consoled him back to sleep.

I lie awake thinking of my thank-you note to Sylla and her second letter to me. Parallel letters, no questions asked this time, none answered, letters meant for the jail superintendent, a false cheer underlying her depression and mine. It's not the same depression. I know what mine is about, not hers, unless she still hasn't got over my abrupt departure. The snippets Vacha has considerately given me about her are more like the Sylla I know. He described how she looked when he met her with friends at the cinema, and one Sunday at the beach. In his meticulous legal fashion he told me what she said, how she said it. I was grateful for the details. It was Sylla as I remember her, busy, desired, admired. I fall asleep near morning to the sound of her voice, the green of her eyes, the glow of her Parsee skin in the sun. And morning separates us from the criminal jungle. We are only nine again, or to be accurate, eight plus one. I'm lucky. I have nothing worse than the boredom and hideous discomforts to cope with. I don't have the uncertainty. There's no battle of wits ahead of me. I merely have to wait. But Vacha has warned it may be a long wait. The prosecution is going to call the same three hundred witnesses we heard in the preliminary enquiry, and they'll have all the time they want to display their theatrical talents. Each of us will be cross-examined, and nobody knows how long that could take. Then the defence will call witnesses. After this the prosecution will start its arguments, and finally the defence. It sounds like the fossil's uncle–nephew title–property dispute. Vacha lays a comforting hand on my arm.

'You have plenty to read, don't you? Keep your spirits up. You're in a special category. I intend to make this clear and cut your case short as soon as I'm given the opportunity.'

After we have walked about the yard, evenings drag and the comrades get down to studying me again.

'You were saying your mother expected disaster for the Tsar's family,' Comrade Pillai reads from his notes.

'Her first nasty shock was the Tsarina's sadhu's murder in 1916, when the miraculous powers that had protected him from three lethal doses of prison couldn't save him in the end. Then came news of the Tsar's dethronement.'

My eyes travel unseeing over the semicircle of comrades. I am inwardly aghast all over again. Her reaction had been so appalling.

Yusuf gently encourages me, 'She was standing at the window, you said.'

Barefoot at the window, grasping its bars. She was nailed to a red and violet night of shooting stars, a sky foaming with firework fountains. Rockets screamed upward and exploded. Clay pomegranates threw whirling crackling showers of colour down the drive to our gate. And these were feathery trifles. The night's drama came from networks of electric bulbs outlining our house and the town's public buildings. They reared up in her window. I had never seen punishment so garishly, graphically lit. I cowered in the doorway to Mother's room, willing her to move, speak, cry. She came from doers, a long line of loud mourners, breast beaters, hair tearers. This was unnatural. I crept to her bed to lie like a little child in the warm tunnel of her quilt, but unable to bear it for more than a few seconds, I flung out of the house. I was out every night of the week-long festivities, only to meet festivity wherever I went.

'You were saying?' Pillai prods me politely.

'That I got out of the house – I had to get far away from the house, from the lights – but everywhere people were chattering excitedly about the electric lights.'

'Electricity is exciting,' agrees Comrade Iyer, 'and crucial to transformation.'

It was the final affront to Mother's grief. I had to hide from its cruel advertising glare. The only place in town without it was the exhibition ground. The annual winter fair was on.

Comrade Pillai sharpens his pencil and one of them asks, 'This third wedding of your father's took place in November 1917. I suppose he was too happy getting married to have any reaction to the Revolution?'

Much too happy, and jumping jubilant for a couple of years after the wedding. His new wife brought him luck. His elder brother said I told you so. He was awarded a jewelled robe and sword of honour for doing more war recruiting than any other *talukdar* in the district. He had taken to wearing all the colours of the rainbow, to kite-flying, boyish games and a French aftershave lotion. The geese reported he was seen night after night drifting down corridors with their sharp left and right turns so confusing to visitors but known to Father since he was a toddler, heading for the newly walled zenana of the third ranee – for on New Year's Day 1919 he became a raja. Late one night when I had diarrhoea and had to keep running to the bathroom I saw him go past my bathroom window. I still wonder if it could have been him I saw, that gleeful apparition, iridescent under globes of frosted glass, more like a heavy hothouse butterfly than a human male.

I have glossed over my personal feelings toward Father and Mother, and the comrades don't push for them, but this business of baring my past is beginning to nauseate me. When Comrade Iyer asks if I had been aware of the Bolshevist takeover myself I want to laugh insanely. I've had enough of their Anno Domini, their public lives, and their politics.

'If you must know, I see no difference between bloody old Russia and bloody new Russia, except Mother Russia's new religion. And that goes for everyone else's blood-soaked history too.'

I leave them gaping in their semicircle and fall on my cot. I am deathly sick of playing Scheherazade. I have no wish to revisit the month of the wretched Bolshevist takeover, but they've brought it upon me. It was when I first saw the girl, if you call it seeing, outside the winter fair.

It was growing dark. She and two other girls in black burkas, with a bulkier burka in attendance, were standing on the road-side. Earlier they had been buying bangles. I had come out of the magic show tent to see the bangle-seller guiding glistening blocks of her ware over three right hands. Wrists were lifted to the blaze of a petromax lantern and airily turned. Where burka flaps had fallen back I caught glimpses of pale sequestered skin above the shining clusters of green and gold-spangled glass. An extension of the magic I had seen. Brightness where black cloth ended, skin come and gone as a hand withdrew tantalizingly into an opening at the wrist so like the magician's hollow device. The girls compared wrists and one of them, the leader of the pack, swiftly decided which bangles they would buy, not the bulky attendant who stood apart and was clearly a servant. The leader of the pack took money from her folds and counted it out. Now they were waiting for their tonga and the leader didn't like waiting. While the others chatted, she fretted. She walked up and down and swung around with such sparkling impatience, I could picture her eyes flashing behind their net panel. In a gesture characteristic of those who are incensed by the fools and slowcoaches they have to suffer, she pushed the hood of her burka off her face to get a good look, her glance coming straight at me, on past me to a bearded tongawallah with his skull-capped head on his knees, asleep in the driver's seat, while a horse not much less hoary, twitched flies off its shanks and stirred half-heartedly between its wooden shafts. The girl pulled her net panel over her eyes, raised the skirt of her burka and ran, hurrying the other two along. She came skimming back to hustle the laggard attendant and helped her to hoist her bulk up beside the driver. The tonga took a lurch forward. They were gone in a slow clatter when my tutor came eddying out of the fairground, all waving tentacles on a papery torso puffed convex or concave by the prevailing breeze. Concave today with the current against him, he had a crazed look that could mean either fear or unhoped for discovery, depending on whether he had lost me or found a rare insect. This time it could have been both. His *achkan* was too loose for him. It was left untidily unbuttoned at the top and hung shapeless over his loose pyjamas. He waited for the lamplighter to finish his job and move to the next lamp, then carefully transferred some form of insect life from his handkerchief to a perforated cardboard box he carried on outings. I caught the metallic gloss of a gaudy beetle before he put it into the box. I stepped back into the shadows to let him rush past, looking for me.

The spider, as I called him, had been engaged to coach me when I was removed from school for doing no work. But now his task became impossible. He droned. I thought of her face. It took me years to decipher its spell and understand why it haunted me. It defied unwritten laws. The Tartar cheekbones of this face should have had slanting eyes above them, but hers were long ovals, the lidded eyes of temple sculpture. Their width took me unawares when they pounced upon her tonga. It was this manifest racial impurity, a mix belonging to a vision of future communal union, that made it unforgettable, and retreat impossible for me. At the time all I knew was I had never seen such a face.

'He is intelligent but he won't apply himself, sir,' Spider complained to Father as if I were not in the room with my atlas open at the land of Eskimos. 'He wastes all day in the library upstairs, reading, reading, reading.'

'Stop him. What are you here for?'

'All day it is his own choice of this or that book.'

'Stop him, I said. Will you blacken my face?'

Deprecatory horror on Spider's face.

'If he doesn't show his intelligence soon, and if my nose is cut, you've lost your job.'

'His reluctance can be overcome, sir.'

'Overcome it at once then.'

I had better things to do than study the geography of the frigid zone. I was scouring the Muslim *mohalla*. After weeks of investigation and elimination I found the house, as shabby, but larger than its neighbours in the decrepit neighbourhood. Her father was inspector of schools. I could see into the front room from across the road, but I could be seen too. I went round to the side from where I had a view of whitewashed wall, a plain wooden chair and a vase of pink and yellow paper flowers on a round table. Whenever I could give my tutor the slip I hung around in the lane waiting for her to come into the room. I waited with such intense expectation I knew she would. One afternoon she did, all animation without her burka, and then several afternoons in a row. I couldn't hear what she said but her gaiety made up for it. This girl was never sad and never still. She flitted about like truant light, hardly ever sat on the chair, and I didn't think any chair would hold her for long. The other two, her sisters, quarrelled, snivelled, obeyed, did what ordinary mortals do. And there were relatives in the recesses of the house, at least two older brothers or cousins. They were not housebound like their sisters. One careless move and I would be caught. I could take no risks.

The day she saw me she gave a cry and dropped what she was carrying. I hunched below window level, not daring to surface for a length of time I had no way of judging. I was stiff with cramp but it never occurred to me to go away. She rewarded me by appearing in the window at the identical hour every afternoon. Now that I was certain she'd be there I could relax and let my eyes leave her face. She had school ink on her fingers, a blue smudge of it on her nose. Her wristful of bangles glinted in a shaft of dusty sunlight at the window where she concocted odd jobs to keep herself in view. She sucked a sore thumb where her needle had jabbed it as she unfolded a cotton square pencilled with peacocks and shook it out to show me their embroidered tail feathers. She stood so close to the window I could see a mosquito bite on her smooth cheek and a single smallpox in-dentation just below it. One day she undid her braids, combed out her hair and languidly braided it again. In moving, enchanting detail she fed me with bits of herself. How did she know what I wanted? Where did she get her intuitive knowledge of me? And had she been born knowing what it was to be free? I wasn't meant for geography and mathematics. I had a vocation. It was this. She and I were so intimately connected that when she stopped appearing in the window I felt I had been cut off at a vital artery.

I next saw her one mid-March morning on the road to the Anglo-Vernacular Female College for Domestic Arts with her attendant. I was on my bicycle and I recognized the hoary tongawallah. He was absent-mindedly flaying the horse's rump. I wouldn't have known it was her if she hadn't raised her hood. I knew she must be on her way to the college. There was no-where else along that road for a girl in purdah to go. The tonga joined a line of tongas turning into the college gates. I cycled past them to the back of the building. The day was warm and hazy, growing hotter. I stood with my sweating hands glued to the handlebars of my bicycle. I didn't have the power to move. They would find me, a blackened upright corpse, fastened to the machine. And then she came, still shrouded, flying out of the back door. The bicycle fell over, its bell clinked as it hit the grass. She unbundled a burka she was carrying, tossed it over my head and made straight for the brambled countryside. Trapped in my folds I lumbered behind. She avoided all the holes in the ground though I was the one who knew this territory well. Low jungle a hundred yards away, where elephant grass grew high, would give us cover. Father's seventy miles adjoined the government's forest. Father and his friends had hunted jungle fowl, wild boar and deer on his tract before the college was built. In the heat I imagined branched antlers shimmering above the tall grass. Where the two tracts of jungle coverged there was a shortcut to the river bed, dry at this time of year. I wrapped my skirts around my waist and raced ahead of her to the monument on our side of the bank. It was on a mound in the shade of an antique tree. Prehensile roots corded its massive trunk and hung in shaggy grey beards from its higher branches. Stray off-roots drilled through the monument's walls. Since childhood I had expected this stranglehold to explode the tree and send it thundering down, but the monument looked nearer collapse than the tree. Every town in the district is named after a fort, some of these mere hillocks of mud ringed by dried moats. The grim edifice that has given Vijaygarh its name dominates the district, keeps its blind vigil for Turk, Afghan and Mongol, and the battle cry '*Allahu Akbar*' from a thousand throats. This small crumbling ruin wasn't part of the countryside's attack and defence mechanism. But it may have been built to commemorate some minor victory where fewer hundreds of her ancestors and mine had fallen slaughtering each other and been left limbless for the vultures. On the other hand it could have been a religious shrine, spared because it had no idol and didn't look like a shrine.

I was there before her and struggled out of my burka. She caught up, whipped hers off and aimed it at a thorn bush where it stuck. A warm wind lifted the edges of her *gharara* and the flimsier stuff of her *kurta*. We were out of breath and laughter made us both incoherent.

'You looked so screamingly funny,' she gasped out.

'How do you walk in that hideous thingamajig, how do you *breathe*?'

'That's a good name for it. Thingamajig!'

I looked at the ugly shroud I was still holding and put it to its first decent use. I spread it on the ground in the shade of the wall, took her hand and drew her down beside me. After all we weren't strangers. We knew each other well. I lay on my back, lifted her by the waist and pinned her against the dazzling blue expanse above us. She was too delicate a burden to test the strength of my arms. An uncaged swallow, ready to fly. It was time for introductions.

'What's your name?' I asked.

'Yours first,' she challenged.

We spoke our names together and stopped dead. These names could not be linked by *and*. We would have been wiser to do without names. But people must call each other something.

'Razia,' I repeated, and lowered her to align her eyelids, her lips, her beating heart and ribs with mine, and there was nothing, least of all the names others had given us, to prevent us from embracing for ever. We stayed fitted together until I felt the weight of her. Then I eased her off and carefully did all I had been taught to do. She was breathless, wide open-eyed with surprise and delight all the way. When we sat up the wind had rippled and ridged the sand on our side of the riverbed. The further bank was sculptured into silvery dunes. Razia started up in alarm.

'It's late. Why did you bring me here? Let go of me.'

'Who brought who?'

She brushed off her clothes and hunted frantically for her slippers.

'Get up! Darning must be over. I don't even know what time it is. They must be cooking. What got into me to come on this adventure?'

'I'm not an adventure,' I said, getting to my feet, 'I'm your destiny.'

Now that had a grand sound but Razia retorted, 'So is my thingamajig and look where it is now.' She picked the sorry mess off the thorn bush, shook it vigorously and put it on.

Yet it was Razia who arranged our meetings and kept track of the time, with her inborn knowledge of when darning ended and cooking began. If occasionally she wasn't sure, we gambled with the curriculum. Neither of us had watches. It's hard to believe we embarked on that dangerous enterprise without a watch, trusting to the sun, and the wind on the sand dunes. Somehow there was ample time. Soldier ants attacked decomposing patches on our tree trunk, burrowing for an opening into the tree. They tore at the masonry of our monument and tunnelled into it.

'Would you believe ants had such jaws!' said Razia in awe.

Cavalcades of them lugged moths, bugs and worms down our tree trunk, found luscious caterpillars and hacked them into shreds with those vicious jaws. And time stayed elastic, minutes seeming gentle hours. We rolled down our side of the steep bank to the riverbed, clinging together like burrs.

'When I go to Mecca,' she announced, 'you won't catch me going like my aunt.'

'How did your aunt go?'

'In the cabin. All the way. Her husband would never let her stand on deck even in her thingamajig. I'll stand on deck.'

Mecca gave me a shock. What were we doing, rolling about, shouting our names at the sky, behaving like children when we should be making plans. Inevitably we'd have to cross the riverbed long before it filled and disappear on the other side, and on to somewhere else from there. If I could have uprooted our tree or pulled the stones out of our monument to build a barricade to halt our pursuers I would have done it. We had to find another place. But Razia was not the worrying kind.

'I like it here. This is our place.'

'We'll find another. This is only a victory site where my ancestors gave yours a thrashing.'

'Or mine yours.'

But where, anyway, our forefathers had bloodthirstily tangled and where soldier ants commemorated the slaughter by shredding live caterpillars and devouring them. In Father's jungle nearby I had once seen a wounded cheetal rocking on her side with tears in her eyes as Father's shikaree deftly scooped her liver out on the point of his knife. It was grilled on hot coals and served to Father before she died. Razia and I wiped out the grief and carnage with our bodies on her burka.

The sun was hotter every time we met.

'Mangoes soon,' she said drowsily. 'Let's bring some and eat them here.'

We dropped off to sleep on that remark and woke to find our shade gone. The sun was directly overhead. Razia sat up and burst into tears. I scrambled to my feet, got dressed and was ready to go, but to my horror she was still half-dressed and on her knees. She rose to her feet and stood in a trance before she bent forward, sliding her hands to her knees. 'Razia!' I begged. She straightened but her eyes were closed and her lips moved silently. She slipped to her knees. Slowly her forehead touched the ground in what I recognized as the lowliest obeisance of *namaz*. I jerked her to her feet but she pushed me away and started the robot sequence all over again, her time sense no longer to be relied on. I panicked. We were in a white-hot furnace. The sun fierily branded my brain. I looked wildly about for a way to jolt her back to the danger we were in, the lateness of the hour, and then, I will never know why, my agitation ebbed out of me. I knelt too, facing Mecca, and prayed in imitation of Razia, yet as naturally as if I had been doing it since birth. My clasped hands burned each other to the touch. The noonday earth scorched my skin as I lowered my forehead to it. There was a hammering in my head. When I could endure it no longer, the fierce heat cooled. A quiet rapture streamed through me. I felt we were shielded by a shining controlling intelligence and knew this was the meaning of our lives. We turned and shuffled to each other on our knees.

I heard the snorting and stamping in the bushes before she did. There had been no sign of wild boar so far. No sooner had I pulled her to her feet than they came from behind the monument to surround us and we were the hunted animals at bay, trapped in a circle of spears, clubs and lathis pointing groundward. I knew two of the men, Razia's tongawallah, nursing old hatreds by the look of him, and the college night watchman who had been a servant in our house and now spent his days in opium slumber under a guava tree in the college compound. His daytime eyes were sullen and furred, but he grinned and waved the others back.

'Don't touch her,' I ordered.

The grin expanded.

'Come now, young master. We are here to escort you home. Lucky you have come to no harm.'

He led. Razia encased in her shroud walked behind me, and the other men brought up the rear. Students crowded the windows as we approached the building. A woman came out of the Principal's office into the hall, said, 'In here, Razia,' in dead tones and shut the door. I tried the door handle, solid brass buried in teak. Iron would have been as bendable. I threw my weight against the door to the accompaniment of shrill screams. Students and servants scattered as I turned around to pick up a wooden bench and drove it into the door. The battering didn't budge it. I went on and on until two policemen overpowered me and took me home.

# Chapter Six

Since my refusal to talk about my background, the comrades keep their gentlemanly distance from me, but they have got it going and my personal life is upon me. It's all I have while they polish their drafts, Bhaiji and the twins spin, and the whole lot cook, sweep, and wash their clothes in the trough in the yard. One of the warders washes mine for a consideration.

I can feel Mother's hand on my forehead, sense her fright.

'Why is his fever still so high?'

Bittan: 'We must be thankful he's not delirious any more. His servant says he was raving. He had a time holding him down.'

'The servant is a nitwit. What was he raving about?'

'He kept wanting to do *namaz*.'

'*Hari Om!*' in Mother's shocked whisper. 'Thank God the Calcutta specialist is here.'

I lay wrapped in a sheet soaked in iced water. A cloth fan above my bed, pulled back and forth by relays of invisible coolies, kept it cold. My painful eyes opened a crack but I couldn't see the speakers in the dim room. My mouth was dry with soda bicarb. I had the bitter after-taste of quinine on my tongue.

A voice I didn't know said later, 'If he has had venereal disease, he must be given iodide of potassium immediately.'

An irritable denial from Father.

The voice went relentlessly on. 'Sunstroke can be dangerous if the blood vessels of the brain have been affected by syphilis.

This could be sunstroke of the spine. I've known village youngsters to get it by running around naked in the summer sun.'

No comment from Father.

The Calcutta specialist prescribed cold-water injections, purgatives, ice-cold sheets and a dark room.

'When he recovers he won't be able to bear much sun exposure. We'll have to guard against after-effects, specially any permanent injury to the brain.'

'Surely not! Sunstroke is so common. There are hundreds of cases every year.'

'Of all sorts,' the doctor reminded him.

When I sat up, drained and dehydrated, days later, my servant broke the news. A mob of five or six hundred had made Hindu–Muslim war with knives, stones and broken bottles on the front lawn of the Female College. Someone set fire to one wing and the mob stampeded in to loot pots and pans and sewing machines with yells of '*Allahu Akbar*' and '*Ram Ram*'. Then they went on a rampage through the town, and the killed and raped count was rising in the hospital. I winced as he spread ointment on my blistered face. The fishmonger's son had his teeth shattered by a lance blow. Another Mussalman had his arm ripped off by an explosive. The Hindus picked it up and waved it like a flag. This morning it was still lying near the lawn's brick border. It sounded the most inventive religious riot in years, each side spurred on by unmistakable signs from heaven. My ass of a servant babbled on, filling my head with the rioters' cries. I shut him up but they returned, wheeling like mounted archers to attack again and again. My head bulged with them.

He sponged me and left the room. I heard the door click, then its echo. But a click has no echo. I got out of bed and tried the handle. He had locked me in. I lowered myself unsteadily to the floor to think this over. I counted the breakables – jug and basin on a wooden stand, light globes, a thermometer, vases, plates and glasses – and smashed them on the red and black mosaic floor. I used a coat-hanger to break the window panes. It was quite effective. The door was pulled open. In the commotion I saw Mother hurrying up the passage. A knot of men servants moved aside, averting their faces to let her pass, but she was oblivious of them. She came in. The debris made a crunching noise under her shoes. Her black eyes and the diamond in her nose glittered. She had a look of violent, voluptuous joy. Behind her Bittan bent to pick up a fragment of Japanese porcelain.

'This was your present from the Raja Sahib's great-uncle,' she cried.

Mother snatched it and dashed it down again, never taking those joyful snapping eyes from mine.

'Food!' she ordered. 'Good nourishing food. Can't you donkeys see he is well?'

She hadn't been so high-spirited since Father brought his third bride home. Father was glad to hear I was getting better but he had his own way of showing it.

'See to it he doesn't move out of the house. Strap him to the bedpost if you have to. Fifteen Hindus, ten Mussalmans and two policemen have been killed in the riot. I have no explanation for the Commissioner.'

'It is most serious, sir,' my tutor agreed.

'Don't talk like an owl's tail. It is a catastrophe. And at a time when we are backing the Mussalmans in their support for the Khilafat in Turkey. Raja Wali Khan is speechless. Next door to his estate my son abducts a Mussalman girl. I am covered with shame. My face is black before the Ottoman government. My nose is cut. My Mussalman tenants are yelling Islam is in danger, when but for my lascivious son, it is nothing of the kind.'

With the cousin whom he called elder brother he came straight to the point.

'What beast have I fathered? What monstrous appetite has he got that the lower half of well-known prostitute can't take decent care of? Don't think he hasn't had every opportunity for over a year now. Why did he have to abduct the inspector of school's wench for lewd purposes?'

Through the keyhole uncle looked morose.

'This is worse than abduction. This is no prank. I'm afraid our child may be one who needs a face.'

'Are you out of your mind?' Father shouted, quite forgetting he was the younger.

'Not merely a face, but a particular face.'

'My only son besotted with the sluttish daughter of a Mussalman school inspector?'

Their own grandfather had been a case in point, uncle reminded him, and had married the woman too, with the predictable disastrous consequences of marrying for love. But grandfather had at least taken a woman from his own community.

Father murmured dazedly, 'One woman and no other? Can the boy be quite sane?'

Uncle counselled looking ahead. Studies. A firm hand. Regular sex.

'The slut's father is disgraced,' said Father. 'He came begging me to get him transferred. I said I'd put in a word for him. It's not his fault, poor man. But wherever he goes, who's going to marry the slut now?'

I kicked the door open. Father mustered a gracious calm.

'Son!' he welcomed. 'You have been under a great strain, son.'

'I won't be kept locked up in the house.'

'Your uncle is here. Greet your uncle.'

Uncle stroked my head. They coaxed me into a chair.

'You are being kept at home for your own protection, until the riot fever settles down. Then you may go where you please. You aren't well yet. And you must understand, son, people have been killed as a result of your little escapade.'

'Is it my fault if wild men kill each other?'

'When men are aroused, they kill,' he soothed. 'It's only natural.'

They stood on either side of me, preventing escape, working their persuasive skills on me, yet making me feel I was responsible for the riot.

'You have work to catch up with, son.'

'Latin and Eskimos.'

'Never mind those. Spend your time with books till you're better. Your owl of a tutor says you like history.'

'If he likes history, there's his own.' This was uncle's inspiration. 'One should be proud of one's family, one's ancestry, of who one is.'

He prescribed family documents and other papers in the estate archives as therapy. He was sure there was a cupboardful right here in the house – or what the climate and white ants had left of them.

'Tell the tutor fellow to sort them out,' he said to Father. 'He doesn't spend all day coaching.'

Even if I took a look at family portraits all over the house, those framed swashbucklers whose jewels, turbans, swords, whose eyebrows, eyes, moustaches identified them as the Rajputs they were, I'd have the thrill of realizing who I was, every inch a Rajput myself.

I longed to be left to myself to decide my next move. I could have taken refuge in Mother's apartment, under the geese's uncritical gaze, where nothing would have been demanded of me except a length of leg to knead. But I was a misfit among the geese, no longer the right age or size to play with Mother's pale green bottles and jars, straddle her stomach and flatten her nose with kisses. Too large to butt one of her geese in the stomach. And Mother's apartment was almost as alien as the rest of the house. She didn't lose her temper any more. Her reviving wrath deserted her when she gave up the supernatural powers brigade. I stayed away unless she sent for me. By a strange piece of luck I happened to walk in uninvited one evening to hear Bittan say, 'He is a certifiable imbecile, I swear, but who else would marry a ruined girl? Here comes your son.'

In the tactful pause Bittan combed hairs out of Mother's silver hairbrushes, wound them ritually around her fingers and placed them in the waste-paper basket with her customary care. She and Mother exchanged a glance and Mother said, 'Go on.'

'About this imbecile? All I know is he's the only son of the cloth dealer whose shop is opposite the tailor who finds your things. There's nothing all that much wrong with him. These first cousin marriages among Muslims sometimes make their children turn out a little queer. The imbecile is soft in the head but he's harmless. His manliness is not affected. They say he is healthy enough to keep two wives busy. She'll be the second. She should consider herself lucky.'

I got up to leave the room almost as soon as I had sat down. They didn't coax me to stay.

I was still at home under supervision and I had no option but clan history. Unfortunately for my therapy it started off with an almighty thrashing for the clan, a Mongol victory over Prithviraj that made Mohammed Ghori master of Delhi in 1192. 'The Hindus became like atoms of dust scattered in all directions, and like a tale of old in the mouth of the people . . .' I read from Al Biruni's *Kitab-ul-Hind*. The scattered clans then spent the next few hundred years fighting their way back to crumbs of their inheritance. This elephant-trampled plain where we lived must have been clogged with arrow-pierced bodies while the Word of God made war on the Word of God. Endless war, for the Muslim hordes had been commanded to wage it until all men cried *'la ilaha illa 'llah'*. And all men never would. When it came to pointless hullabaloo jihad certainly took the cake. And the Hindus, instead of getting off their elephants on to something small and fast, kept getting a hiding.

My tutor tried to rescue the situation. There had been no surrender to the sword of Islam, he droned in obedience to his orders, though the conqueror came with the force of a roaring gale. Hasan Adib took Badaun. Aghul Bak took Oudh. And eclipsing them all came the terrifying exploits of Ikhtiyaruddin Mohammed bin Bakhtiyar Khilji . . . Unfortunately Spider could reduce the whole roaring gale of conquest to a bee-drone. Embattled ranees who rode war horses, defended citadels and destroyed themselves by fire to escape the conqueror's lust never got quite clear of his Adam's apple.

To me Spider's voice was a godsend. I could forget it and concentrate on the imbecile's murder. When he hesitated, my unblinking stare got him going again. In my mind's eye I saw crowds and confusion as its best setting. The Dussehra festival would be ideal. It was a lavish affair and this would be Father's first Dussehra after his third wedding. New relations and their minions would come. The procession had horsemen, swords-men, spearmen. Father in his finery led the train of elephants on his own painted, gorgeously caparisoned one, flinging coins to the people from his majestic swaying height. Drummers and dancers made way for him. After him came elephants carrying family members and estate officials. Then horses, camels and servants. Every child knew the route of the march. Some ran alongside the brass band setting off firecrackers from the house to the grain market outside the Shiva temple and back again.

Crowds there always were, but no confusion. I had never heard of an elephant getting out of line. It was unthinkable that one of these well-trained obedient creatures would let itself be led away by a stranger to lift a mammoth foot and crush a body in gunny-sacking to pulp under it. At Dussehra ten-foot-tall effigies of Rama and Ravan were brought to the exhibition ground, ready for burning. The townspeople assembled in the evening and Father lighted the torch. Surely the imbecile could be trapped in one of those effigies. Someone could take him sightseeing during the day, gag and truss him and cram him into the hollow of one of them. But who? I had no helper, I was under surveillance, and Dussehra was months away. I couldn't wait till October. It was true the time for haste was long past, and haste now would bungle it. This job had to be thoughtfully done, but I didn't want to waste a moment.

Mohammed Ghori's Indian possessions passed to Qutb-ud-din Aibak, first Indian ruler of Muslim India, and the scene shifted to Delhi. Spider's instructions were to stay close to Vijaygarh. He pulled out an old estate file. My family had a praiseworthy record, he intoned. Did I know Father had supported the Age of Consent Bill which had raised the marriage age for females to twelve years? Mother had been betrothed at five, but she hadn't come here as a bride until her thirteenth birthday. And during the past fifty years the disposal of female children had definitely been on the decline, Grandfather had reared three whole daughters. A less liberal family in those days would have – disposed of them – at birth. The cost of marriage was astronomical. No daughter of a Rajput could marry beneath her. The right grade bridegroom wasn't easy to find. One's nose couldn't be cut, or one's face blackened. So it was a hazard bringing up females. Regrettably one had to do away with half one's infant daughters. It was custom-ritual.

'High and low were driven to it,' Spider explained. 'Here in Vijaygarh the inspector of police in your grandfather's time was known to have dispatched his three daughters in the pious hope of being blessed with a son.'

Yet in spite of their allegiance to custom-ritual my own family had been broad-minded. My grandfather had attended the meeting in 1861 when *talukdars* had been asked to keep records of female births and deaths on their estates, so that no one could say hundreds of girl children had been carried away by wolves. But I was engrossed in the police inspector's daughters.

'You have a question?' Spider asked warily.

'How were these infants dispatched?'

More and more I liked this neat and tidy word. The imbecile needed to be dispatched with the same sorrowful ease as the police inspector's daughters. In a town where so many females had been so piously dispatched, why not one flawed male? Why should he present such a problem?

'These matters were left to the women,' Spider mumbled vaguely, but goaded, he remembered the command to keep me interested and occupied.

'One must understand it is a stunning shock to be told of a female birth. The police inspector was not a rich man. I know another family where the poor unfortunate lady kept giving birth to females. They were forced to dispatch all eight one after another.'

'How?' My tight smiling grip on myself troubled him.

He said hastily, 'There are records of strangling with the umbilical cord. Another popular method was a pill of bhang.'

Very safe and simple this was. The midwife put the pill on the infant's tongue and it slid down the throat like a sweetie, or she smeared the mother's nipple with it and the infant swallowed it with the first suck. However, if they buried the infant alive as some did, first they filled the hole up tenderly with milk.

I slumped in my chair. Spider, the fool, thought my apathy was disgust. Infant slaying was old sport. It was too late for squeamishness, but also much too late to strangle the imbecile with his umbilical cord or poison him at his mother's nipple, or bury him in a milky hole. It did start me wondering if the two girl children Mother had had before me had been stillborn after all, or lay buried in milky holes under ground I bicycled over every day. Frankly I did not trust Father. And would any guilt-free woman be so determined to turn herself into stone?

'See how your son has settled down,' Bittan fondly remarked to Mother. 'He goes about with the half-closed eyes of a saint.'

Wonderful how a study of the past, of ancestry, family, lineage, could give a young life a purpose, they said. I had discovered my duty. I knew who I was. Actually this was what I didn't know any more. Mother, I discovered, had been an identical twin. So devoted had they been, their parents couldn't risk parting them. Out of compassion they were both married to Father and as twin brides had refused to be separated. Then one of them had died. Which one, when, of what, the chronicle didn't say. Whoever wrote it, skipped the details. What do flies die of? A swat, most likely. And they don't have names.

I would have harried someone for an answer if anyone I knew had been in the habit of giving straight answers. But in Vijaygarh the spoken word ballooned, or was left suspended in a fug, neither hidden nor divulged. If I had cornered Father on his heavy butterfly trail one night, pressed him to the wall under an ancestor and hoarsely demanded the truth, he would have been shocked to the core, sent for a doctor, and had me nursed till I was well again. And then perhaps he didn't know himself which of two little girls, alike as two peas in a pod, one on either side of him, with him rollicking from side to side on the big bed like a weather vane tickled by a breeze, was the girl who died, and which was the girl birth-ravaged by me.

At last I got out of the house. The servants were told there was no harm in my prowling a little so long as I didn't go out when the sun was hottest. The day I reached the bazaar a dead buffalo lay at the traffic crossroads, where it must have baulked at its brickload and buckled. It must have lain there for days judging by the sunken tracks bullock carts had made around it. It was so long since I had felt unwatched I had to get my bearings. I rode my bicycle round and round in the wheel tracks. A flock of belled goats and one or two dirty white sheep trotted jingling past the animal's stiff hind legs. I swerved to avoid them and knocked against a man carrying stacked cages of hens hung on a bamboo pole across his shoulders. He staggered and the hens set up a tired friendless cackle of surprise. A cartload of squatting women went by. Their heads were bowed, their faces covered and they were monotoning some tale of woe. I rode through the bazaar and located the imbecile's father's shop as well as his house.

I followed him about between home and work. He had a distinctive gait I would have recognized in the dark. Imbecility had blurred and jumbled his movements. They were shapeless and uncoordinated. His limbs flopped. His head moved turtle fashion in its cavity. Compared with the bazaar average he was not deformed, but he gave the impression of being patched together, his vertebrae carelessly strung. I was certain his tongue lolled in his mouth instead of staying put behind his upper gum. He must have dribbled when he ate. His work in the shop consisted of taking bales of cloth from shelves lining the back wall and handing them to his father in a series of awkward balancing acts. One evening he climbed a ladder to slide a bolt of artificial silk from the top shelf, came down all right, but tripped on a bump in the floor matting. A customer waited patiently while the old shopkeeper helped the imbecile up, steadied him, and holding the foolish face between his hands, seemed to be breathing a breath of revival into it. Turning to the customer he said with fierce proud tenderness, 'A fine boy, this only son of mine, but Allah Most High in his wisdom . . .'

Nausea forced me to the gutter behind the shop. A monster sow rooting for garbage lifted her snout and waited placidly for me to finish retching. A low invisible moan, an eerie forewarning of sound, came from the heart of the bazaar. Then '*Allahu Akbar*' threaded nasally through vendors' calls, above the crack of tonga whips, never too far above the ground for men to hear. '*Allahu Akbar, La ilaha il-Allah, Mohammed-al-rasool Allah*' and on and on in shining wires on the air. I cling to the hem of, I grasp the handle of, I am girt with the sword of. Words I had heard times without number and could have chanted with the muezzin, an untaught inheritance I was surer of than I could be of who had given me birth.

That night Father had a music party. There is an abject streak in all of us. Father's was made of music. It alone could reduce him to tears, fill him with tearful exaltation. His temple and his brothel met in music. He was high priest, devotee, wet nurse and lover to musicians' hands, singers' throats, dancers' feet, and generous about keeping vocal chords, joints and tendons in prime condition with gifts of money, pepper, unguents and honey, though he wouldn't have known their owners if he met them in the street. They were hands, feet, voices. After dinner I joined his guests in the big room grandiloquently called the durbar hall. Near midnight a visiting artist gave us a long low ethereal note as introduction, slid up the sale and slipped into the most startling vocal arabesques I had ever heard. He sat as the other performers had, on a red carpet in front of the marble grille. A breeze came in from the rose garden. The moonlight and his voice made living white flowers of the marble lilies decorating the grille, and the tabla beat conjured silences as hypnotic as sound. Without warning his voice broke free of the known classical scale and soared into a passionate 'Ya la, ya la la, ya laley', a sublime invocation to deaf gods that flooded the hall and stunned me with its tragic beauty. I crept out of the room. Spider, at the carpet's edge with other estate retainers, saw me and got to his feet, yawning, thankful he could go to bed.

The imbecile's house was a fortress like every other house. It had a stout, scarred, permanently closed outer door. Here in these lanes a man had killed his wife because he had seen her through an open door. I judged this one to be six or seven inches thick, tough with age, on rusted iron hinges with an iron chain and latch. It was not howdah-high for an elephant to pass through, but too high for me to look over into the courtyard, even from the raised bank on the other side of the lane. But one day, as I knew I would, I found it swung outward on its hinges. A woman in a burka came out of an interior room into the courtyard, pulled her hood down in a swift reflex action, and hunched over a bucket under the tap. She lifted sodden clothes out in slow motion, twisted water out of them and pegged them to a rope. Which one was she, could she be mine? Mine was not this hump in deep dark black, bowing and bending mechanically over a bucket. Or had captivity so wearied her, she no longer looked up when a shaft of light came through an open door?

There was nobody in sight. I could have rescued her there and then if I had been sure it was my beloved and not the co-wife. But we had no future with the imbecile alive and it was dangerous to linger. The whole problem narrowed down to the courtyard and the lane, to something as workaday and easily available as a crowbar. And I was alert again, making practical plans.

# Chapter Seven

The conspiracy prisoners in Lahore jail have been on a hunger-strike since July. Our newspaper tells us they are being force-fed and putting up a gruesome resistance. They jerk their arms and legs, lie on their faces, bang their heads on the floor and against the iron grating on the door. When they were too ill to sit on chairs in court they were stretched on mattresses in the court-room, and when they couldn't attend court at all the government passed a Hunger-Strike Bill so that court proceedings could go on without them. One of them, Jatin Das, is resisting hypo-dermic injections too. They're protesting against the treatment they're getting in jail and court.

Comrade Dey says it is disgusting, the difference between Indians and whites. A European criminal is entitled to a ward like a bungalow, with fans and table lamps, a proper bathroom, milk, butter, meat and toast to eat, and suits and ties to wear. Our politicals get shirts with cut-off sleeves and pyjamas with cut-off legs, and food unfit to eat. He's all for the protest but a hunger-strike is worse torture than hanging.

'A tough warder throws you on your cot, sticks a rubber tube into your nostril and pours milk through it.'

It's the first I've heard that he served a fourteen-year sentence in the Andamans in his youth. He and the man in the next cell swallowed chillies to make their throats sore. When the tube was inserted it made them cough and had to be pulled out in case they suffocated and couldn't be tortured any more. It only worked for a day. After that they were closely watched and couldn't lay their hands on chillies again. Two men died that time, one on the ninety-second day, and one of torture during interrogation.

Bhaiji's reaction to these sombre facts is to say we must all go on a sympathetic fast. It will bring us public sympathy, too, and where will we be without public sympathy?

'Exactly where we are now,' retorts Comrade Iyer. 'And if we do support the Lahore prisoners, who's going to hear about it anyway?'

Iyer always sounds more injured about being in this jail than about being in jail. But I can see his point. No one in his senses would wear himself down to a shadow when he needs his wits about him. The comrades can't afford to go on an energy-sapping fast. They all agree there's no use if only the jailer knows they're fasting, because he won't care. Sen pipes up to say he can't stand the public. The public couldn't care less when a worker dies of malnutrition. As for him, he's not joining any fast. The whole idea stinks of self-denial and obscurantism. This starts Bhaiji and the comrades on one of their bickerings. They're off like snorting steam engines at the slightest provocation and it doesn't take much to provoke them. Bhaiji is a diminutive engine but quite a snorter.

One of the subjects they snort about is Gandhi. The comrades make him sound like a comma in the middle of a sentence which would read a hell of a lot faster without it. If he hadn't called off the last civil disobedience agitation just because it turned violent, his party would be in better shape today. But with the stab in the back he gave it, it is thoroughly demoralized, and Gandhi's influence is waning. And what else could you expect of a machiavellian Utopian? Most of all they clash over what free India will be like. The India of Bhaiji's dreams is a country of vegetarian capitalists and rural handicrafts. A few machines such as sewing machines, that won't corrupt the economy or the moral fibre, will be welcome. They'll make way for leisure but not too much of it. Silk, wool and cotton will be spun in cottages. Citizens will abstain from sex and turn the other cheek. Independence will be the dawn of an era washed clean of drink and lust.

In fact, Bhaiji expounds, man's reproductive fluid (as he calls it) will be saved up to regenerate his body and brain and, as yogis know, extend his life beyond the normal hundred years it should be by twenty-five more years. He will attain the Vedic lifespan. Who these days lives to even a hundred years? Bhaiji pokes his chin challengingly at us.

'Well? Do any of you know a hundred-year-old? There you are then! The precious fluid is being squandered.'

Civilizations have declined and disappeared because they frittered it away. Iyer tells Pillai independence might come sooner than we think, since he's pretty sure the bureaucrats have not been conserving their precious fluid.

The comrades' India is going to be forged out of steel, concrete and electricity, glorified by nuts and bolts. Men will make love to throbbing machine parts. Machines will shiver, groan and respond. The sun will be made of molten metal, the stars of iron and steel. Machine-tool grease and factory smoke will perfume the air. It seems entirely possible that men and women will turn into machines. To each his own paradise.

Even Comrade Yusuf, who claims to read poetry, is a machine addict. He sits Bhaiji down and reasons it out. A machine takes an hour and thirty-four minutes to manufacture a twelve-pound package of pins, while a man would take a hundred and forty hours and fifty-five minutes. But Bhaiji doesn't think it's all that important to produce pins in such a hurry, so Yusuf says all right, two hundred and thirty-four hours, twenty-six minutes to make a hundred pairs of shoes by machine; one thousand eight hundred and thirty-one hours, forty minutes by hand. Obviously the future depends on machines. One must control nature in the service of humanity. No answer from Bhaiji.

'How can you avoid the logic of it?' Yusuf demands.

'Oh, it is all very logical,' admits Bhaiji readily. 'What I am saying is, what *use* is it?'

The Lahore prisoners are in a bad way. Since August they've been locked in their cells, no fresh air, no outing. News of them is blacked out. The news we get is from Bhaiji's lawyer. The trial has become a *cause célèbre*. The prosecution's key witnesses have turned hostile and it looks like becoming a fiasco for the government, so a special tribunal has been set up to try these men. The government is also using mediators to try to persuade the hunger-strikers to eat, and Jatin Das to take medicine. But Das says he wishes to die. Why should you die, asks the mediator. For the sake of my country, replies Das, for the treatment and status of other political convicts. All this in a whisper because he's dying. And then he gets his wish. On the sixty-first day of his strike he dies, only nineteen, the same age as Sen.

We read of the public outcry, huge demonstrations, shop shutters down, protest hunger-strikes in other jails. And Bhaiji's lawyer smuggles in clippings from other newspapers. He's not exaggerating. It seems there's a mood of national mourning. On September 14, 1929 Motilal Nehru moved a motion censuring the government in the Central Legislature.

> Sir, the charge is that the government stood still while human life was ebbing away . . . When there was time for government to realize that these devoted, high-souled men, however long they may have been hunger-striking, would not surrender their principles, what did the government do to save their lives?

Amar Nath Dutt said:

> Sir, I rise to offer my tribute of tears to the memory of the great departed . . . Sir, I charge government with the murder of Jatindranath Das who laid down his life to vindicate the elementary rights of political prisoners in India.

There are more. We pass them around. My companions are grim and subdued. The night after Das's death I woke from a disturbed sleep to hear some of them talking while the others slept and then changing places in their joint vigil for the dead youth. We are all troubled that the Lahore trial has been dispensed with and the accused when sent for at all, are brought in handcuffs.

'Good God, suppose that happens to us?' I ask Vacha when he arrives with his own information confirming all we've heard.

He brushes aside my anxiety. 'It won't happen to you. Two of those men threw smoke bombs into the Central Assembly.'

'Was anybody killed?'

'No, they were smoke bombs. But one of the men is accused of shooting the British policeman who beat up Lajpat Rai. Unfortunately, as you know, Lajpat Rai died of his injuries.'

'And what are the others supposed to have done?'

'Now, there's no reason to panic. We have to see it from the law and order angle. There is no comparison between that case and this case. And if the worst comes to the worst, remember you are in a special category.'

Bhaiji reopens the question of a protest fast. This time there's no argument, but the comrades get into a huddle at their end of the barrack to discuss it. Before lights-out Iyer announces their decision. They are prepared to go on a fast provided it is called a hunger-strike. They don't want the issue confused with puritanical twaddle. My remark, that I will get just as hungry whether I go on a fast or a hunger-strike, is coldly received by all eight. I have never seen them so united. With all eyes on me I haven't a hope of refusing. I'm not sure it would be wise to refuse. One never knows how a conspiracy trial may go. The way this one is stretching out, I may need a reprieve as badly as any of them, never mind Vacha. I can't be the only one to forfeit public sympathy, always supposing the public hears about us. But my companions are determined the public shall hear.

Bhaiji sends for his lawyer and briefs him, and I've never seen a lawyer look so thrilled. The project fills him with ghoulish satisfaction. He says he understands the issue perfectly and will draft a statement for the press the minute he gets to his office. Two days later we read it. In solidarity with other political prisoners, it informs us, and in memory of the martyr who gave his life in jail, we, too, are prepared to make the ultimate sacrifice for our sacred motherland. It is too late to back out of the rendez-vous with suicide he's landed us with, and the comrades launch their hunger-strike in a rage. I feel extremely nervous myself. On the other hand Bhaiji and the twins already have a sacrificial glow about them.

The rest of us are in a foul temper and giddy with hunger when we return from court the first evening. We are forbidden exercise in the yard, our newspaper has been stopped, and we have absolutely nothing to do. Comrade Pillai says reasonably enough it's silly to take it out on each other when the fault is that nincompoop lawyer's. He suggests we form a circle and play a game. He has it from a slimming expert that concentrating on food works on the subconscious to substitute for food and stave off hunger pangs, so let's take turns describing the most memorable meal we've ever eaten.

'We'll proceed clockwise, shall we?' He points to Bhaiji.

'Cornflakes,' says Bhaiji.

We wait, but this is it. Bhaiji has found this English foodstuff most unusual, chiefly because it is completely tasteless. Most food has taste.

Dey, the force-fed comrade, comes next, and I learn he is well-travelled. He says he's going to tell us about a meal he ate on his visit to Moscow two years ago. He made a tour of restaurants among other places, and is pleased to report that the famous Yar, where the bourgeoisie used to blow up fortunes on drunken gypsy entertainments, has been converted into a motorcycle garage. He came across several restaurants that have been turned into old people's homes and young people's communal parlours. Finally he discovered a restaurant that was still a restaurant. Here he had crayfish soup, salmon à la monastery, cauliflower à la Polonnaise, lamb-filled *pirozhki*, boiled potatoes, sour-cream pancakes, butter, cheese, tea and a bottle of wine. The menu glides off his tongue with the fluency of hours of mental practice. His face is alight with memory. We are all too desperate to utter, except Bhaiji who beams as he waits for the game to continue and is disappointed it has ended so soon.

Comrade Dey offers to relieve the gloom by enlightening us about the non-culinary aspects of his Moscow trip. We listen – there's nothing else to do – but the various celebrations in honour of the Revolution's tenth anniversary leave our stomachs growling. Only Sen responds with pleasure. He's still at the stage where a story is as good as food. The dullest driest facts delight this boy. I am certain it wouldn't have made me leap up and slap my thigh if at nineteen I had been told the west had boycotted the tenth anniversary, but fraternal delegations from Persia, Turkey, Afghanistan and Mongolia had hailed it. Sen is such an ideal audience that Dey goes on to tell him the story of a film he saw about mutiny in the Tsar's Black Sea fleet. Sen is enthralled. The ratings' revolt, their enthusiastic reception at the port, the spectacle of Cossacks pouring down the great flight of steps and firing volleys into crowds of people who scatter and flee, keep him engrossed after the rest of us have gone to bed. I'm so hungry, I'm the only one who hears the happy ending. The Tsar's ships sail by with sailors waving from the rigging, a sign that they have joined the Revolution.

By the third day of our hunger-strike we aren't talking to each other. We could be two rows of newly caught fish gaping at each other all the way to court and back in the lorry, and eight cooked fish laid out on our cots on our return. Bhaiji, compared with the rest of us, is cheerful if not spry. He slyly admits he's used to fasting once a week and eating lightly the rest of the week. On his tours to convert the population to khaddar and sexual abstinence, he's used to getting by for days on a handful of peanuts, so he hasn't felt the strain. Comrade Iyer glares at him and controls his wrath with an effort.

'At least when Gandhi goes on a fast he doesn't trick his associates into going to death's door with him,' he says curtly.

On the fourth day we have no more sense of solidarity left than famine victims. There's no such thing as a communal yawning chasm, and Bhaiji does not win the comrades' hearts by pointing out we are now one with the hungry peasants. The twins slump against a wall when they are not lying limp on their cots, content to be led to the last gasp and too far gone to raise an eyelid. The hairy twin manages to raise his, nudges dumpy, and asks him to watch him cantilever his right arm up listlessly a few inches and let it drop again – to demonstrate, I suppose, how feeble he has become. We have suspended our food orders but tin plates of gritty jail mishmash keep arriving at mealtimes. Nothing would prevent me from swallowing the mess if the other eight weren't there. I've made up my mind to do so if the jailer decides to force-feed us. He has been round to say the government doesn't want us to think it can't discriminate between respectable middle-class people and ordinary low-class persons. If there's any lack in our lives we should tell him, and our social position will be taken into consideration. He's met with silence and goes away.

I try concentrating on the hollow of my throat. I try thinking of Sylla instead of food but a smoked haunch of lamb intervenes. My Afghan host plucks out its eyes and offers me, his guest of honour, this delicacy for a starter. Before I fall asleep I train my mind sternly on Sylla.

Being a Parsee she wears frocks, swims in a bathing costume, and has bobbed hair, all of which account for the informality between us from the start and the ease with which we became friends. Outside of foreign parts, Sylla's Bombay was the most foreign city I had seen. It had trams and a few taxis. Half the people in it were English and the Indians might as well have been. I had never seen so many short-haired, dog-owning women. They gave their dogs names like Bonzo and Mr St Clair, and said 'Woopsie-daisy' when they spilled ice-cream on their blouses. Their saris were made of English crêpe and French chiffon, and I heard about ice blue and tango orange for the first time. Sylla had a chic older friend, a leader of fashion who smoked through a foot-long holder, wore tango orange saris whipped twice around her tightly instead of once loosely, and looked like a better brand of cigar. She had that brown wizened look, too, from sunning, which I thought rather a shame as I liked her, till I heard it was dreadfully smart.

When Sylla wore a sari at all, she wore a transparent wisp of a blouse with it that would have scandalized Vijaygarh. I often begged her to do just that. I longed to toss her like a lacy hand grenade into the centre of the bazaar and enjoy the consternation, or set her down among Mother's geese and watch them flap and squawk in amazement while bare expanses of Sylla's skin turned faintly delectably green. But Sylla was too clever to set foot outside Bombay. When she travelled it was west. Her refusal to come to Vijaygarh was not why we didn't marry. I think she understood as soon as she met me that I was a man just off an operating table and the anaesthetic hadn't worn off. When it did, she didn't like what she saw. It upset her. She wanted to know, 'What are you thinking?', a question a man never asks. But we were happy going to tea dances and the races, and she introduced me to the editor of a magazine with a minute circulation, who published some of my poems. She was keener on dramatics herself and her tableaux were well received. She composed one for a party at her grandmother's house. It was a scene out of Sarojini Naidu's rhyming poems. This was about a flute-player. It went:

> I pray you singing girls refrain
> From music and be mute,
> O laughing Flute-player restrain
> The rapture of your lute . . .

And so forth. An obvious reference to Lord Krishna and his adoring milkmaids dancing to the Divine Orchestra. But Sylla jazzed it up and made it contemporary. I don't know how an Italianate temple as a backdrop was supposed to help. I was the Laughing Flute-player and had to keep my mouth open in a laugh while six shingled barefoot girls in clouds of tulle balanced Grecian urns (on loan from someone who collected urns) on their hips and gave me the glad eye. Sylla's ivory figurine of a grandmother sat in the front row. Her sari had a French fleur-de-lis design. She wore pink pearls, a broad silk headband and chandelier ear-rings. The chain of her Austrian *petit-point* evening bag kept slipping off her wrist and being put back on it which distracted me terribly from my laugh. She had been educated in France.

After the tableau, when I had rearranged my jaw, Sylla introduced me all over again and her grandmother studied me through her lorgnette and enquired how His Highness my father was.

'I told you Jumbo's father is not a highness, Grandmother.'

'You told me he is the Raja of Vijaygarh,' said my hostess firmly.

She hooked her *petit-point* bag on to her wrist, led me into the dining room and put me on her right. Grandmother asked. I answered. I had the distinct impression I must speak when spoken to, and not natter randomly. At the end of the meal I cautiously broke the rule. I asked her the name of the Parsee confection we had been served for dessert. She lorgnetted me for a split second and said it was, in fact, caramel Pavlova, but it had been discerning of me to perceive a difference. Her cook, an accomplished pudding-and-pastry chef, had authored crushed cardamom in place of a European essence, and had transformed the dish at one stroke. I complimented her on her cook. She measured my worth through her lorgnette again and gave me a little smile. Grandmother had standards. She knew when appreciation was genuine.

After dinner Sylla told me her grandmother thought I had Rudolf Valentino's profile, but what she completely adored about me was my *politesse*. It was important for anyone in Sylla's intimate following to be adored by her grandmother. This imperious ninety-five-pound lady had supervised Sylla's upbringing and educated her abroad. Her parents, having done their job by producing her, had been bypassed as soon as Sylla was weaned so that no time would be lost in making her her grandmother's child. Nobody owned Sylla but her grandmother came closer to it than anyone else. Sylla had parents who were content to be nice and rich. Her mother was a roly-poly twitterer who played mah-jong. Her father went to the Ripon Club every Wednesday in his high Parsee hat to eat the Wednesday speciality, mouthwatering *dhansak*. Every Tuesday he played bridge. They welcomed you to their home and let well alone. There was nothing to distinguish them from other nice rich people. Grandmother was grand, partly because she firmly believed she was. She had an eye for celebrity and a nose for finance.

Sylla's house was down the road, walking distance from her grandmother's, but that night she was all dolled up in a scanty sari and high heels, so I offered to drive her home.

'I've got to feed Crème Brûlée first. She's ill.'

I had not yet had the privilege of meeting Grandmother's golden retriever but I knew her floor cleaner walked and fed the other dogs.

'I'm the only, only one who can feed her, Jumbo.'

Sylla has to be taken very seriously when she repeats a word in a sentence. Otherwise she despises repetition. I went with her. Crème Brûlée's inert hulk lay across the satin bedspread in the guest room. A dreadful smell came from Crème Brûlée. She was a wreck of a retriever, apparently on her last legs, the front ones. Her hind legs were paralysed. Her tail was dead. Her dinner

77

bowl of bread and broth steamed its own knockout odours from a corner of the room. Sylla got down on her knees, put her face close to the ancient bitch and spoke to her in a whinnying soprano. Overpowered by the reek of Crème Brûlée and the fumes of dog dinner, I thought the squeak was ventriloquism, but it was issuing from Sylla's own mouth.

'How's the boofle nittle baby girl, Sylla's own pore ta-hiny darlint?'

The strange dithering squeak pulled what remained of Crème Brûlée's consciousness from caverns of comatose sleep. She unglued an eye. It had a permanent static pool of tears she could neither roll out nor blink back.

'Is the poochie-pie ever so hungry then? Come!' shrilled Sylla, seizing the stinking hulk's shoulders and hauling her forward to the edge of the bed.

'Now then, Jumbo,' panted Sylla in her lively normal tone, 'you catch her front paws. I'll lift her from behind.'

The paw padding felt hot and dry, the hair around it scraggy, and I could have sworn Crème Brûlée hadn't had a bath since she was young, Sylla coaxed and heaved. It took all her strength and a piece of her sari to lower the retriever's behind to the violet roses and golden deer of Grandmother's carpet. From here she took over, inching the rigid hulk forward, front, hind, front, hind alternately like a stalled centipede, off the carpet to the dinner bowl, where with shrieks of encouragement she fed bread and slop sideways into the clamped antique jaws. The bitch had then to be centipeded to the garden to do her nittle wee-wee before beddie-byes, but this part of the operation was entrusted to the dog servant. And this went on every day.

'You've been such a help,' said Sylla in the car. 'Crème Brûlée is quite ill.'

Only my newfound friendship with Sylla prevented me from saying Crème Brûlée was not ill, she was in rigor mortis.

'You should have seen her when Grandmother first got her, Jumbo. She was a dark honey colour with the most aristocratic expression you ever saw, and so lean and long she was like a lovely leaping gazelle.'

I failed miserably to visualize Crème Brûlée in her gazelle incarnation.

'She can't move,' I said guardedly. 'She can't see. Wouldn't it be a good idea to have her put down?'

Sylla was shocked. 'Didn't you see her open one eye at the sound of my voice? No matter how ill one is, Jumbo, one doesn't want to die.'

'Poor old Crème Brûlée doesn't want to live, Sylla. She's half dead already.'

'That is an unpardonable thing to say. Thank you for the lift. Goodnight.'

Sylla's kindness was categorical. I couldn't make a dent in it. It was the only issue she wasn't willing to compromise on. She was the most intelligent person I knew, but I hadn't counted on her being quite so kind. She had strict views about killing. It filled her with unspeakable sorrow and anger. Except for war, which was war and had a background, causes, heroes, etc.

'Don't make excuses by harping on war. It's different,' she once told me because I did, I confess, worry the subject. Killing had the rare fascination of being both classic and contemporary. The best and the worst people did it. It never went out of style. A clean sweep of how many had Herod's pogrom resulted in, though the one he wanted got away? No wonder Jesus ended on the cross. You couldn't live much past thirty knowing you had triggered a pogrom.

'You're proving my point,' said Sylla.

But Lord Krishna, I reminded her, had triggered one too, and he had lived to a hundred and twenty-five, nourished on amorous adventures, butter and curd.

'All I'm saying is there can be two views about killing.'

'No there can't,' said Sylla.

I drift into sleep composing a letter to Sylla. 'Sylla, dearest girl, my lawyer must have told you it's going to be a long trial . . .'

Bhaiji is showing signs of fatigue and failing stamina but it doesn't keep him from his disciplined schedule of spinning, reading, talking and not-talking at their assigned hours. His timetable has the advantage of giving him something to look forward to every second of the day, even if all he's looking forward to is not-talking. The Congress lawyer shows up on the fifth day at Bhaiji's non-talking time and is brought to the barrack so that the nine of us don't get prison publicity parading to the superintendent's office. The twins who can talk if they try, don't dream of doing so. Starvation has collapsed what remains of their identities. The comrades are livid with the lawyer for misrepresenting them, and are determined not to say a single word he can distort again. That leaves me, but his gaga reverence is so off-putting that I'm damned if I'm going to pander to it. Nothing daunted, he sighs at each of us in turn, shakes his head, and begging my pardon (as I am nearest) he puts his fingers on my pulse and catches his breath in excited alarm. He promises to draft another statement for the press praising our indomitable courage in the face of approaching death. Comrade Iyer's eyes flash.

'The wretch's reputation now depends on finding us dead next time he looks in,' he says when the wretch has departed.

Bhaiji signals the twins for a piece of paper and writes down some advice. We are to breathe slowly. The slower one breathes, the longer one lives. He demonstrates a very long, very slow breath.

'And if it gets so slow that it stops, one lives to a ripe old age,' says Comrade Dey scathingly.

Bhaiji is delighted. He writes that Dey has grasped the secret. When Sen's turn comes to read this, he is incredulous. He can't believe anyone that old can be that daft. If we're in possession of all these secret formulas, like this one and the precious fluid, how come we don't share them like science? Bhaiji gives him a scornful glance and writes, 'Why tell it and be burned at the stake? If you have a secret, keep it, I say.'

On the sixth day the lawyer is with us again, so downcast that we expect more bad news from Lahore. But he's brought a message from the All India Congress Committee. It's an appeal to all political prisoners to end their hunger-strikes on the understanding that the AICC will spearhead the campaign for jail reform on their behalf. Bhaiji listens impassively to these tidings and harasses the lawyer with questions to satisfy himself about the integrity of the offer, as if we had all the time in the world before we passed out. He nods at the replies. Then instead of getting on with it and accepting the offer, he sinks into a two-minute silence to consult his conscience. The tension is awful. He surfaces, lifts his eyebrows at Comrade Iyer who with admirable restraint lifts his own at his comrades before nodding a wan assent. While the lawyer cools his heels Bhaiji signals us with a weak forefinger. We limp into the centre of the barrack to pass a resolution that we are breaking our hunger-strike in response to the AICC's patriotic appeal. This done, we crawl to our cots, hoping we'll last out until the next meal. The lawyer who must have been hoping for a fast-breaking ceremony with a candid shot of him holding a teaspoon of orange juice to Bhaiji's lips appearing in the local press, takes his crestfallen leave of his breathing clients.

We're let into the yard for exercise again and Sen soon starts sprinting with maniacal energy to make up for the past cooped-up week. I've been meaning to ask him about his nightmare since we've been forced to share it with him. When he stops for a rest I enquire what the great escape is from.

'My father and mother.'

This marathon by rail, this huddling and hiding and forgoing bananas along the way is an escape from a chubby bald-headed clerk in a government office – this is how Sen describes him – who wants him to be a clerk in the same government office, and a doting mother who is scouring Calcutta for a bride for him.

'What are you laughing at?' he scowls. 'It's no joke.'

'I thought you'd committed murder.'

He shudders and vows he will if they make a married clerk of him.

'Why are you here then?' An idiot's question by now.

Sen says he got politicized while he was doing his BA. He joined a youth group that met in a big airy house with pictures of Bakunin and Kropotkin on the walls, to have discussions and sing songs. The police had raided the house, arrested them all, parcelled them out to different jails, and taken away the pictures as evidence. He knows much more than I do about current events. The last subject they discussed before the raid was the

Kellogg–Briand Pact, signed in Paris. There have been so many pacts, treaties, conferences and wars since the War – and now there's a League – that I've lost track of them. This pact, says Sen, is an agreement not to go to war to settle disputes, but the British have said it's not to count as war if it's connected with their empire. He treats British statecraft to a gust of amusement.

'The British would capture the whole Middle East if it were not for Kemal Pasha and the Bolsheviks. Like they tell us the Afghans are savages 'who will plunder and loot us if they go away.'

But I'm more interested in the nightmare.

'So you weren't arrested on the train?' I ask.

'What train? The train is in my nightmare. I tell you I was arrested under Kropotkin's picture, singing a song.'

He sings it:

> It is the final conflict,
> Let each stand in his place
> The International Party
> Shall be the human race.

Sen has a beautiful voice. It has a heart-rending lilt. The jailer leans against the stoutest pole of my toilet enclosure, closes his eyes, and with an aggressive wag of his head, cries *'Wah!'* If such is Sen's transporting lilt when the words are English, he says, replacing his fez, where would it not arrive in our own Hindustani, or even Sen's Bengali? He suggests concerts.

I realize I am being rather slow-witted but I want to get this straight. After his encore I ask Sen, 'So why do you go on having the nightmare?'

'Because the day I get out of here they will make me a married clerk.'

Is this the time to be married, or a clerk, he demands? The American stock market has collapsed, capitalism is doomed, and life is about to begin. He's as jubilant as a boy scout who has struck flint to make a fire in the wilderness and stands back in rapture to watch the blaze.

So we get into a phase of singing and story-telling. Sen sings and Dey, normally aloof and taciturn, becomes chief story-teller.

*The Battleship Potemkin* has whetted Sen's appetite. But now Dey's tales have the beat of a muffled drum. They begin, 'Once upon a time there was a young revolutionary'. His revolutionaries are born in Midnapur, Bengal, in and around the same small hamlet near a railway station. There is something in this soil that breeds them. They have a thirst for higher education and for freedom. They have sworn to rid their motherland of the British lion while they still lisp, as the Carthaginian general Hamilcar made his son pledge eternal enmity to the Romans. In Midnapur the British lion is the District Magistrate. In these tales he is shot, the revolutionary mounts the gallows with '*Bande Mataram*' on his lips, and another takes his place. Criminals, forgers, drunkards and pimps are procured to bear witness against these patriots, for no decent man will. They are tortured, their families are hounded, but the gospel spreads and the dying declaration of a Punjabi martyr becomes its testament: 'May I return of the same mother, may I re-die of the same cause, till the cause is successful.' Dey's drum beats in my head long after his story finishes, but Sen falls asleep like a milk-glutted infant at his mother's breast, serene as he dreams of the milk and honey of revolution instead of the nightmare of marriage and clerkdom.

'I'm telling you about them,' I hear Dey say to Sen late in the night, 'so that when you are old, and the struggle is won, and a few survivors are hogging the glory, you will remember the ones who went to their death but never went down in the annals.'

Tonight the tale is Garibaldi's. Dey, it appears, stores knowledge in every crevice of his formidable brain. Fourteen years in the Andamans gave him time to memorize chunks of culture in English, German and Russian, besides his native Bengali and a garbled Hindi in which he remorselessly mixes genders. Thanks to my freak forebear who collected books I, too, am familiar with the words of Garibaldi's hymn:

> That their dust
>    may rebuild her a nation,
> That their souls may
>    relight her a star . . .

# Chapter Eight

This time round the prosecution witnesses' stories don't sound so hair-raising. We know what's coming, and it keeps coming through the winter, with some new embellishments. This room is big and draughty. The gravel outside where the judge's and lawyers' chauffeurs squat to smoke and play cards is sunny and warm. The sun glances off the judge's Rolls Royce. Sen sits next to me at the end of our row. He has his shoulder to the wall and his cheek propped on his knuckles. He is as oblivious of the tear trailing down his cheek as we are in sleep, and only when we wake do our sticky, salt-crusted eye rims tell us we've been crying. A snuffling slumber has overtaken one of the twins at the other end of the row. He has no wall support and his head in its wool scarf nods and jerks. The comrades want to be in court every day regardless of the agenda, so we all attend every day. Solidarity. Vacha says I needn't be here at all but the empty barrack would be worse than court and my credit with the jailer has dwindled since I hunger-struck with the others. His enquiries after my health and comfort are noticeably less gracious. In court the voices in my head have courtroom voices to dilute them. The trumpets and drums of welcome for Father's third bride are less raucous, the electric lighting less lurid.

It was a long time since I had been to Mother's apartment. Not since I heard about the imbecile's impending marriage.

'Where have you been?' Bittan upbraided me out of Mother's

hearing. 'Why haven't you been to see her all these weeks? Too fond of your studies to remember your mother?'

She didn't know what to do about Mother. Nor did I. None of us knew how to cope with her silent stationary grief. I would rather have seen her gin-drunk or dancing herself into collapse. The geese stood frescoed against her bedroom walls. Mother saw me and gave a loud cry. She threw her arms around my neck and wept stormily. The geese stirred and returned to their tidying and I braced myself to let Mother cry herself out. My chin rested on top of her head, her tears soaked my muslin *kurta* and her breasts felt warm and comfortable against me. I was holding an adult woman in my arms. I never had before. Her hair had come down and when her shivering sobs subsided I wiped her eyes with a thick strand of it. We sat down together on the bed.

'You must go to the Commissioner for me, son.'

A goose who should have known better, blurted, 'The second household is also sending a message.'

Mother's wet lashes drooped in contemptuous dismissal.

'The letter will go from me,' she said. 'She can join my request if she wants to. It makes no difference whether she does or doesn't, the unfortunate woman has no son's future to protect. If she was going to have one, wouldn't he have been here by now? It's this latest marriage that may produce one.'

Her red eyes were on mine. Black chaotic hair tumbled over her breasts. There was a wild unearthly beauty about her, but she had control of her features.

'I must be certain the title comes to you.'

'But Mother, there's no title yet.'

'There will be. Haven't we moved heaven and earth for it?' She sounded bruised and bitter. 'When your father gets the title, the Commissioner can use his influence to make it hereditary if he wants to. If he doesn't do this for us, what's the use of anything?' And she was near breaking point again.

Her sycophants murmured their submissive approval, happy to be making a contribution again. I asked for a writing pad and drafted some kind of a letter for Mother. But the Commissioner was not in Vijaygarh. No one knew how long he had been away. A substitute was officiating. Father had been married ten months when the Commissioner got back from, some said, a long leave extended by illness, and I finally found myself on his veranda with the letter. Mother had sent me in her carriage. It was the only way I could leave the house on a confidential mission without the household knowing.

Father's *taluk* was the divisional headquarters. The Commissioner's house had two sets of wrought-iron gates, for entry and exit, and several acres of wooded compound with tennis courts at the back and a sort of pavilion to one side where the *hoi polloi* waited early mornings with their requests. The veranda was for dignitaries. Mother's coachman took her brougham into the shade and settled down for his afternoon nap while I sat out my obligatory wait on the machan as the famous veranda was known, where the gentlemen bearers of appeals and offerings dozed, woke and slept again until the beast in the shape of the peon on duty appeared in the clearing, to say the Commissioner was ready to receive. There was no one but me today.

Since I had first heard of the Commissioner, who hunted with Father and his cronies, vetted lists of candidates for rajahood, and was chief guest at their parties when he wasn't keeping them fuming or snoring on his veranda, he had been three different men. The one who received me didn't look elderly enough to be as furrowed and desiccated as he was. His eyes had a deep brooding absorption when he raised them from the diagram of swirling spirals, loops and curlicues on his desk. Reluctantly he put his pen down.

'Ah, it's you,' he said in Anglo-Saxon surprise.

He knew it was me. My name had gone in to him half an hour ago.

'You're – what – seventeen now?'

'Eighteen.'

'And turned over a new leaf. Working hard at your books, your father tells me.'

I wished he had been like the commissioners I had heard described, the commissioner with the bedside manner, or the sporty one who had waded into the crocodile-infested bend in our river in a sola topi, with an umbrella in one hand and a gun in the other, or any commissioner but this bloodless one. I said I had a letter from Mother and wanted to take home a reply. This gave him a real surprise. He broke the seal and unfolded the letter. My glance went from the bookshelves lining one wall to the wall behind him. It blossomed with guns, daggers and sabres glossy with wood and steel polish. The small silver tray on his desk had the same high sparkle. It was indented for pens and had two square-shaped glass inkstands with silver lids, one containing royal blue, the other bright green ink. An assortment of paper knives lay in a neat row beside it. His peon came in with a message. The Commissioner went to the back of the room with him, climbed a step ladder and ran his finger along the two top shelves until he found the title he wanted. He took the book out, gave it to the peon and came back to Mother's letter. The top of another letter showed under his curlicue diagram. It was upside down but easy to read in his broad-nibbed, bright green handwriting: 'for the devoted care, and the perfectly marvellous rest in your home afterwards. Kindest regards from Marjorie and myself to every member of the staff. And once again our grateful thanks. Yours, Gilbert.'

He finished reading Mother's letter.

'I'm sorry your mother is so distressed. She sounds quite distressed, doesn't she? I don't really see how I can help her. I gather you know what this is all about. The title would ordinarily pass to you, except that at the moment there's no title, is there?' His pale lips extended in a smile. 'Your father has, of course, made a splendid contribution to the war effort in men and money. Should he be rewarded for his services, and should the title be made hereditary, there's no problem, is there?'

As I couldn't think of answers to his queries, he took pains to point out again how hypothetical the case was, did I see what he meant? *If* there was a title, and *if* it was made hereditary, I would presumably succeed to it. If I *didn't* – for some entirely unforeseeable reason – only *then* would Father's third wife's son, *if* she had a son, be the next raja. *But*, if I carried on as I was doing, working hard at my books and keeping out of trouble, well my mother had nothing to worry about, did she? Well, then! Did I think I could explain all that to my mother? He brought his white-knuckled hands together in a clasp of dismissal and smiled his wintry smile.

After this curiously Vijaygarh conversation about a non-existent title coming to me (if I was good) and not to a half-brother who might never be born, considering Father's feeble sperm, I got into Mother's curtained brougham to make the journey home. The sultry heat and the horses' steady trot put me in a narcotic daze. I felt entombed. I shifted uneasily on the seat but I couldn't escape its slippery buttoned surface or the thick dark smell of enclosed leather. I saw what Mother saw of Vijaygarh through the eye-width panel between the curtains. I pulled them apart, leaned out and ordered the coachman to drive me to the bazaar, expecting he had instructions to take me straight home and would ignore mine. But he blandly reversed direction. Twenty minutes later he put me down at the traffic crossroads where the dead buffalo had blocked traffic for days. I told him to go and have his tea while I shopped for ping-pong balls.

I can see myself now, racing to the high door in a wonderfully elated mood. There are days when anything can happen. Did I expect the door to swing open of its own accord to admit me? Or would she unlatch it to go on a veiled errand, and come flying out to me instead? I don't know what I expected this day, but as a precaution I moved further down the stony ground to wait where the building's scabrous yellow outer wall ended. The door opened. It was the imbecile who came out. He stepped backwards over the wooden ledge with ungainly care, sneezed up a hurricane, lost his footing and reached for the doorframe with both hands. Swivelled his head, saw me, his face a pure puzzle. He let go of his support and sketched a wavering, querying salaam. My head, my neck, and most of all my legs were soldered to the ground. I couldn't move a muscle. It was he whose eyes lit up, he who came bounding and tongue-lolling toward me like a dog to its master. Kept coming, would have scraped my chest with his floundering paws if I had not pushed him away in violent revulsion. He stumbled and fell in a big soft heap. I remembered I had to buy ping-pong balls. I ran all the way to the shop, bought them and went home. There I sent for Spider to play a game of ping-pong with me. He was nowhere to be found. He blew in, flustered and apologetic, his usual demented self. I really made him run for the ball. His game was worse than usual. He stabbed empty air, rose and fell like a wounded bird. He would never learn ping-pong. When I'd hammered him I let him go. His diary had slipped out of his satchel and I turned the pages, curious about his private affairs, and what sort of women haunted his spidery dreams. Spidery writing, close together, but one page was readable:

She is stout, short and thick-set. Her body is clothed in delicate hairs. Her colour is brownish yellow with black stripes on her thorax and abdomen.

Wrought up as I was over the day's doings, I got hysterical over it. There were two more entries below:

She is half an inch in length, black tinged with green. Her bare body is granular, and prettily ornamented with a pattern of spots.

A body of bronze with a green diamond patch on its lower back.

When he came back for it I was rolling with laughter, flinging it about. He lunged to rescue it but I hurled it up and caught it. We had a five-minute game and it was in sorry shape when I got bored and tossed it to him, then went to Mother with the Commissioner's verbal reply.

Mother took it stoically but it was a mortal blow to her. After that she cared little what went on around her. I don't believe she would have known the war across the seas had ended if its official end had not been so mystically tolled on the eleventh hour of the eleventh day of the eleventh month, as if the allied governments had consulted the stars when to stop fighting.

I am called to the jail superintendent's office on a February evening. Vacha gets up as usual to shake my hand. He looks disturbed.

'I guessed they would try to make you sound irresponsible. It's what they do, attack a man's character when they can't get him any other way. You don't fit into their categories and they have no evidence against you. But this is worse than I anticipated. If they go on like this they'll have the judge believing you are violent and unstable, if not insane. I've never heard such wild allegations.'

It has been warmer in the courtroom, warm enough for flies.

I sleep so badly at night that I've been too sleepy in court to pay close attention. I ask him what he means.

'Did you, in fact, assault anyone?'

Inanimate objects – doors, windows, china – plenty of that. I'm a person who kicks a drawer he can't open. Many of us do, in temper. My personal servant is a fool, a typical nitwit. I frequently box his ears. Vacha gently brings me round to the day's proceedings. I explain I punched the imbecile without intending to. There had been no quarrel. It just happened spontaneously. One of those powerful instinctive revulsions.

'But this man died of it later?'

I had never thought of the imbecile as a man, but it's true he died later. Vacha's gaze flickers over my physique and rests on my hands. I can almost hear him thinking they are a respectable size and shape, but hardly lethal weapons.

'Where did you punch him?'

'How do I know? I just hit out. It must have got him in the liver.'

He looks grave. 'It must have. Great pity. The groin and liver are particularly vulnerable. Persons have been known to die of blows directed at these organs.'

'This one did.'

'It's most unfortunate,' he says, and I agree.

'This Hindu–Muslim riot afterwards, was it the frightful orgy of killing they made out it was? Some of these communal incidents are grossly exaggerated.'

'They weren't exaggerating. There was a riot the year before, too. Same sort. Howling mobs on the rampage.' My head aches with recall. I plead, 'Can you tell me why ordinary people go so raving mad?'

'I wish I knew,' says Vacha, his doubtful tone implying that an upcountry backwater has to be judged by different standards from the rest of the country.

'It is peculiar,' he worries. 'Ten, eleven years ago, there was a Hindu–Muslim *entente*. They had a common grievance against Britain's treatment of the Ottoman empire and the Caliphate' – he uses the anglicized pronunciation in place of Khilafat – 'so why should Vijaygarh have had two murderous outbreaks at that time?'

He goes on looking quizzically at me. In fairness to him I explain the background. I find it painful to lay open this deeply private part of me. Visions, I say slowly, have their origin in the souls and bodies of men and women, in bed-and-board love, everyday human love. After all, what other kind *is* there? I myself believe in Hindu–Muslim unity and my commitment to it has cost me dear. People who practise what they preach get labelled lunatics. If that is what I am, so be it. I tell Vacha what happened all those years ago.

Vacha's face shows comprehension. He reacts with the sensitivity of a man who cares, a man to whom words like love and brotherhood are not mere words. He understands what crimes against one another mean. He pays me the tribute of looking profoundly moved as I speak. I feel I am meeting Nauzer Vacha, the human being, for the first time. It is somehow refreshing to note he has clothes of superior cut and is well-groomed. His hair lies liquidly on either side of his ruler-straight centre parting. He is a man of the world. His presence brings the world into the superintendent's dingy office, cracks my leaden indifference to the life I will lead after my release. I still can't imagine a future that matters, but he stirs an active nostalgia for the life I've left behind.

'A boyhood love affair,' Vacha comments thoughtfully. 'Let them dig it up if they want to. It has no bearing on this case. Thank you for telling me about it.'

He adds that the impetuous punch in the liver might well throw a new chivalrous and idealistic light on my character.

'How much later did the man die?' he asks.

'I don't know. About four days afterward, still unconscious. We only got the news after the rioting stopped and the bazaar reopened. The police had to cordon our house to protect us when they found our compound walls defaced and stamped with the crescent, and scrawls of "Be ready, we're coming". They warned Father they wouldn't be responsible for any member of the household, all three households, who ventured out. The mob was in a lynching mood. So at home we didn't know exactly what had happened.'

'Death as the result of an accident,' Vacha muses.

'Maybe so, but I feel like a criminal whenever I think of it. Father wanted to help the family but he couldn't do anything for them. By the time we got the news they had packed up and disappeared.'

'Where did they go?'

There were two bazaar versions of where they had gone. Aren't there always? No one knew for certain. Either they had gone to Bombay or Lucknow. One reliable informant said Bombay. They had relatives in both cities but Lucknow was probably too close for comfort. Vijaygarh never saw them again.

'You didn't go abroad until almost a year later. I thought you said your father wanted you safely away as soon as possible after the riot. Why the delay?'

'The war had to end first. Then passports came in. We got the application forms from the provincial government office but they asked a lot of questions about me and why I had become a target for the rioters. Father had to go to Lucknow to answer them. My mother was convinced it was the Commissioner who was delaying my passport on purpose, hoping my presence in Vijaygarh would start another riot. She didn't trust him. She called him a mischief-maker. Her theory is the British need a Hindu–Muslim riot now and then. No riot, no raj.'

'Your mother sounds a shrewd and clear-headed lady.'

'She is. She doesn't read or write, you see.'

'Why didn't your father send you to Europe? America is the other end of the world.'

'That's why Father chose it. It was the furthest point on the globe from Vijaygarh where he had a friend. A man who had taken tiger pictures in Vijaygarh before the war.'

The delay was partly Father's nervousness. Every time he got ready to book my passage he would hear something that would change his mind. Names like Lefty Louie and Gyp the Blood of the Five Points Gang of New York, for example. He had heard America was a violent, dangerous place where it rained bullets, and gangsters in dinner jackets with guns under their left armpits gave orders to politicians. Another Hindu–Muslim riot on home territory seemed much safer by comparison.

I walk back to the barrack with a convict warder under a warm, starry February sky. It is spring in north India. I am calm and quiet. I remember what Nauzer Vacha said at our first meeting. The prosecution would try to invent charges and we would have to counter their tactics with inventions of our own. But I sleep worse than ever, dream of the imbecile dying of his fall, of men clubbing each other to death in the second riot, of bloody scraps of Hindu–Muslim flesh and clothing frying to the same crisp unidentifiable brown under the sun. And finally my dream transports me to an inflated rubber mat beside a pool of turquoise water. A girl lies on her stomach beside me, wearing a polka dot bow in her hair and little else. She waves her nude legs and tries to curl my wet hair round her finger. This is Wilhelmina Goldberger.

'Why do *you* have to feel guilty, for goodness sake, if a bunch of men went crazy and killed each other?' she asks. 'I can't see how it's your fault.'

And in my dream it's not my fault at all.

# Chapter Nine

The comrades have decided to annoy the authorities by learning Russian. Dey is teaching them to conjugate the verb *ostanavlivat*. The twins are holding literacy classes. I can hear the convicts in the next barrack stuttering, 'A – aah, ee – eee, oo – ooo.' The alphabet comes incongruously from throats well past their prime. What a waste of time instructing middle-aged illiterates in a skill that will be no use to them when they get out of jail in ten or twelve years' time. Two are lifers who won't see the outside again. But I suppose it helps to pass the time.

Bhaiji sticks to his spinning. He's going to donate his yarn to his 'fallen sisters' in a red-light district somewhere in this area where he does 'social uplift' when his tours bring him here. He has taught his fallen sisters to spin in their spare time, of which there's plenty during daylight, and praises the head sister who has become quite expert at it. They've all been kind enough to patronize the khaddar shop he has set up in the locality. I don't know why even a fallen sister would want to wear the stuff, except that it's cheap, but Bhaiji counts this his major triumph in the district.

'If these ladies take to the livery of freedom,' he says, 'can anything be impossible unto us?' One of his gems, akin to the Vedic lifespan and the precious fluid.

I lie on my cot and stare, mostly upward at the iron hooks along the top of the wall. There's no ceiling, only a V-shaped tile roof with a gap below it where the wall ends, to let in bats, blasts of weather and the phases of the moon. None of it adds or subtracts from this uncanny sensation of an eternal present made of insect bites, insomnia and the state of our bowels. Bhaiji has remedies for every ailment of the large intestines. One of these, powdered charcoal, does double duty, for clogged as well as watery bowels. Our sudden spate of black stools confounds the sweeper. This afternoon in court it dawned on me we were not spending an interminable, preposterous interlude cut off from real life. This is our real life.

Comrade Pillai believes it's a matter of days before our trial is shut down like the Lahore trial, and our cases sent to a special tribunal to make sure we're found guilty. Comrade Dey rules this out. This time the government has picked prosecution witnesses who aren't likely to defect. This rock-bottom bunch would sell its own grandmother. When I last talked to Nauzer I asked him if there was any chance of our trial being suspended and he said not to believe such irresponsible talk, especially as our cross-examination was now under way.

'But is it true the Lahore prisoners are kicked and beaten for shouting slogans when they're brought before the tribunal?'

Nauzer confirms this. 'There have been incidents, and the public is revolted by the behaviour of the police.'

'How d'you know it couldn't happen to us?'

'Believe me, the government is well aware of the difference between one prisoner and another. After all, it is the British government we are dealing with, not a corrupt oriental despot.'

Still, he can't explain why he hasn't been able to get me on the witness stand and out of here by now, as he said he would.

I have read Sylla's books and started on the jail library. Yesterday I finished *A Manual of Family Medicine and Hygiene for India*. Absorbing (though slow moving), with a section (there's no getting away from it) of bowel diseases of Englishmen and their families in unhealthy localities. The author got a Government of India prize for it in 1873. I've put it under my cot across a bowl of water to keep white ants and other crawlers away. Now I'm reading *Esmeralda's Lover*, a book you can't read slowly.

'Oh ho,' sighs Bhaiji, 'I have lost a tooth.'

He holds it up over the edge of my book.

'Half a tooth,' he amends. 'Only the top. By any chance do you know if a broken tooth should be left in or pulled out?'

I put my bookmark in the page ending 'Esmeralda, he whispered hoarsely' and fish out the medical book.

'I'll see what it says here. I know it has something.'

Bhaiji waits with a kind of shining eagerness.

'If the remaining half is hollow,' I say, 'it has to be filled with beeswax.'

'It is not hollow,' he tells me with mounting excitement.

'A broken tooth means decay, in which case it has to come out. Let's see – yours is a back tooth.'

Bhaiji points out he has forbidden himself (and the twins) any favours from the government and these include a dentist. A satyagrahi must be prepared to suffer. By the grace of God he's not suffering yet.

'Well I could take a bash at it. I'd need a forceps with in-turning claws. All I do is grip the neck of the tooth, give it a twist and yank it out. Easy. But if you want it painless, I'll have to paint your gums with a ten or fifteen per cent solution of cocaine. I can ask for it. It's not against my principles.'

I try to infect him with the novelty of tooth extraction but now he's mulish about keeping it. He hoards the broken bit away in his *takli* box and goes back to his spinning wheel. For a while I watch. He is sitting on his cotton mat in the aisle between his bed and mine with his legs crossed in their spinning posture. His right ankle rests on his left knee, his right foot jerks rhythmically to the turn of the wheel. In no way does Bhaiji resemble the butcher in his vest and dishevelled lungi who keeps a goat's hind leg tucked between his big and second toe as he saws at it. The meat piles up in soft red lumps on a sheet of newspaper under his knife. A sawing motion for heavy flesh, swift lightning strokes for bone. The red pile grows, a presentable offering that has no connection with the skinned carcasses hung behind him. As a boy I was riveted by that masterly accuracy, no waste of meat or motion. I wanted to be like him. Laughing, he let me try. But my knife bounced on gristle and scraped bone. I sank it in further up only to feel the flesh spring and bounce elastically under the blade. Clearly it was a matter of practice. You'll get it right when you're older, young master, the butcher promised. All these years later I feel slightly sick.

I am relieved when the comrades stop conjugating and their mascot, Sen, stretches, touches his toes, swings his arms around his body and takes a running jump toward us. Bhaiji gives him an encouraging, affectionate smile. Young men should be active. Old men should be honoured. Widows should eat blood-cooling food. Jail is an honour. Freedom will come of spinning thread. He believes it all.

I have a letter dictated by Mother saying she has found a yogi with three lungs to teach her to sit still. While the comrades are conjugating one day I ask Bhaiji why anyone would want to sit like a block of wood for hours on end.

My ignorance baffles him. He says it is the supreme quest. In every generation countless people embark on it.

'And it is not for blocks of wood,' he says severely. 'Please realize the dangers of this path.'

For every rare individual who sits still long enough to rouse the life force in his coccyx and send it hissing to his brain – where it explodes into the light of a million suns and liberates the sitter from all bondage – there are any number who fall ill or go mad. No one should experiment with the path of fire and light. The best candidates are those who have a sweet non-violent nature and realize their utter insignificance. Mother doesn't fill the bill. It's worrying.

'If it's so dangerous, why would it be worth the risk?'

For the rush and roar of liquid light up the spinal column, explains Bhaiji, for the exquisite incomparable sensation as it floods the brain. For the bliss of ten thousand orgasms, who wouldn't take a risk? I see his point. I see Mother's too. All of a sudden I see it only too well.

'The precious fluid is directed upward, you see,' Bhaiji continues. 'But it does not mean ladies cannot achieve highest bliss. Ladies can, and do. And whoever attempts it has nothing to lose but his chains.'

He chortles at having stolen the comrades' copyright. Tit for tat. Their men sabotaged his Congress committee work. I add one more gem to the sayings of Bhaiji: Highest bliss comes of a petrified posture.

By April we have more variety in our lives than dentistry would have provided. Gandhi has marched to Dandi beach, a distance of two hundred and forty-one miles from his base, to disobey the Salt Act and manufacture salt on the seacoast. A civil disobedience campaign is in full swing. Our newspaper says immense crowds cheered him on and thousands joined the march. People are manufacturing salt in tin pans all over the country. Overnight our jail is full of Salt March prisoners, four in our barrack, I don't know how many opposite, and a dozen half-grown schoolboys who arrive last and sleep chained together in the yard. My barrack mates congregate at the barred door to greet these latest arrivals. They grasp each other's hands through the bars with outbursts of mutual rejoicing. One of the boys sees me on my cot and calls out to me with a warm appealing courtesy it would be churlish to ignore. My hands, too, are caught in congratulation by each of the boys in turn. They have invited me to clasp hands, but their handclasps are more like a fervent unearned embrace. My hands are trembling. I don't know if it's their ardour that makes me so emotional, or an axe to my grave that will stand me up whole and resurrected, a man among men. The thought, God give me my life all over again, sears me and is gone.

Now we have such a wealth of news from the outside that adult literacy and Russian verbs have been forgotten. At night a baritone across the yard sings:

> With dear old Gandhi
> We'll all march to Dandi
> And break all the salt laws
> That a white man ever made . . .

This voice belongs in a gilded auditorium. I wonder at the men and, from what we hear, the women, who marched to Dandi or made salt in tin pans to get themselves arrested. The prisoners in the opposite barrack get their daily airing on the other side so we don't see them. But they love to sing. The warder who hits prisoners on the head and bellows their numbers all night now gets hymns and national songs, and defiant slogans shouted at him as he passes. Most often it's 'Mahatma Gandhi ki jai'.

Bhaiji, after consulting his conscience about the ethics of disturbing jail routine, announces his decision to join the slogan shouters from tonight. He doesn't have much of a voice but he makes a valiant effort. The comrades, who are lukewarm about the Gandhi slogan, join in for solidarity's sake, and introduce one of their own, 'Victory to the Peasants and Workers', which the yard boys take up lustily. I join in self-consciously at first. Oddly enough I've never raised my voice to this pitch before, or in unison with other people, and it takes getting used to. But it's an alchemizing experience. It goes to my head. It's a positive improvement on counting sheep. We keep a continuous uproar going for about an hour every night, staggering our chorus with the one across the yard. Bhaiji leads our lot in his reedy voice and the rest of us echo the second half of the slogan. 'Inquilab Zindabad' has a rhythm the others lack and soon becomes our favourite.

We're just getting started on the third night when we hear the clangour of chains dragged over stone and lathis hitting the ground. Someone unlocks our barrack door. The jailer straddles the entrance with a horsewhip. He's left his fez at home. In the lantern light his face is puffed with sleep, smeared with sticky black eye make-up. A restless night has daubed his nose with it too. But for the whip he looks like a clown or a circus bear, shifting his weight from foot to foot. His whip, it seems, is for decoration. Behind him in the shadowed yard an active horse-whip swings in an arc and descends on a boy, unchained from his companions and roped to a tripod. The boy is still screaming when the whip rises again. The tripod is in shadow but a shift of the lantern shows us a row of rifles behind it. There is no beginning or end to the screams, they are joined together behind the jailer's sleep-coated smile. He has come to request us earnestly not to join these misguided boys in their mutiny. We are senior. We are better class. We are here to set an example. The whip descends whistling and now the boy's screams end in shrill wails of 'Mahatma Gandhi ki jai'. My companions push forward but can't get past the jailer. Sen, beside me, raises his fist and hollers,

'Murderers!' But Bhaiji forestalls a stampede by nimbly stepping out in front of the jailer.

'We also have an earnest request,' he says curtly. 'Stop this at once or we will stop you.'

The jailer goes into an elaborate explanation. We cannot hear a word he says above the whip's whine and that penetrating scream congealed like another whiplash on the air. Sen tugs my sleeve and jostles me to the wall. He is in his underpants with his dhoti hung around his neck. I brace myself as if to ski and he leaps on my shoulders, flings the knotted end of his dhoti up to an iron hook, is up it silky as a snake and over the gap. I hear his landing thud on the other side. The lantern crashes, there is pandemonium and we surge out in the dark with Bhaiji in the lead. The whip is suspended in the confusion. Then another lantern is lit. I see Bhaiji lean close to the boy's face to hear him gasp, '*Baba*, is freedom coming soon?' 'Soon,' Bhaiji promises, 'upon my oath.' The next whiplash welds their two bodies sickeningly together. Bhaiji is plastered over the boy like protective armour, and his arms dangle on either side. Someone shouts an order followed by rifle fire and bedlam. We bump against each other, catch our feet on the jumble of chained bodies groaning on the ground, stumble and fall, for the rifles have broken ranks and are among us. A pain so excruciating, I feel my head is severed, rips through me, as a rifle butt hits the side of my neck. I crumple where I stand. Alarm bells are ringing. More lanterns arrive. The boy has been untied from the tripod. He and Bhaiji have slipped, still grotesquely stuck together, to the ground. A warder strips Bhaiji off the boy. 'I am not dead,' says Bhaiji matter-of-factly as he is carried past me to the barrack. He doesn't say another word for the next twenty-four hours. We stagger into the barrack, lie down and sleep for what is left of the night. In the morning we discover Sen is not with us. A warder comes to remove his belongings. The whipped boy and one of his chained friends are dead of stray bullets. A few have been removed to the jail infirmary. Comrade Dey, who is the least battered and swollen from his injuries, or the toughest of us, harries the warder for news of Sen and is told he is in a solitary cell as punishment.

Our yard exercise and newspaper have been stopped again. The jailer informs us mutiny will not be tolerated. Drastic steps will be taken if we shout slogans. The comrades demand news of Sen. They surround and threaten the jailer. They hurl their fury at his retreating back. He strolls through the yard at a leisurely pace, leaving them to a tongue-torn silence more agonizing than their anger.

The heat is worse this year, or has a year of jail worn our constitutions fine and delicate? Dust gathers and whirls along the ground, rises and whirls in through the gap, and hangs like a curtain. After a month of duststorms, clouds loom black and rugged and sheets of water inundate the yard. Bhaiji's thrashing has enfeebled him. He is deaf in one ear and he can't sit comfortably in his spinning posture. They've all lost their combative zest. They keep their energies for court. Sen is not brought to court. And now the sweeper says he's not in solitary confinement. He cleans the holes in the solitary cells and Sen is not there. Under Comrade Dey's intense cross-questioning he cowers, recovers and offers an array of alternatives. He waits to be rewarded, but Dey turns away in anguished disgust.

Nauzer, who is not required here these days, does his best from Bombay to keep my spirits up. The wheels of justice turn slowly, he writes. The legal process cannot be rushed. It's a piece of irony, my telling Nauzer about the delays before I went abroad in 1919. Compared with the legal process my trip was arranged in the wink of an eye once the passport was issued. The government prosecutor is correct when he harps on the efficiency of networks. He means the underground, but networks are much the same, under or over ground, in the magical ease with which they convey an insider to safety from scenes of crimes. In the limbo called America I inhabited for a year, I see myself beside that pool of turquoise water. Father's friend's half-naked daughter, Willie-May, asks me, 'You know what fascinates me about you, don't you?'

I'm pretty sure I know, but it seems I don't when she supplies the answer, 'You just don't have ambition.'

# Chapter Ten

Willie-May really believed I had no ambition. I seem to give this impression when in fact my single-minded zeal compares with Mohammad or the magi.

'I don't blame you for hating school,' she said, meaning college. 'Daddy can't get me to go. He wants to send me to a girls' school. Can you imagine what it would do to my sex life, living with girls for four whole *years*?' She took a sip from her teacup. 'You could get a job. Any day of the week there are about fifty men who look like you lined up outside casting directors' offices.'

'There are fifty men who look like me?'

'You know what I mean.'

During the past year I had got used to heads turning for a second look. At college I had been told I was the image of Antonio Something or Something Cortez. The taxi driver who had brought me here from the railway station had gaped, 'Jesus, it's Ramon Novarro.' It was a country where resemblances counted. Now that I had made up my mind not to go back to college to be sucked into a retarded adolescence, the country was growing on me. In some ways it was an inner landscape, not a country, a dream sequence where a man and a woman lay naked in broad daylight drinking a fiery concoction called a cocktail out of teacups, with neither guilt nor innocence between them. The women of this country had the mathematical proportions of buildings, a dome-and-minaret beauty that made the beauty of other races look unplanned and haphazard. Their anatomies knew where to grow and stop growing. I doubt if the houris got better results on a diet of goat and dates. The milk Willie-May poured into her body by the glassful seemed to flow directly into her curves. Her skin glowed with chicken gravy, creamed corn and blueberry muffins. Every line of her had succulent meat juices and fruit juices locked into it. Foods I had never heard of had gone into the moulding of Willie-May. Her daddy was away in London, England, but she had done so well as hostess that I was enjoying myself for the first time since I arrived in the country. I told her my father was upset about my refusal to go back to college. There were plenty of other colleges, he had written. One of them would take me. He was anxious for me to stay away from Vijaygarh.

'And you want to go *back*?'

Pleased as I was to be with her, I had never been so acutely aware of Vijaygarh as during this last lap of my exile. The morning was almost as hot as a Vijaygarh morning. Our breakfast fruit had been Vijaygarh fruit. The mansion and its ornaments were different from ours but hovels and shanties look the same everywhere and I had passed some on my way from the station.

'I have to go home.'

'Leave here? You'd have to be crazy. Wait a minute, there has to be a woman in this somewhere.'

'How do you know, Willie-May?' I felt the agony of pressure on an aching muscle. The relief of it, too.

'How do I *know*? Hey, everybody needs sex. Sex is good for you. We'd go crazy if we didn't get enough of it.'

I hadn't heard, but beside this earth-shaking force the ghost of Razia seemed insubstantial as smoke.

'This isn't exactly sex, Willie-May. I haven't seen her for three years. She's disappeared.'

'Not exactly sex?' she echoed. 'I don't know what you're talking about.'

'I'm not sure I know either.'

Willie-May stared. What I was talking about, she made her meaning clear, was a woman who wasn't there, a woman I hadn't seen, heard or felt for three years, if that wasn't the darndest, weirdest nonsense. I admitted it wasn't sense.

'So this is why you want to go back to Vijaygarh?'

'No. This is not why. She's not in Vijaygarh. I told you, she's disappeared. I don't know where she is.'

I could see that this warped fantasy of mine clothed me in an aura, ensouled and anointed me for Willie-May. It was the crowning touch to my lack of ambition.

'Anyway, you want to go hunting for her like a needle in a haystack, is that it?'

She handed me the key to my future with a lighthearted giggle. It was obvious – this clean-cut lifelong quest for the impossible – so obvious, I marvelled at not having thought of it myself. Willie-May insisted it would be a waste of time, and of me. She was convinced I was meant for the movies. But first I'd have to see one. That very evening she took me to the Wonder Palace. We entered a carpeted ante-room called a mezzanine with mirrored walls, pink marbled pillars and pink-shaded electric chandeliers. It seemed a pity not to sample one of the plush velvet chairs but the mezzanine was only for passing through. A Hungarian gypsy whose teeth glinted under the chandelier took our tickets. Girls in gypsy costume sold us programmes. After a fast comedy the movie began.

It was grippingly tense. In the most suspenseful scene the gypsy lover who looked like me scaled a creeper to get to the countess's boudoir while the count was out hunting. He flung a leg over the balcony where she was waiting for him in a low-cut gown with one bare arm around the front of a pillar and her face and neck turned sharp in the opposite direction. The gypsy knelt and wrapped his arms about her waist, looking straight up at her. She put her hand on the nape of his neck. He buried his cheek in her navel. Her nostrils flared. So did his, the one we could see. On Willie-May's whispered advice I paid close attention to these professional details. Then they went into her boudoir to make gypsy love to the sound of violins in the orchestra pit below us.

'See what I mean?' said Willie-May afterwards. 'You'd look great in a role like that and it doesn't need a whole lot of practice. You'll need to see more movies though.'

When the programme changed we went to another movie. A

scene in this one had a man like me dressed in skin-tight trousers flared below the knees and a shirt with long frilled sleeves. He strode into a dance hall cracking a rawhide whip and asked a girl to dance with him. Her escort rolled up his sleeves, bunched his fists and bounced. The frilled fellow's whip slashed all over the room. This cleared it, except for the girl. He slashed the whip once again with lordly disdain, belted it around her and pulled her to him. They went into a glide, glued to the floor. For some reason I had thought dancing was a variation of jumping, with your partner held at arm's length.

'That's a tango,' Willie-May enlightened me. 'You'll have to learn to do it.'

If I could learn to dance, her daddy could help me get a job in a studio. He had entered the business in 1900 with a nickelodeon and made his reputation with a wartime movie called *The Virgin and the Hun*. Now he financed movies. I didn't want a job but learning to dance with Willie-May for a teacher was the most alluring prospect I had yet been offered. By way of rehearsals for movie roles we spent several days making acrobatic love. It was so gloriously simple having one's field of operation in full view, not having to grope for apertures through voluminous clothing, not worrying about the perils of going overtime, and so relaxing to know it wouldn't result in a massacre.

'Sex is *good* for us,' Willie-May assured me. 'It keeps us healthy.'

People who didn't get plenty of it went crazy or got wrinkles. She'd read it in a book. When we weren't on top of each other beside the pool's brilliant water after the servants had served lunch and gone, we were holding hands side by side on a banquette at her favourite restaurant, numbed into a teacup languor, with our dark mirrored reflections for company. Every time the door opened to admit other lunchers we realized it wasn't midnight. The hour didn't matter. Her daddy was still away and there wasn't a picture of him in the house to make me feel uncomfortable. At home when we weren't keeping ourselves healthy, we were busy dancing.

'We'll start with the turkey trot,' said my instructress. 'It's old-fashioned. Nobody does any of the animal trots any more but they'll limber you up and sort of get you into doing steps. First of all you have to run me backwards. Keep your legs straight. *Then* – I'd better show you.'

She demonstrated and my heart sank. It was hopelessly confusing.

'It's easy as pie,' said Willie-May, humming the tune. 'Four trots and a hop on your right foot. Then hop on your right foot again while you kick your left foot in the air behind you. Got it? You better bend that knee unless you want to break your leg. Now do two more trots. Come *on*.'

We did it together and I tripped all over myself. Then Willie-May produced another version. I backed Willie-May, hopped on my *left* foot, and kicked my *right* foot in the air behind me, never forgetting to bend that knee. This done, I hopped on my *right* foot, kicked my *left* foot in the air and backed her in four trots.

'You should be lifting your elbows and flapping them like a turkey when you do the backward kicks,' she reminded me for the umpteenth time. 'It's optional, but if you don't do it, it could be any other trot.'

I was so discouraged I begged her to stop, but Willie-May was a hard taskmaster. If I didn't like this one, there were two other variations. Painfully I progressed to the Yearning Saunter. I did as I was told, walked four slow steps, ran seven quick steps, and brought my right foot to the back of my left foot on the eighth beat, always remembering to keep my expression pleasant and polite. But all this arithmetic slowed me down and the delicious sensation of Willie-May's kneecaps bumping mine made it impossible to think of my leg alignment. I had no choice, however. She wouldn't stand for interruptions and wouldn't let me miss a lesson.

'Let's go! Feet well apart!'

And off we went. We rose and fell on the balls of our feet. We dropped our heels. We dipped and spun, crouched for a jump, jumped, landed. I don't have a mobile face but Willie-May looked arch or cross or roguish as the steps demanded. Suddenly she broke from me and spun on her own and I quickly did likewise. Carried away, we flapped our elbows to breathless little cries.

'Now you're dancing!' cried Willie-May.

In a few more days there wasn't a step I couldn't do. We did the Duck Waddle with our feet turned out and splayed apart. I liked the Camel Walk best of all the ragtime dances. In this dance Willie-May leaned way back and I leaned way over her as I walked her backwards. Then I leaned back and she leaned over me going the other way. She saved the Bunny Hug for last in which we did a quick one-step hugging each other. She told me some dance teachers and Pope Pius X had not approved of these ragtime dances. Pope Pius X had called them immoral and said Catholics should dance the ancient furlana instead, but why would a Hindu and a Jew have to bother with what Pope Pius said? And we went directly into the Grizzly Bear, walking bow-legged, swooping and swaying on our toes and ending the dance with a crushing bearhug that had to be tighter than a bunny hug. Guided by Willie-May, one wonderful day I fell effortlessly into the foxtrot and became an outstanding ballroom dancer. Willie-May and I flowed smoothly forwards, backwards, sidewards through the half-dark, forehead to forehead, hypnotized by the saxophone and each other's huge, magnified, multiplied eyes.

She took it for granted that all women spent their summers somersaulting from diving boards into turquoise pools, and that being fully clothed meant showing arms, calves and shinbones. With all this glorious freedom she longed to be slung over a saddle and kidnapped by a Bedouin Arab, or belted into a dance by a ruffian Argentinian. She listened spellbound to stories of Mother's closed carriage, her walled-in apartment, and Father's other wedded wives. She yearned to be hand-delivered to a rude man and locked up for safe-keeping. She had never heard of anything so romantic, exotic, or erotic as a yashmak. She was thinking of the programme girls in the Salome movie we had seen.

'You can't see through a veil,' I corrected, 'and it covers a lot more than your nose. It's a shroud.'

We were not at the pool or on the banquette. We were in bed having a lazy Sunday morning. The servants had Sundays off. Willie-May pulled the sheet off us, draped it around her and crouched, showing only her eyes.

'Is it like this?'

I gave the sheet a savage tug, toppling her.

'What's the matter, didn't I do it right?'

I hung over her, twisting the sheet into a rope. 'Don't do it again. I'll kill you if you do.'

But this healthy girl had lived so far from danger, she crowed and crooned with delight, brought my head down to hers and whispered, 'If we don't get up right now, we won't get any lunch, and I'm starving, how about you?'

So we went to the banquette to eat, and drink out of teacups. This time, after thanking her for everything, I said I must be going home soon, but Willie-May no longer believed in my ghost-hunt, or that I'd leave, not after all we'd been through together.

'I guess you really love your home,' she said.

It was useless to explain that home is not the place of one's choice. There is nothing sacred about home. One is born there choiceless as a parrot in a cage, or those boxed grey hens whose startled sleepy croak is half-conscious of the neck-wringing ahead. Home is where, for some unfathomable reason, the slaughterer utters, *'Bismi 'llahi 'r 'rahmani 'r rahim'* in the act of raising his knife to kill. In the name of God the Merciful, the Compassionate, he plunges it with scientific precision to jerk the animal to its lawful death. Home is where the clue to who I am is not hidden in life before death, but in lives before this one. It's where every other turnip I have eaten has been fertilized by Hindu–Muslim bonemeal, and salvation is a prayer for release from repeated death.

Our teacup brew was particularly numbing that afternoon. Willie-May soon had the long sad cheeks cocktails gave her. My speech ran down like a clock and had to be rewound. Words came ponderously out of me. Willie-May was intrigued by my twin mothers and Father flopping flaccidly between them. Father, I said, was no good at any sport except blood sport. He could point a gun all right if it was loaded and handed to him. It didn't surprise me Mother had had to go on two pilgrimages and pray up a storm from the southernmost sands to the northern-most mountain top to beget me.

'Gee!' sighed Willie-May. 'She must have been glad to get to the top and come to this cave and have the caveman let her in.'

If I was chasing a ghost, Willie-May's fantasies had bulging biceps. In every man there was a caveman and every woman wanted him. The mysteries were too mysterious for Willie-May.

I took a long nap after our heavy lunch and didn't know Mr Goldberger had returned until I got a message from the great man early in the evening inviting me to his study before dinner. It was hung with paintings of primordial jungles. Ferocious carnivores prepared to spring out of thickets, and snarled over torn prey in clearings. There was no sign of my host in the big revolving chair behind the desk. I was well into the room when the gnome in the chair got up and held out his chilly little hand for me to shake. Not all of us resemble our fathers, but Willie-May was another species.

'Not only is Wilhelmina not like me in face and form, but even her brains must be of some other substance. It is the air, the food, the freedom. Frightening, is it not?' he said in German English.

He poured me a fruit drink and himself a glass of ice cubes.

'One thing she is right about. You have a remarkable likeness. And there is a big demand for high-powered oriental passion. I don't know what's the matter with women but suddenly they don't want plain honest love-making in their own beds with the husbands God gave them, they want to be drugged and dragged into a tent by an oriental.'

I could see the women's point. Later, when men of action began to make news, it struck me that Willie-May and her friends would rather be dragged into a tent by Riza Pahlevi than by Hitler or Mussolini. I wouldn't have given any of them top romantic rating but there is something to be said for finesse.

Mr Goldberger drank from his ice cubes with a shiver. He drank ice to remind himself of never being able to get warm in the ghetto. It prevented his body from softening and his brain disintegrating from limitless opportunity.

'Your father is anxious for you to stay here some more time. But now we are face to face, I see this is not your intention.'

My intention, I told him, was to go to Vijaygarh.

'Your father will be disappointed. Also it is a big pity. The future of movies is here. Europe has been using its celluloid for explosives as well as film. They will remain far behind America. By the end of this twenties decade, I estimate American movie audiences are going to total a hundred million a week. How is that for a career prospect?'

Willie-May had come in and sat on the arm of his chair, a flowery sunshiny bower shading a gnome.

'You can't tempt him with a career, daddy,' she said admiringly. 'He doesn't have ambition.'

'It doesn't look like,' Mr Goldberger conceded. 'It is a pity. The money is not all. There is fame. There is power.'

'I told you it's no use, daddy.'

'Willie-May doesn't understand I want to go back to Vijaygarh.'

'Yah. Who does not?' remarked the mournful millionaire. 'Only Wilhelmina. She has no Vijaygarh, poor girl. But your father has written you should not be in Vijaygarh. If you must go, go somewhere else in India. This Vijaygarh which has the ancient hatred between Hindoo and Moslem is not the place for you. Yah, there are bloods which do not mix.'

If blood could be sent for that kind of analysis, I said irritably, we'd know how mixed they already were. Pure cuisines and dress maybe, or the way people said please and thank you. Those could stay pure, not blood. Mr Goldberger had not expected this vehemence from the son my father's and the college principal's letters had described. He sat back with his ice cubes and reverted to the 'Hindoo–Moslem problem'.

'Do not the Hindoos say, "They put us to the sword"?'

'Not *us*. Other Hindus. Centuries ago. Who hasn't put who to the sword at one time or another? That's what ghastly old history is all about. And at this point what does it matter who killed who in the year dot? In any case, no one ever killed for religion.'

'But people kill. We just had four years of it. Why?'

I shrugged. 'It's a quick solution. As you say here,' and I whipped out both hands in playful imitation, '"Bang! You're dead!" End of problem.'

Willie-May giggled and waggled an impatient foot.

'Daddy, let's eat.'

'Such total dedication as Wilhelmina has to her appetite, better she should use it for her studies. For Wilhelmina a girls' school. Her mother knew best.'

We went into the dining room, where surrounded by canvases of wild beasts in their natural habitat – not a tiger skin or a stag head on the premises – and one artistically conceived dinosaur, Mr Goldberger entertained us with stories of the Canadian moose he had photographed last year, and the African hippopotamus the year before. You could only see the flat top of its head and its nostrils above water. It surfaced after one hour, and the men with Mr Goldberger were annoyed he only wanted to take pictures. They said hippo jelly was as delicate as consommé and hippo-fat pastry was the best in the world. He described the ritual shoot Father had organized for the Commissioner during his own photographing visit before the war. The jungle was thick with birds, so they were no problem. But a tiger couldn't always be counted on to get itself shot. Awkward, if the honoured guest was a lousy shot, as this one was. The tiger earmarked for the Commissioner must have had to be doped. Mr Goldberger had scrambled down from his elephant as soon as the beaters heard the dreaded cough and smelled tiger in the bushes. He had set up his camera and started turning the handle furiously and then it had dawned on him there was no hurry. The beast was a sitting duck.

'What was the Commissioner like?'

'A nice man.'

He sketched a genial giant, revealing yet another aspect of the multi-headed thousand-armed deity known as Commissioner. The only Commissioner I had known – the one who had received Mother's letter – had apparently served the district with such distinction that Father had written he might be transferred to Delhi instead of to another division in the province. It would be a city tailored to the likes of him from what I had heard of Delhi. I could picture him walking the deserted streets of the desolate imperial capital. He would be at home in that wasteland with monuments and mausoleums for company, looking for trouble among the jackals.

Mr Goldberger had work to catch up with. Willie-May and I were left to ourselves to dance, go to banquette lunches and the movies, and keep ourselves healthy. At dinner he would complain how worried he was about the strikes in the building trade, and every other trade. Longshoremen, carpenters, stockyard workers, telephone operators, you name it. It was catching and the movies would catch it.

'Here's this Red menace,' he brooded, 'and President Wilson is off in Europe telling the Europeans how to make peace. War and peace is what they've been making since time began. I say let them make any mess they want, but what we're doing in these United States with a president who is off making peace in Europe when his own front yard is on fire, I don't know. The Bolsheviks are coming, does he care? They could be infiltrating the movies. They've crashed into the Russian Famine Relief Fund. This country could go socialist in the middle of Wilson's next speech.'

I had never seen a socialist but they sounded like religious maniacs with bristling beards. I said I thought the emergency was being dealt with. I remembered reading soon after New Year's Day this year of round-ups of radicals. The Attorney General's office had unearthed a gigantic conspiracy against the country and found three pistols. Details of the plot were to be divulged at the proper time. Mr Goldberger confirmed that the Attorney General, known as the Fighting Quaker, was wide awake and on the job. His men were tracking down Bolsheviks with a fine-tooth comb.

Mr Goldberger was almost as concerned about drunkenness, gambling and skirts getting higher. And most of all about crime, which unlike the Bolsheviks already seemed to have taken over. Johnny Torrio of Chicago's underworld was out to capture the city's bootlegging business, and he had just put a disciple of Gyp the Blood and Lefty Louie, called Al Capone, in charge of it. Mr Goldberger had seen the sign outside his office: 'Alphonse Capone: Second-Hand Furniture Dealer – 2220 South Wabash Avenue.' And now anything could happen in Chicago. He wished he didn't have a distribution agency there.

After turning down Mr Goldberger's movie offer and saying

I was leaving for home, I had stayed on. Mr Goldberger was so understanding and I could talk to him so easily. We had more in common than either of us had with Willie-May. I think he felt the weight of my unutterable sadness, and I completely understood his ice cubes.

'If you must go back, you must,' he said one evening. 'The knight must look for his lady. The search must go on. Even so, the chances of finding her are greater outside Vijaygarh, are they not? You yourself say she is not in Vijaygarh.'

The problem really was to lose her, that incomparably impure face, her impetuous running walk, the unforgettable way she parted her burka with both hands, stepped out into the startling light of day, and walked away free. The wind on her face, her every gesture was engraved on my sleep. If I could have slept for the rest of my life I would have been a well and happy man. But on nights when I couldn't sleep I watched the sequel in terror. The burka she had tossed on the thorn bush skulked up to enshroud her again. The hood descended like the lick of a long black tongue over her face. She was sucked back entire into the monster, beyond the reach of love or rescue. It was unthinkable, unacceptable that as long as she lived she would live in that coffin, and however long I lived I might never see her again.

Mr Goldberger knew a sick animal when he saw one.

'I will write to your father. He has suggested Bombay. How do you feel about it?'

But he extended his offer once again.

'It is the chance of a lifetime, making love on the silver screen. You have what it takes for the camera. Do you think love scenes come easy? We have to train an actor to lift his hand, smoulder. To you this comes naturally. It is the caste system. And oriental love is big business right now.'

But what was big business compared with the magic fire? Or perhaps I was basically a hand-to-mouth man. Sufficient unto the day. I didn't seem able to conceive of the infinite, whether it was wealth or the pantheon's dizzy choices. Too much sounded a bit obscene. Just a matter of taste, I suppose. So Bombay it became, an exile nearer home.

# Chapter Eleven

The Salt March prisoners have been removed to another part of the jail to prevent a second 'mutiny'. Our newspaper has been restored but it does not report conspiracy trials. We have no news of other political prisoners and our links with the outside have become so tenuous that the news we read may as well be from Saturn or Mars. Mussolini is Prime Minister, Minister for Foreign Affairs, Interior, Colonies, War, Air and Labour. He is also head of the Grand Fascist Council.

Since our battering we have run out of talk. No more guesses about why we are here. That subject has exhausted itself and there is no other subject. We read our quota of books, write our quota of letters, wear scummy grey clothes. Our laconic comments have a statistical sameness. I get the impression we are beginning to look alike the way boarding-school children do. Each of us could substitute for any of the others in the dock and the judge wouldn't know. Bhaiji does not have the strength to attend court. Some sort of slow deterioration has set in. He lies like a rag on his cot with scarcely enough energy for the racking cough that has plagued him since the rains began. We have urged him to petition for parole, if not his release.

'Why should I petition? Have I committed a crime? It is for them to admit their fault and release me unconditionally.'

He will lie on his cot, grafted to his principles, until he dies. He refuses to see a doctor. Nauzer was going to bring a specialist all the way from Bombay to examine my neck, which I still can't move easily from side to side, but in the circumstances I've asked him not to, as if I'm outlandishly grafted to Bhaiji. It makes no sense, but none of this does, and I don't expect Nauzer to understand that though I'm no longer in pain, I will never forget that night. He writes regularly, as a friend, not a lawyer. He sympathizes with the indignity of that anonymous blow in the dark, but he points out there's no need to feel humiliated by it. It was not a blow aimed specifically at me. If I had not been in the mêlée I would not have got hurt. I can't make him realize we're pigs in a pen. We're a blur. We're what a crowd looks like, anybody, nobody. Sen's removal has depleted us, Bhaiji's illness has crippled us, and the bullets that killed the boys we hardly knew have riddled our vocal chords so that we haven't got one complete sentence to say to each other any more. Our sole claim to separateness is the lives we once lived and which each of us seems, in our long-drawn-out silences, to be reliving. Sylla came into mine when I settled down in Bombay, in the flat Father had rented and furnished for me. Servants were sent from Vijaygarh and I was writing poetry.

At the time Sylla and I were warm but not intimate friends. She was never in one place long enough to get intimate with. She was a modern girl, full of enthusiasm. Vitality, because I have so little of it, has always been hard for me to resist. I am its natural follower. And Sylla was a natural leader. Right after her Laughing Flute-player tableau she took up the Khilafat cause with a fervour all the more remarkable because she wasn't a Muslim. The Ottoman Caliph and his empire became as dear to her as Parsee widows and orphans to her grandmother. I hadn't known Sylla long or I would have heard the venture had her grandmother's blessing. If Sylla had sent for a barber, had her head shaved, and gone into public mourning over the Allied occupation of Turkey, as Gandhi had done, her grandmother would probably have egged her on. But the old lady was sold on this venture herself. And it had nothing to do with Gandhi's espousal of the cause, or with the Muslims. The only Muslims she knew, apart from the Aga Khan, who was a variation, and a skinflint – his Ascot lunches were deplorable – were Bombay merchants and shopkeepers. A Parsee girl whose family she knew had married a well-known Muslim lawyer called Jinnah, but that was more reason for Parsee foreboding than rejoicing as he was far too old and busy with briefs to be much of a husband for their fresh young blossom. As for Gandhi, a Middle Temple lawyer who preached sedition, threw off his vest and topi, and reduced himself sartorially to a loincloth, was in her opinion quite beyond the pale. What incensed Grandmother was the British government's treatment of the imperial Ottoman dynasty, older by far than the Hohenzollerns and the Romanovs, and as old as the Habsburgs, and it made no difference that none of these was exactly reigning. The Sultan–Caliph had been grievously wronged. Allied fleets and armies occupied the Straits and Constantinople and were giving him orders.

I went to Sylla's house to read her a short poem I had written and was directed to her grandmother's down the road, where the old lady sat in a Habsburg sort of chair she reserved for giving audiences, with her feet on a footstool, listening to a delegation of wealthy Muslim merchants who had come to seek her support. They wanted to organize a meeting to highlight the Khilafat cause and her help in collecting funds. Sylla was at her grandmother's side. I beckoned her into the garden and told her Khilafat was all nonsense.

'What do you want to support some old Caliph sitting thousands of miles away for? What use is he to anybody?'

Sylla lost her temper.

'He is not some old Caliph. He is the Shadow of God on earth.'

'Rot.'

'How dare you call it rot?'

'I'm not the only one. It was rot to the Moguls. They were so rich and powerful they didn't have to kowtow to the Ottoman Caliph. Akbar refused to. He said he was the Shadow of God on earth himself. He had "The great Sultan, the exalted Khalifa" inscribed on his gold coin to prove it, and he named his capital *dar al-khilafat*.'

'Whatever that means,' she said crossly.

'It means Abode of the Caliphate.'

'Well the Abode is Constantinople now and the Hindus and

Muslims are all supporting the cause. It's a big Hindu–Muslim cause. And what do you mean by calling me out here. Those merchants are saying Indian soldiers are being used to crush the Turks. Don't you care about *anything* that goes on?'

She was marching into the house when I shot back, 'Of course I care about Turkey.'

As so often happens in a hectic argument we didn't realize we were talking about different Turkeys. Sylla was defending her grandmother's imperial Turkey headed by a Sultan–Caliph who was being bullied by the Allies. I was referring to Mustafa Kemal Pasha's Grand National Assembly at Angora which was thumbing its nose at them all. I didn't know much about either, but I would have backed the king of the pixies against a caliph, more so a man who didn't care that he had been excommunicated by one. The Shadow of God had declared a jihad against the pasha. He had promised the faithful rewards in this world and heaven in the next in return for the pasha's dead body. I was betting on the pasha, who now controlled three-quarters of Anatolia and had the officers and governing classes with him. Subconsciously I must have been waiting for him all my life, this prelude to all pandits and ulemas being pulled up by their combined roots and sent packing. In the words of that crafty courtier, Al-Biruni, I was counting the hours till they were 'atoms of dust scattered in all directions' and became 'a tale of old in the mouths of the people'. I followed the pasha's progress as keenly as Sylla's friends followed cricket scores.

'Jumbo? You truly care about Turkey?' Sylla made sure. 'If you mean it, you could speak at our meeting.'

'Now, just a minute. I don't make speeches. I don't know how to.'

'You don't have to make a speech, Jumbo. Talk naturally. Be yourself. You're a poet. If you don't like the Caliph, never mind. You can concentrate on a beautiful theme, like Hindu–Muslim harmony. It'll be a perfect contrast to the speeches. It'll put you on the map, too. Don't you want to be known?'

I didn't specially. But her suggestion had a breathtaking audacity. I had spent the last two years in virtual quarantine, being forgotten. They had hidden me to keep me safe from a lynching mob. Then they had pushed me out of sight on the other side of the world. Now they wanted me to stay under cover for the rest of my days. I was tired of being shunted around, disgusted with tiptoe and *sotto voce*. In future I would do as I pleased. I felt I had taken on a dare.

A colourful crew we were on the dais. There were Hindu and Muslim politicians whom a kindergarten babe, or a clever cat or dog, would immediately recognize as a Hindu or a Muslim from miles away. It was impossible not to, they were so careful not to be mistaken for each other. Their dress, greetings and mannerisms had been handed down intact through the ages, masterfully pickled and preserved, each in its own brine. Their speeches were pickled too. They applauded each other's cussedness and defended each other's dogmas. The room grew clammy with their sentiments. A pandit and an ulema sat in the middle seats of the row in a purely ornamental capacity, providing mute evidence that cultures, like sexes, can grow up unmet and unmixed. I was the last on the speakers' list, being the youngest (by about forty years) and least consequential person on the dais.

All my poems are about Razia. I had chosen one that opens, 'I am you, there is no other way'. After the political speeches it got off to a ripple of expectant applause. I had planned to recite only the first verse, but the poem took over. It poured out of me with a primal force I could not control. In the prayerful stillness of an evening I had prayerfully put Razia on paper. But aloud these very words rose up and danced, reeled and rejoiced, celebrating the matchless mix of her culture and mine. From the sublime to the ridiculous, we were fatally, finally wedded, we who ate and got drunk together, outbid each other to deflower the next accomplished *kotha* virgin who came of age, fêted each other with traditional elaborate insults at poetry time. Fate meant the two of us for love, not war or separation. It meant us to roast our dogmas in the same bonfire.

I saw Sylla's warning frown and wondered if something was going wrong but I couldn't stop. I determinedly covered the landscape with Shiva temples sprouting minarets. In the mosque of my creation, *Om* flowed calm as a horizon along the muezzin's call to prayer. The poem ended but I went on. This is where my natural talk was supposed to charm them, but what could be more natural than my interwoven life, and I herded them through the weave right down to my entrails. I challenged them to extricate my Hindu from my Muslim self, if they could. And then I gave a clarion call for Hindu–Muslim marriage. Sexual unity was the acid test of unity, I said.

I heard myself declaring, 'Should Islam tell you how to treat your wife and carry your handkerchief and trim your beard, and what colour your shroud should be? Should Hindus and Muslims lock up their women . . .' Two men in skull-caps and jellabas loomed out of the audience like genies from a bottle, and started up the aisle waving their fists, roaring for an apology. 'If these men have their way,' I pointed, 'we'll have a songless danceless universe. They'll banish everything, from music to a woman's face and limbs and breasts.' In the noise and confusion, Sylla told me later the pandit and the ulema got up as if they were manacled together and left the dais in outraged protest. People milled in the aisle. Sylla and the Muslim merchants made frantic appeals for order and one of them tried to pacify the genies, but the meeting broke up before the chairman could announce it was over. Within minutes I was alone on the dais and Sylla was in the auditorium, in her corner seat in the front row, staring glassily ahead of her. A pin dropped would have made a deafening racket.

'Well, you're known now,' she brought out at last, 'as a raving lunatic.'

I was aware this was not Willie-May-land, but I was so exhilarated I couldn't help stretching out a hand and covering Sylla's. Hers was stone hard. Pointedly she removed it to her lap.

'Who is this Razia person?'

'A girl I knew. Sixteen years old.'

Sylla, who was expecting an apology, an explanation, anything but this quiet elation, turned to face me uncertainly.

'It's hideously hot in here and I'm dead beat. I'm going home. If you want to talk about it, you can come to dinner.'

We had prawn curry at Sylla's with her father and mother,

and sat the required time on ornately carved black furniture among fringed lamps and beaded cushions. There is a clean private beach behind their house. When her parents said goodnight, Sylla and I went there to cool off in the sea breeze. It was there on a rock, with my shirt sleeves and trouser legs rolled up, my shoes off, and the waters of the Arabian Sea lapping the soles of my feet, I made the discovery that Razia was no longer sixteen. It was the end of 1920. She must be nineteen. Three years ago I'd seen her spangled wrists at the fair. Much longer ago I had held her in my arms. And it was an eternity since we had been viciously wrenched apart. In these matters time is no more reliable than a sheet of scrap metal. Memory gets dented, twisted, scarred, and you can't tell the last scars from the first.

Sylla was strained and distant – it's hard to relax on a rock – but she gave me her fair-minded attention. When we parted she had become my doctor. She treated my memories of Razia like patches on a lung that rest and a dry climate would cure, and she was confident of a cure. It was a matter of the right prescription. She became so involved with my symptoms, they became her symptoms. Gradually she fell in love with my love for my beloved, and we drifted along in a tender close companionship, highly prizing each other's sensibility, until one day it dawned on her I wasn't getting any better. Then we started arguing.

'You're making a holy of holies out of your monomania. That's what it is, monomania.'

If this was the word for it, there were days when only my monomania convinced me I was really alive. I couldn't get her to understand it was our ally, Sylla's and mine. She was determined to have it out of the way, and I to nurture it. If I retreated into a week's silence, she wanted to know why, and my sudden bursts of laughter bewildered her. One afternoon she worked herself up into an uncharacteristic scene about it. We quarrelled and emerged lovers, but lovers with this insoluble problem between us. And talk about it she did. Constantly. Coolly and rationally.

'How many months did this go on?' And, when I told her: 'Is that all? You can't feel so strongly about one speck of time such ages ago.'

Her views on the subject, as on all subjects, were clear. She delivered them without a trace of rancour. Every word she said was true. 'You can't make a profession of being in love.' 'You've built this up into a mountain, a girl you only knew for a couple of months.' 'Actually, you're all mixed up, Jumbo. The first time you told me about her, you couldn't even remember how old she was.' 'You're obsessed with your obsession, not with her.' 'Has it ever struck you you're so self-sufficient, an absent woman suits you best?' And, on occasions when her patience ebbed, leaving her defenceless: 'Jumbo? Jumbo! You *couldn't* have come to a stop in 1918.' But at last she learned I had. She had to face the fact that this was all there was to me. I opened and closed and lived and died over and over again around this wound. My relationship with Sylla had formed a scab over it, but naturally Sylla didn't want to be a scab. She was hurt when she couldn't heal the wound, cure me, make me her kind of normal person. She wouldn't accept the only explanation, that loving might be a vocation like medicine or the priesthood, that perhaps the worshipper in all of us must have the last word.

Men have mistresses and enough has been said on that tired topic, but if anything, I was Sylla's. I was more feminine, more gentle and compliant than her. I was the one who waited at home for her visits. She came when she wanted to, like the independent little green-eyed cat she was. I was the one who loved to linger, loved to perform small services for her comfort and pleasure, made love to the lofty monotheism and the simple ethics of her tribe as much as to Sylla. How could Sylla know, or I ever explain to her, that just as Razia and Islam were non-detachable, so were Sylla and Zoroaster. It was true I wasn't having this lyrically passionate affair with Zoroaster, but in a way I was. This particular affair might not have taken place without him. Women don't realize they are our states of mind. Sylla was my peace, my haven from the furies of Hinduism and Islam, because she was a Parsee. With her I was never afraid of being swept off my feet, driven out of my mind. I was safe where I stood. I was allowed simply to be. Her drop-in-the-ocean sect believed in a God of Light and Good, who pre-dated Islam in Persia, and they fled when that storm came. Peace be with you, all religions say. Only Sylla's means it. These pale people who have devoted themselves to creating culinary masterpieces, making money, and dispensing charity, have done no one any harm. Of whom else on earth can this be said? The city of their religious origin seems to have vanished, its name lost. It could be Rhages? Rhei? Rei? Ray? No matter, they do without a Ganges and a Mecca. But you cannot tell a woman you are her devoted servant because her prophet was a decent sort, and the origin of his ism is obscure. Sylla would not have appreciated the point.

We did our utmost to sort out what love and in-love meant, how much or little of it would do, what per cent of my divided self – and hers too if she had admitted it – we could put into our common pool. I genuinely believe lovers should enjoy what they can of each other, the one-fifth they can willingly surrender without haggling. We managed beautifully, but always in single file. We took turns being aggressor or pacifier, flirting with the idea of marriage, not wanting it, wanting it. We never simultaneously wanted anything. And never would Sylla at any stage agree to come to Vijaygarh, while I spent more time at home every year.

It is a strange feeling, going back to the room where you were born. Once again an eye-shaped single ellipse – made of half a dozen pairs of eyes – is on you. Its owners encircle the cushion you lie on, as humbly entranced by your gurgling struggles with speech as they are with the mystifying babble of priests who preside at ceremonies using language they can't understand. They lean in ceremonial adoration over your loud, louder babble of Mmm-mum-mum-mum until you force out *Ma* to their wonderstruck applause. They couldn't all have adored the babe, could they? How could they, the young goose with the jaunty walk as much as the warm-lapped widowed goose with nothing but the babe in her life? Yet they hurry and dawdle similarly over you, chant in the same tonal scale. And when your gurgles burst into an exasperated yell at being able to go no further than *Maaaaa*, a pair of hands, but whose of that half-dozen, whisks you up, the little trophy of them all.

One or two of Mother's present geese attended my birth along with Bittan, when Father's mother had written '*Om*' with honey on my tongue. Earlier, when my sisters were born, no goose of this batch had been there except Bittan. And unless my sisters had been stillborn, as I had been left to infer, Bittan it must have been who had put soft opium pellets on their tongues, or done the other crueller thing. Her strong wirily veined hands suggested strangulation, and strength was surely needed. No infant woman born of Mother would have died without a struggle. I could walk into the rooms of Mother's apartment – that realm of story-telling and withholding, of tales invented to lull and divert me, and tales concealed to spare me, of aunts and great-aunts strangled with care and kindness – I could walk in and find nothing changed. Here, at home in Vijaygarh, lies were a lulling imitation of life, and fiendish imitations of war made do as war. This kingdom seen through haze and gauze was where I belonged. These people and I were bound in alliances that Sylla and I, her Bombay and I, modern times and I, could never be.

I drove about Vijaygarh by myself, parked my car at the edge of the compound behind the Female College. Now it had an iron palisade as a boundary and a garden of modest flowers, phlox, nasturtiums, petunias, nothing enterprising enough to bloom in blazing clusters or make a perfumed splash. Black shapes walked past me, hoods off their faces, saw a stranger's stare and scuttled ahead. I wandered into the low jungle where, since Razia's capture the undergrowth had been cleared and tree trunks stood out all the way to the riverbed. The ground was deeply cracked, leaves crackled with papery dryness. But at the shrine the foliage bowed, lush and heavy with rain-anticipation, so that I fully expected the stones jutting from the riverbed to gush water and submerge my ankles. A donkey with its forelegs tied together was grazing the greener patches. What else had I never been told? Which rosebud had Father blown on to as they lay on either side of him? And now, incuriously, which of two wombs had grown me? If the key to life's puzzles lay in childhood, mine was too wriggling a labyrinth to yield it up. If only I could blast a tunnel through reality to the dream.

I walked slowly up the riverbed, back the way I had come, to the car, and drove it to the bazaar. Shop owners greeted me with feigned obsequiousness, pity or malice tucked behind their smiles, depending on how charitable they were, as it was now known I was a bird of passage. The title would not pass to me, and not because Father had another, preferred heir. He had none. The gossip was I preferred a western lifestyle in Bombay.

'Were you looking for someone?' an uninhibited ragamuffin I had never seen, and who had never seen me, ran up to ask.

I tossed him an anna and said I was looking for the tea stall.

'There's no teamaker here, never was,' said the child with the absolute certainty of one for whom never is five or six years.

A man behind a barrow of fly-infested cucumbers spoke up.

'He's no more here. He's been gone since the second riot. They set fire to his stall and threw his son into the flames.'

The street killing had been fiercest here. A number of shop-keepers had fled, including the cloth dealer, but that shop had survived and had a new owner.

I found the door to the imbecile's home swung outward on its rusted hinges. The courtyard walls had sprung moss and greenish black stains of old mildew. Grass stubble pushed up between the cobblestones. The interior doors were latched and locked. A swollen rat edged exploringly along the drain from the tap enclosure to a bed of rotting potato peel thrown over the wall. She crawled to the peel, lifted her forepaws in a dainty pirouette and voided a wormy black litter with fluid ease.

I strolled back to the bazaar, observed my human body walking, smiling, greeting. I chatted with the clairvoyant tailor, grizzled now, with an arthritic left hand. Fortunately the right hand could stitch and turn his machine handle. His clairvoyance had worn smooth with the demands made on it. It was said he had sidetracked true bliss by dwelling on this minor gift, and then blunted it by taking payment. In his own lane the butcher's genius reigned, his cleaver a wand of split-second accuracy. One of his customers had had a dream of a flock of goats on their way to the slaughterhouse before sunrise. Suddenly they had known where they were going, elevated their horned heads in horror and frozen in their tracks. Unhappily this customer had been a rare connoisseur of this animal. The butcher would have been delighted to carve his orders with a diamond saw to achieve the cut and precision the gentleman required. He hoped his customers wouldn't catch dreams from one another or he would be out of business.

Mother had become uncannily balanced of mood, a tightrope walker who would plummet to her destruction if she didn't watch her step. I missed her desperation. I felt queerly bereaved. I mourned the woman who had been on fire with love for an unborn son, on fire with grief for a Tsarina. Every moment of every visit home, my heart cried, Come back to me. But even this did not signify change. Had there ever been a time since her first cry when I had not grieved for her? And all of this, would Sylla understand? She knew she would not. It was why she never came to Vijaygarh.

'Life, I saw you in a dream.' A line of poetry I had scribbled, an idea for a poem really, and left under the teapot when Sylla came to tea, to keep the fan from blowing it away. Generally she ignored these crayon scribbles on red-lined paper until I was ready to read them to her, but that day she picked it up.

'What is this supposed to mean?' she demanded.

We were in a touch-and-go phase when a line of poetry could become an insult to our relationship. Which was the dream and which was life, she asked, or didn't I know the difference? Tea and cakes are no help at this emotional altitude. I regretted the chocolate éclairs I had specially ordered from the Taj. Sylla wouldn't touch them.

If there is no love but Love, said Sylla, in other words if there's only *one* destined love in every life, and it is perfect, omnipotent and omnipresent (Sylla's words – a poet's are much simpler), then where in Hades did she and I go from there? If every other love was a fudged copy of the One, she was sick and tired and fed up to the teeth of being a fudged copy. Valid points. I viewed them from a towering height where mist transformed them into fields of meadow flowers, or on days of sharp clarity. into humps of grazing moving cattle. A Vijaygarh trick, or habit, never to meet a question head on. It's more considerate, for truth is such explosive stuff. That was a meadow flowers day. I held Sylla's left hand – she was pouring tea with the right – and begged her to eat an éclair. She called me a narcissist, got up and left.

This was unfair. She knew I was not in love with myself. I'm not very lovable and I have no illusions about it. Narcissists don't, in any case, get attached to another person, as I certainly was to Sylla. She and I were a definite improvement together on either of us alone. We were so critical of each other's motives, it was obvious we were terribly involved. We rarely quarrelled, but when we did we behaved like a childless drunken couple who don't care how loud they shout, and know exactly how to hurt and humiliate each other.

When Sylla was still my doctor, she had said, to reassure us both, 'Worshipping at a shrine is not a twenty-four hour business, Jumbo. Even the uniquest lover has to eat, go to the bathroom, socialize. You've made a cult out of your nympholepsy.' Which when I looked it up in the dictionary I couldn't do without since I met Sylla, meant a longing for the unattainable. 'Make up your mind and snap out of it.'

Make up my mind, as if mind had anything to do with it. Try telling a contemporary foetus to snap out of the womb. How could I be matter-of-fact, recant, start leading a life of Reason while I fought to free myself of torturing possibilities, each worse than its alternative? What if I never found Razia? What if I found her – soul-destroyed and brutally used in some human kennel of a slum? I dreaded finding her, and I dreaded abandoning all hope of finding her. Either way I was in a trap. My profoundest instincts told me there was no simple solution for mysteries rooted in magic.

# Chapter Twelve

Bhaiji makes a big effort to hobble about on a curtailed parody of his strict schedule. He says he has to be in court to answer for himself when his turn comes. The Congress lawyer made a hash of the hunger-strike, and can't be trusted not to make another mess. By the time Bhaiji's turn comes he has to be carried into court on a stretcher, covered wth a brown jail blanket, and supported to the witness stand. He stands in the dock with his good ear angled toward the cross-examiner, frowning and straining to catch his words, while the cross-examiner strains to catch Bhaiji's reedy voice over the thudding rain. It is immediately clear that Bhaiji, who makes a fetish of good will, has taken a violent dislike to the man's dark Indian face. A white face he could have scorned and pitied, for what else could you expect of a white face? But he will give no quarter to this traitor to Bengal.

Bhaiji describes himself as a khaddar worker. His leader's motto is, 'Clothe the nation in khaddar'. Consequently he has been given the task of setting up khaddar shops and enrolling volunteers who go from door to door in towns and villages all over the province, collecting foreign cloth from householders and replacing it with khaddar. He also goes about reasoning with people to give up drink and curb their carnal lust. He gives his deaf ear a shake and glowers.

'You are not before this court for clothing the nation in khaddar and reasoning with people not to drink,' the traitor reprimands, pointedly ignoring Bhaiji's third mission.

Bhaiji is furious. 'So – aha! – *now* at last you intend to inform me why I am here!'

The cross-examiner chooses to ignore this outburst.

'You are a local Congress leader of known extremist views. You have given your name as Gandhi-*bhakt*, your occupation as freedom fighter, your caste as no-caste, your address as India, though these are not your name, occupation, caste and address.'

The main facts having been correctly stated, Bhaiji sees no need to contradict them. The lawyer swings his robe in a half-circle to tell the judge that this is the camouflage now fashionable among conspirators. Jail lists at Allahabad, Agra, Azamgarh and Rae Bareilly have numerous such entries.

'You and your so-called volunteers,' he swings back, 'are responsible for inciting the peasantry of this province to withhold the government's revised assessment of land revenue.' He produces a pamphlet and reads, ' "*Kisan* brothers, how long will you let these leeches suck your blood?" This single sentence will suffice. Do you deny you are the author of this pamphlet?'

'Why should I deny it?' asks Bhaiji haughtily.

'So you do not deny fanning revolt in the countryside?'

Bhaiji flies into a weak rage.

'Who is fanning, you or me? *You* are raising revenue. *You* are seizing buffaloes. *You* are forfeiting land and auctioning it. Will you take this land to England, answer me? We are telling the dumb millions, remain on your land, sow your crops, tie up your buffalo, we will see who takes it!'

'Precisely,' confirms the lawyer in his Harrow-on-the-Hooghly accent.

He dismisses Bhaiji and addresses an eloquent speech to the judge who taps it all down on a typewriter. They pause for each other like partners in a minuet. When it is all down, it is read by the court reader in English and Urdu. Bhaiji's sins are on record. So is the government's determination to show no leniency to peasant uprisings and their instigators. It expects the revised assessment of land revenue to be paid into the treasury immediately. The minuet is over but Bhaiji is still on the stand. He is taken by the shoulder and hustled to his chair. It is the dumpy twin who, after intoning Gandhi-*bhakt*, freedom fighter, no-caste, and India in reply to who and what he is, reveals why the three of them were arrested. They were sitting with eighty-nine other men on the roadside, watching the Collector's house.

'Proceed!' orders the irritated cross-examiner.

The twin, about to step down and return to his seat, is ready to oblige but not sure how to. Then with surprising insight he describes himself as a lump of common clay, a mere clod whom Gandhi has turned into a man. Therefore, he and his brothers in khaddar had sat watching the Collector's house, on the lookout for confiscated buffaloes and other movable property belonging to their *kisan* brothers, which the police were seizing, so that they could seize it back and return it to its lawful owners. They had not been sitting in the middle of the road holding up traffic. They had been on the side. So had the patriot, Lajpat Rai, been on the side, when the English policeman hit him in the chest, the blow he died of. The cross-examiner cuts him short as if he had all the ammunition he needed for the present.

'And that is not all, my lord.' Elbows out, he gets into his minuet with the judge. 'This band of so-called volunteers ran amok with the peasants, surrounded the homes of landlords and moneylenders. There were cases of arson. This so-called No Tax Campaign has wrought havoc.'

Dumpy smiles disarmingly. Asked if he has anything to say, he pleads that a mere clod has few words. If permitted, he will use a poet's words, and he does.

> 'You claiming it, I ask: Who owns this land?
> You? Your forebears? Tell me who rears
> The seed in earth's darkness, who lifts
> The cloud from the sea, who brings the rich
> Westerly wind and the rain?
> Who owns the sun's streaming light, who
> Fills the field with pearls of wheat,
> Who taught the seasons revolution? . . .
>
> I say: It belongs to him who rears
> The seed, lifts the cloud, brings the rich
> Westerly wind . . .'

'Enough! This is not a poetry festival, my lord.'

The lawyer takes up the revolutionary situation in the country. It is perilously close to the Mutiny mood. The government has taken a hundred thousand Salt March prisoners. The English police officer who struck Lajpat Rai in the course of his duty has been shot dead by an assassin, and the public has reacted with joyful excitement. The assassin and his colleagues are now in Lahore jail and the public has made heroes of them. Their ringleader has called for a revolt with torch and dynamite, though fortunately the bombs he threw into the Central Assembly chamber had been harmless. Can such a mood be ignored? Add to this, agrarian revolt and a chain of strikes that lost the country thirty million working days in a single year, 1927–8, and worst of all, on April 18 this year, the raid on the great arsenal at Chittagong . . .

A convulsive gasp, a shout goes up in court. It wakes me from a doze in which I have been picturing an elephant carrying revenue in a stately procession to the vaults, halted by Bhaiji and the twins, who scamper up its trunk, take the silver horde from under the howdah and pelt it on the crowds. Beside me in court my companions are cheering, calling, 'More! More!' They are electrified with the news. And the cat is out of the bag. But the lawyer manages to twist the news into his own triumph, egged on by his own impeccable diction. So can one doubt the conspiratorial links, he demands, and grandly tells us the whole story.

'At ten o'clock on the night of April 18, my lord, a gang of terrorists wearing British uniforms, carrying bombs and revolvers, surrounded the Chittagong armoury, overpowered the guards and took possession of all arms. A second gang disrupted the town's communications. A third gang gained control of the police barracks. Then this so-called Republican Army of Chittagong was joined by the townspeople who with the utmost audacity went in procession to the city centre singing their so-called national anthem, and held the city for several days.'

The judge does not ask what this audacious feat has to do with my companions, or perhaps he thinks they've pulled it off by remote control from their barrack like wizards of old. But the cheering has upset him. A wilder cheer goes up when the lawyer says there were disturbances in hundreds of towns after the raid on the armoury. In Sholapur mobs took control. In the North-west Frontier Province the government had to use tanks and aeroplanes to restore law and order. His last words get a terrible drubbing. He can't be heard above the comrades' slogan 'Inquilab Zindabad' barked in unison to the rhythm of their stamping feet. The judge threatens action. Two policemen come in and tussle with them. Yusuf and Dey are thrown on the ground, rammed under the policemen's knees and banged about the head. Pillai and Iyer fall on their tormentors and claw ineffectually at their backs. One tormentor turns to throw Iyer off and kicks him in the testicles. Iyer rolls over with animal howls of pain. The kicking stops on signal. The policemen salute smartly and depart. The lesson is there will be no slogans in court. The Lahore prisoners' behaviour will not be repeated here. Iyer is still lying with his knees drawn up to his chest, his whole face clenched. He opens his eyes and sees the sweat running down my face, a horrified spectator to a crime. He is helped to his feet by his comrades and they take their seats. But this is no longer a court or a make-believe court. It is enemy territory. We listen dully to the rest of the Chittagong narrative – what a near miss it was, how the first train taking reinforcements to Chittagong was derailed by the rebels. It was only because the gangs had not captured the port that the commissioner (yet another) could make his way to it and telegraph Calcutta. The lawyer then leaves it to the judge to figure out cross-country links of treason from this mass of incontrovertible evidence.

I shut out the court, think of Sylla. We'll meet again, I command myself to believe. She hasn't written of late and her last letter gave me no idea how she feels about seeing me again. I remember her saying, 'I'm not a log and you're not a drowning man. There has to be a better reason for being together.' But a man who is really drowning she would rescue.

At night I find myself involuntarily muttering prayers, to Sylla, not God. I mumble Sylla-Sylla-Sylla. I begin to understand how a mindless mumble shields one through the dark. The Word, they say, has properties. What they don't say is any word will do. Repeat and repeat it to keep evil at bay. At night I repeat her name. In court I summon the separate visions she and I had of love and togetherness. The system works. One wonderful vision we co-authored comes back to me, a jewel of a memory I had mislaid, or never seen in its perfection.

Sylla's work for the Khilafat cause fizzled out – not because I had disgraced myself at her meeting, but because the Khilafat movement was fizzling out. There was civil war in Turkey and the Sultan–Caliph's imperial Turkey was getting the worst of it. The Allies had forced a treaty on him, chopping the prize of Asia Minor into bite-sized pieces under their own command, but forcing the treaty on the Turks was another matter. They had demonstrated against it under the very guns of the Allied occupation. And no one – not the British, French, Italians or Greeks, who were attacking in the hills – had reckoned with Mustafa Kemal Pasha. This military inspector-general turned generalissimo had routed the Greek armies in the hills at the Sakaria river, and driven them east of Eskishehir. Turkish territories I knew nothing of, but names that would live in poetry. A year later when he drove them all the way back to Smyrna and the sea, I gave a party. I invited Sylla and her friends to celebrate Kemal Pasha's victory at the battle for Afium Quarahisar along with my birthday at a moonlight picnic on Juhu beach. Sylla looked ravishing in cherry-coloured beach pyjamas. Her birthday was just a couple of months away.

'Why are you celebrating your birthday with this battle for whatever it's called?' the lady who looked like a cigar wanted to know.

Sylla's friends' tongues cavorted in Latin and French but foundered on eastern syllables. I explained this battle was the birthday of my heart. The cigar laughed throatily and lit up through her foot-long holder, missing my eye by one inch.

'I thought you were a peace-loving chap, Jumbo.'

'Oh, I am.'

Ordinarily, I told her, I wasn't rhapsodic about wholesale slaughter, and this had been an epic one. On its retreat from Ushak to Smyrna the Greek army had razed towns to the ground, killed every Turkish man, woman and child and burned fields to ashes. And the Turks had repaid them in kind. There had been vengeance galore. In the sea at Smyrna Greek and Turkish corpses bobbed among the European battleships. But it was over! I caught the cigar around her drum-tight sari and spun her around. Her holder lacerated several cheeks but she joined throatily in the fun. I threw back my head and laughed. God, how I laughed! Kemal Pasha, the Ghazi, the Victorious, was master of Turkey. The days of Sultans and Caliphs were numbered. Islam would have no sole Vice Regent of God on earth. I clapped my hands for a servant and when he came, ordered him to fill everyone's glasses. I raised my own in a toast.

'To Turkey, the new Mecca!'

We drank.

'To the Ghazi Pasha and his ideas!'

We drank again. I jumped up on a table as the Ghazi had done in his Grand National Assembly.

'"Civilization pierces the hills!"' I cried. '"soars in the skies, sees and illuminates and studies all things from the invisible atoms to the stars."'

'Your poetry?' the magazine editor enquired.

'Not mine, the Ghazi's!' I kissed my fingers and blew the kiss into the sultry night. '"Civilization is a blazing fire that burns and obliterates those who will not acknowledge her."'

But what with the champagne and the sea and the gramophone where a rich rough Negro voice took turns with a trumpet, I doubt if they heard me. My guests were dancing. I struck my palms above my head and revolved in a slow sinuous dance I hoped passed for Turkish. The cigar called, 'Hear hear!'

'What a gorgeous mood you're in tonight, Jumbo,' murmured Sylla, making satisfied burrowing noises into my chest as we danced.

The sand prickled our ankles. We kept sinking into it, slowed to a laggard beat all our own. Sylla laughed giddily into my chest. After a while our feet gave up their contest with the sand. We sank them into the first warm smooth hollow they found and stood still, holding each other in the lunar light. The tide filled our ears, sea sulphur sprayed our faces. Sylla sang. She is never more endearing than when she sings, for she can't sing. I rubbed my lips against her hair.

'I think we're in love,' I said.

'You think! You monster! You *know* we are.' And she murmured other broken sentences that made perfect meaning.

When we had had enough of the party we trailed along the shore hand in hand, our fingers entwined. Far away from the others we lay down in the moonlight and made sweet disembodied love.

# Chapter Thirteen

I am called into the dock as our second jail monsoon tails off. It is August 1930. The English are people I have never given a thought to, and scarcely seen except in Sylla's Bombay, yet here is one of them deciding my fate, and I am 'the accused'.

'Your name.'

'Bhushan Singh.' And in my thirty-first year.

'What do you do for a living?'

'Nothing.'

'I understand you write poetry.'

'Not for a living.' You funny fellow.

The enemy lawyer complains to the English judge. My lawyer raises an objection. The judge holds forth.

'The question is legitimate,' he says. 'The court is interested in how the accused spends his time. Though one's circumstances in life may be fortunate, life cannot – or should not – be aimless.'

'Mine is.' From your point of view, all you judges.

And deliberately so, of course. I have not survived these thirty years without realizing that the burning zeal of a Mohammed or the magi marks one for the madhouse if one's name is merely Bhushan Singh. The seeker who has a star to follow, learns to follow it with his eyes to the ground. Keeps trackers off the scent and the bloodhounds at bay. I don't deny I have goals, specific reachable targets. Getting a ball over a net, driving from one part of the city to another, making love to Sylla, any line of action that delivers a result. But I'm not mentioning these examples as I doubt if they will interest the court, or throw light on a plot to overthrow the King Emperor.

'If you insist you do nothing,' prods Harrow-on-the-Hooghly, 'how do you spend your time in Bombay?'

They stick to Bombay. The bulk of the iceberg doesn't worry them.

'Well?' the enemy badgers me. 'Do you not spend several months of the year in Bombay? How do you spend it?'

'I used to drive around in my Bugatti until I sold it. After that I drove around in my Hispano Suiza.'

Replies the comrades would have jeered a year ago, and Bhaiji would have hiccuped like a rabbit at, but now my companions accept them as the literal truth. Only the judge and his accomplice object. The pink-cheeked dignitary who comes to court in a Rolls Royce should know all about a leisurely lifestyle, and the blackish one should mellowly agree since he is there to swing and sway with the judge, but I am lectured. The judge says my flippant attitude will not do in a court. He seems to be implying my answers have a hidden purpose that I am refusing to reveal. He tops up his sermon by asking me whether I don't care for the praise or blame of my fellow men.

This needs thought. Then I reply.

'Not particularly, because I've never known why my fellow men praise or blame me. Take my awful poem "The Bridge". I haven't the slightest idea why it got published, and so many good ones didn't. It leaves one in a quandary about praise and blame. In the end it boils down to whether one is pelted with flowers or fruit – if one considers the tomato a fruit.'

I see a grin of satiric amusement on Comrade Iyer's wan, wise face, and the others brighten, too, exept for Bhaiji. The deaf smile on his exhausted face is one of general support and encouragement. The enemy lawyer now points out it is all much as he feared. My lifestyle, may it please the court to note (meaning himself in cahoots with the judge), is totally aimless and unstructured by my own admission. It is exactly what may be expected of an anarchist. And he sits down well pleased with himself, fluffing his robe like hen feathers and mopping his curls. Yet there has been no lack of purpose in my life, and nothing hidden about my poetic purpose. I have poured it into every poem I have written. It's not my fault if some have been published and other's haven't, as the Potter or his whimsical counterpart, the publisher, wills. I have laid my cards on the table at every conceivable opportunity. How can anyone who reads pretend not to know my purpose? I have stood stripped in its glare, and at times it was so harsh I had to shield my eyes from it or be blinded. My search, which I've taken care to keep hidden, is something else. It is curious it was discovered in spite of my infinite precautions by – of all people – Sylla's grandmother.

She had had her reservations about me since the Khilafat meeting fiasco, but this, she confided to her tableau circle in astringent French, was the last straw. She was more vividly voluble up and down the Parsee-Gujerati scale to everyone else in her vast acquaintance. People talked, all the way to Vijaygarh, and Father's nose was cut. He wrote in spluttering indignation, telling me how it bled and how black his face was. In Bombay the Zoroastrian community was told what Grandmother would do with her diamonds and Part Two of her last Will and Testament – Part One being committed to a charitable trust for the support of deserving Parsee widows and orphans – *if* her granddaughter were fool enough to marry this impostor, this scandalous loafer. But since she couldn't have her Sylla connected even in scandal with a common and garden loafer, she somehow managed to convey I was a debauched grandee in my early forties, a disinherited son of an upcountry maharaja. And this happened when Sylla and I were happiest, in the serene aftermath of the Ghazi Pasha's greatest battle.

We might have slipped quietly into marriage any week after my beach party, if the beckoning finger in my dreams had not lured me to nightly tours of Kamatipura. I didn't take my Bugatti. For midnight brothel cruising, as for my tenement tours, I hired the same horse-drawn victoria. And if I did this when Sylla and I were idyllically happy, it must have been simply because our unalloyed happiness was the first premonition I had that the search for Razia might be Sylla's search as much as mine. When it was time for us to part one evening and we couldn't bear it, I wanted to beg Sylla, as I drove her home, to come with me to Kamatipura. But a dream explained would have sounded absurd. It would have amounted to saying I was endlessly falling, or that I struck out but my fists went feeble. So I said nothing but a tender goodnight. The brothel district was one place where she and I could not go together.

I had by then completed my dawdling tours of Muslim localities and bazaars, thankful this once for the clear communal divisions that made my search easier. I had even combed a respectable, largely Muslim suburb, perambulating it street by street until the horse's feet hurt. I wanted to see and be seen, to get a sign or a signal. Now my victoria cantered through Gandugali, eunuchs' land, rowdy with sailors on leave, groups of millworkers among them. The red-light district was a world of fabulous promise those nights. Bellasis Road and Foras Road were the dim smoky yellow-blue of illumined manuscripts whose wondrous or monstrous revelations one has yet to decipher. Somewhere in there the clue to my seeking lay buried. Or as the mystics have it, that point of central awareness in or outside the mind which leads one to the clue to all creation. I stood in front of those caged and cubicled women with a humble exaltation. I don't know why I felt reasonably certain she was here, and here my search would end. There is no fathoming the contortions an ordinary life can be driven to. Mother's, her sister's, mine. The lowlier circumstances of Razia's life made her more of a pawn, a pitiable fate that much more possible, unless she had gone to a common tubercular death. But something in me would not accept her death.

I was befuddled by the variety. I loitered outside each cage on Grant Road as in the antechamber of a prince. I studied each occupant through the bars, willing my imagination to penetrate the layers of cheap bazaar powder and paint that altered the true contours of a face. I lingered longest before the cages of hill women from Assam and the north-east who had the light colour and Tartar stamp of Razia's facial structure. Caged women in frocks had names like Annie and Ida. I closely inspected every one. It would never do to glance and pass on. A life in Kamatipura could change a woman drastically. And there are disguises without number – dirt, fatigue, dress and expression apart from paint. Blankness, too, is a disguise. The imported white women, rouged and frocked, could have been any vintage, any land. It took me longer to rule them out than the squat dark creatures who didn't remotely resemble Razia.

Sometimes I didn't move until a crowd pressed round me and an impatient customer shoved me aside to negotiate and be let in. I spent a portion of every visit outside the Japanese cages where Japanese clients decorously signed the books of Mama-san and paid at the end of the month. I was prepared to believe that Razia's features, suitably trimmed and rice-powdered, might have landed her here, though it was a far cry. Razia's eyes were undisguisable and I, in any case, could not get in. The kimonoed women were specialists meant only for Japanese shoppers. Yet I never passed them without careful scrutiny.

Elsewhere I was welcome, a fixture you might say once they got to know me. I dare say I was a change from drunken sailors and the rest of the rabble. The aged beggar at the entrance to the sari cages waved his stubs and cackled a gleeful salaam as my coins rattled into his plate. He knew I needed no guide. I was one of the jostling regulars. Hope has its own branchline of agony, and these visits were no pleasure for me. They were too emotionally fraught. No aesthetic pleasure either. The women were ugly and, however young, they had an old indifference to their task. All but one, that is, of the Annie–Ida group. She had a furtive, faltering grace and a few gestures she had salvaged like trinkets secreted from a kinder past. When I had gazed long and searchingly at her for several nights in a row, it was she who invited me in and I lay with the wistful creature for two seasons of nights.

Sylla's reaction was a surprise, though considering her modernity it shouldn't have been. She came to lunch with me after spending the morning at her grandmother's and walked straight into the bedroom where I was sitting at my desk, staring at my red-striped scribbling pad. She lowered herself into an armchair without saying hello and said with weary resignation,

'I wish you'd told me about it, Jumbo.' I turned my chair around and studied my nails.

'You can't think how dreadful it was to be told by someone else, and Grandmother of all people. You've disillusioned her most horribly.'

'I'm sincerely sorry. I like her.'

'You can't expect a person of Grandmother's age to understand it's all part of your nympholepsy and that you're not a lascivious old lecher.'

'Is that what she thinks I am?'

'Goodness, Jumbo, what else is she to think? Besides, she feels at your age you should be settling into a position of responsibility. She's right. If you'd been to university, you'd have graduated by now and been a junior executive in your father's firm.'

'My father's "firm" is Vijaygarh,' I reminded her, 'and he doesn't want me in it. It's his idea, not mine, that I should make myself scarce for months of the year.'

'Only because you never showed any interest in the estate. You told me so yourself. You don't cultivate anybody there. You spend hours wandering around the bazaar. And basically your father has nothing to do with it. You are odd, you know. You could make more of your Bombay life, but you haven't even *got* a Bombay life. You're living *my* Bombay life. Why can't you make more out of *life*, Jumbo?'

My servant came in with a glass of coconut milk for her, which she drank distractedly.

'You could have been the world-famous film star instead of Valentino.'

Not that she wanted me to be one, she said, and I believed her. I must be the only man to have earned an Order of Merit for not doing something. She respected that decision. And there was not a trace of disapproval in her now. I perplexed her, and myself too. My mind ranged over Vijaygarh in search of an answer to my oddness, and stuck at a run-over dog in an alley, squashed so flat by a succession of vehicles that it lay levelled and pounded into the earth in a design of black and muddy white chalk. I said it must be the environment I had grown up in, its low level of oxygen – or aspiration – same thing. If you didn't fight for more, you were all right. The only person I had ever seen raving for more life to live was Mother. Always beating her brains out, in the old days, not now.

Sylla nodded, sadly sympathetic. 'What else can you pin it down to?'

Analysis was not really my line but pushed to it I came up with the whopping lies I had been fed with Mother's and geese's milk. Lies of omission and commission.

Sylla was taken aback. 'Deliberate lies, you mean?'

'That's one of the things I can't pin down. But it's a wonder they didn't go cross-eyed telling lies. Bloody liars!' I said vehemently. 'One whopper after another. I tell you, they don't know the difference between fact and fiction. It all flows down the Ganges together.'

'Everybody knows the difference,' said Sylla firmly.

I would have had to start at the eleventh century to explain to her how mentalities got ingrown toenails and warts under the skin and tumours as big as toadstools and suchlike. And then she wouldn't have been convinced. It's funny how the universe, for people of Sylla's straightforwardness, is made up of their papas and mamas multiplied a millionfold, and then there's the occasional oddbod.

'When I look at you, Sylla, I wonder if there's a human nature common to us all. You're so straight. But never mind all that. What did your grandmother say this morning?'

Sylla sat up straight, as though in the Habsburg chair, hands clasped in her lap, and copied her grandmother's imperious manner.

'"I educated you in England and Switzerland, Sylla. Why do you imagine I did so?"'

'"To be a success, and to make a brilliant marriage, Grandmother."'

'"Exactly." And then, Jumbo, she looked all old and tiny and said with a tremble in her voice, "And to be happy, you wilful girl. I will not have you unhappy." I rushed to kiss and console her and promised her I'd be happy. It was awful seeing her in that state. It gave me goosepimples. When we'd both cheered up, she said about you, "I suspect he is lazy at bottom." Which is the most damning thing she can say about anyone. "Doesn't he realize how old he is?" '

I held up my hand in a pledge-taking gesture.

'I do, I do. I'm twenty-three. The same age as Al Capone was two years ago when he took on the Chicago speakeasies and smashed them up if they didn't buy his brand of booze. Rumour has it he's been killing off the competition and making a roaring success of his career.'

Sylla began to laugh. I held out my hand and she came and sat on my lap. 'Anyway, Jumbo, do stop cantering around the red-light district in a victoria.'

'Would your grandmother prefer me to go in my Bugatti?'

We shrieked like children, silly children.

Sylla wiped her streaming eyes. 'Grandmother doesn't want you to be as successful as Al Capone. There are other successful men.'

Bombay was teeming with them. She named six Parsees off the cuff. Between kisses I named three more Parsees. But we both knew I had wrecked my chances with Grandmother.

'Stuff her diamonds!' said Sylla in a scintillating spurt of disloyalty that we both knew had nothing to do with loving her grandmother and being her precious pet. Sylla and I knew each other so well, so very well, that in the instant she streaked off my lap and stood over me, a taut arched cat, I knew she was going to say, 'And how do you blasted well know Al Capone is being such a roaring success? You've had a letter from your American chum.'

Modernity is not all open house. Sylla could be philosophical, analytical and medical about Razia, and an appeasing angel when it came to local prostitutes, but her hackles rose at the mere thought of a woman eleven thousand miles away with whom I'd never had the tremor of a romance. Plenty of healthy exercise, yes. I ordered lunch, and over lunch I told Sylla I had heard from Willie-May about Al Capone, and Willie-May should know. She had run away from home and married one of Al Capone's boys – who were helping him smash speakeasies – and Al had done them proud. She and her beau had driven to their wedding in an armoured car with a bodyguard car in front and back, followed by a fleet of shining gangster cars. Chicago's most prominent citizens had come to the wedding and what a wedding! Police had had to control the fans waiting in the snow outside the church to shower confetti on them. Al had given them a ten-foot wedding cake and a honeymoon in Rio de Janeiro for a present. Her daddy had been desolate about the match, but the connection was proving so valuable, he was gradually coming round to accepting Al's big, dynamic, result-oriented family, closer to each other than blood brothers. Willie-May's husband was an insanely jealous hunk of a man and she was divinely happy. Altogether it sounded a good second best to being lassoed, or drugged and galloped to an oasis. And this very Willie-May, I said to Sylla, had once admired *me*, a man with no ambition.

'Say what you like, all women worship success and ambition. How can I blame your grandmother?'

I got up and put my arms around the only exception. She put hers around me.

'I know why I need you, Sylla. You're sane. You're my nest from storm, plague, pestilence, not to mention the Hindu–Muslim love-madness that rages in my middle ear.'

'Silly,' murmured Sylla tenderly.

'Yes, Sylla mine, that's why I need you. We might be the same age, but you're young and I'm old, you're clean and I'm a cesspool. But why in God's name would someone like you need me?'

Most men would not have felt flattered by the length of her pause before she said, 'Mm, now let me see,' and paused again.

'I know why, Jumbo. I think it's because if you were successful, you'd be busy every minute of the day. And this way, look at us! We can be together whenever we want to, in the middle of the day or the night. I can jump into my car and pop over any old time.'

So, what women want more than success and ambition seems to be a round-the-clock lover.

I was wrong if I thought I could block out the court with a mutter of Sylla-Sylla-Sylla. Some nights the enemy lawyer's interrogation goes relentlessly on in my sleep, but these are questions he has with deliberate cunning avoided asking in court, to keep the court in ignorance.

'What is your religion?'

'I am a Hindu Muslim.' Or put it the other way round, lawyer.

'Your mother tongue?'

'Poetry. But if you're going to finick about it, my mother tongue is Hindi, and my father tongue is Urdu, she – illiterate though she is – hailing from the Sanskrit script and paraphernalia, and he from everything that hit us when Islam rode in. Let me assure you, Father wouldn't know Hindi letters from a crab's crawl. His tongue doesn't rise to the higher pillars of Hindi pronunciation. The glories of Sanskrit are Greek to him. The capital of his culture is Persia. For Mother it's all tongue and no script. She's forgotten how to read and can't write. The Ganges valley has other plans for its women.'

'This levity won't do,' raps the lawyer. 'Which language do you speak at home? What are you, a Hindu or a Muslim?'

Now this requires reflection. Then I say I've dreamed in both languages. My diet, and therefore my digestion, are mostly Muslim, but my blood seems to circulate in Hindu fashion, and my heart beats alternately to each.

I must have foreseen the trend his attack will take because in court he introduces what he calls the Hindu–Muslim Question. It becomes an issue, problem, obstacle, impasse and dilemma as he goes along. It winds up a riddle of the Sphinx: What goes on four feet, on two feet, and three? But the more feet it goes on the weaker it be? Against the backdrop of this insoluble riddle, he launches a frontal attack on my politics. Nauzer is on his feet to remind the court I detest politics, have none, and have said so on oath in the witness stand. But this, claims the enemy, is a typically evasive, deceitful and misleading reply, the type of reply I insist on giving to throw justice off its track. Isn't politics the same as religion in this country? And aren't I up to my ears in religious intrigue? Does the court know, for example, that I was responsible – solely – for instigating a Hindu–Muslim riot in Vijaygarh in 1917, and another in 1918, the two most barbaric religious riots in forty years? As he claims and declaims, the court starts its journey to the interior, the path winds inexorably, fatally backward to

Vijaygarh. It is almost a relief. How long can it be avoided? He has a mass of information about the riots. He describes them, especially the second tornado, for days.

'Picture to yourself,' he says, 'this seventeen or eighteen-year-old nearly adult male, to whom the kindest epithet we can apply is delinquent . . .'

Another day he addresses me directly. 'Does it not strike you as peculiar that you should be among these agitators whose confessed aim is to overthrow the raj?'

'Very peculiar indeed,' I fervently agree, which annoys him because he takes no notice of my reply.

'Aren't you afraid to cast your lot with those who would dispossess you and throw you on the rubbish heap if they had the opportunity? The Bolshevik creed makes no secret of this.'

It's an Anglo-Indian sergeant who cast this lot and threw me on this particular rubbish heap, I want to remind him, but here come the Bolsheviks again. As the enemy lawyer expands his thesis I see them coming, rather like Comrade Dey's description of the Tsar's Cossacks hurtling down a flight of steps to mow down the fleeing crowd in *The Battleship Potemkin*. But as the lawyer warms up my Bolsheviks warm up too. They thunder down through the Khyber Pass on horseback, with their horned standards, five-foot iron bows and iron shields, steel-tipped arrows and scimitars. From Kandahar to the Indus they plunge through gorges, passing the tower of human skulls erected by their lame ancestor, Timur. Coming, in other words, in the time-honoured way, on the beaten path, to douse the plain in a time-honoured bloodbath. But the enemy lawyer seems to be waiting for an answer. I give a foolish shrug.

'What's the difference? If they're coming, they'll come, won't they? Inevitable. Everyone else has. It's probably their turn next.' I glance across at the judge who is as pale and tense as if he had been looking at the same images I had, and say to him, 'Your lot, of course, came the longer way round, by sea.'

Insomnia is an old complaint. I've never slept well, and I can't after the wearisome hours in court. But I do feel I'm jogging homeward and soon will arrive. The lawyer's diatribe, the judge's censure, are so familiar, they don't daunt me. Father.

Uncle. Tutor. To some extent, Sylla. In their way, each of them has made the same point, a lack in me, some vital ingredient left out. But I don't have to worry. Nauzer, rising star in his profession, knows his job.

# Chapter Fourteen

Mother was the only person who didn't think there was anything wrong with me. She was unperturbed about my bachelor life. Bachelor life was whatever a bachelor chose to make it, and the stars were not propitious for my marriage yet. On a visit home I told her it was just as well, as the only woman I wanted to marry didn't want to marry me. I had to repeat this blasphemy, then she said, 'Bittan, hear this?' and made me say it again.

'Explain!' commanded Mother.

'It's quite simple. Sylla and I don't have much in common, and for a while I was seeing another woman.'

They waited for the real explanation, these being incredible reasons for not marrying me.

'Sylla is not one of us. She's a Parsee.'

Mother greeted this with distaste. She had heard Parsees were people who had a hankering for cold fried eggs.

'Sylla could never live in Vijaygarh. She doesn't observe purdah.'

'Describe this Parsee woman to me.'

I did, to Mother's mounting amazement. I guillotined Sylla with every sentence.

'She has short hair. It's brownish. She smokes cigarettes. She has green eyes. She wears beige. Mostly English clothes – frocks – and to be perfectly honest, much less for swimming. She swims.'

When Mother recovered she said, 'The Commissioner's wife

dresses in this style. I don't know if nature or her garb has flattened her chest but she looks positively ironed. How can one wish to have no bosom whatsoever, and hair like a man's?'

I wanted to ask, despairing, Where did your beautiful bounteous bosom get you? What guarantees were your eyes, your glorious hair, your fruitful womb? Did any of it save you from damnation, even the birth of a son? But I said, by way of rescuing Sylla from the mire, that these were modern times. Mother cared nothing for modern times. She'd never heard of them.

'Marriage can wait until you find a modest woman or I find you one. Astrologically you mustn't marry yet. You'll marry when the constellations are right. Your horoscope says so.' Said she with a smile of smug satisfaction, forgetting her own and every other experience of marriage within recall.

'Times are changing, Mother. Who would have imagined the Turkish Khalifa would be sent on a permanent holiday and there'd be no pope of Islam?'

She hadn't heard, and received the news gravely. She wanted to know what was being done about it.

'King Fuad of Egypt is canvassing to become the new pope, but the Egyptians don't approve. Emir Ibn Saud now controls Mecca and Medina and he probably has a better chance of succeeding to the papal throne, but he knows better than to try. The popeship is finished. Turkey has the right idea.'

This stung Mother into retorting she had heard this new Saudi champion of Islam belonged to an upstart puritanical sect that had destroyed the decorations on some tombs at Mecca. What was religion without incense and flowers, even if it went off the deep end at the sight of an idol? But faraway changes didn't affect her. Hejaz was so far off her pilgrim beat that it didn't matter one way or another if it was getting motor cars, telephones and a railway. Let those who had gods to propitiate there rejoice. It was useless talking to Mother about change. No one could have set out on the journeys she did if she hadn't believed her own world was going to stay securely in place till the end of time.

Mother's occasional dictated letters to the jail have no spark. Father's fossil has taken them down through her curtain and put them into his own withered prose. Sylla doesn't write, and I feel strangely abandoned as I face interrogation in court.

'This man who says he has no politics, addressed a political meeting in Bombay.' The lawyer gives the date, and the address of the hall.

Now he wants the court, keeping the Vijaygarh riots in mind, to pay close attention. (As if the court had any choice.) The meeting was held in support of the Khilafat movement, that celebrated cause of the early twenties, jointly backed by the Hindus and Muslims in their reverence for the Ottoman Sultan–Caliph. But what does the accused do? He sabotages it. He appears on that platform to betray his hosts and set fire to beliefs both communities hold sacred. He calls these 'baggage' to be 'dumped'. He goes so far as to say there is no difference worth preserving between them. They are one.

'I put it to you, my lord, these communities have lived honourably apart, preserving their differences under British protection. Yet the accused shrieked obscenities at them, calling on them to destroy this status quo and mix.'

Nauzer plays with the top of his fountain pen. He seems to have the matter well in hand.

'It is not at all clear, my lord, whose agent he is,' the enemy continues, 'a Hindu agent to subvert Islam, or hired by the Mohammedans to poison his own traditions, and let that remain a hypothetical question. The country well knows His Majesty's Government is committed to holding the line between the communities, and Muslim loyalty has been rewarded with special protection. Does the accused fancy himself as the prophet of a new era?'

The tirade rolls on into winter. There is a certain comic aspect to it if any of us had been in the mood for comedy. The enemy lawyer can't have enough of my 'political' performance and keeps referring to it. He says I ranted about hats replacing turbans when the Prophet himself ordered turbans. He can prove it: 'God and the angels give their blessing at the Friday prayer to those who wear turbans.' 'Two prostrations with the turban outweigh seventy without the turban.' 'The turban is the barrier separating belief and unbelief.' He says I advocated clean-shavenness when the Prophet himself said, 'Distinguish yourselves from idolators; let your beards grow and trim your moustaches.' Had I or had I not said – he turns to face me at last after showing me his back and regaling the court with turbans, beards and moustaches for an hour – that a man with a beard cannot think clearly? Had I not made fun of the martial traditions of my own caste? If I was not the agent of a foreign power, he said, showing me his profile, then devout Hindus and Mohammedans were justified in believing I was an agent of the devil sent to unite them. The government would never permit it.

It has never occurred to me that the Bolsheviks – this scourge like a misfired orgasm that continually seems to be coming and never comes – are going to find another mention in my case, but here they come again. We are told they are out to storm the citadel of Islam.

'Incredible as it may seem, my lord, there is a Mohammedan sitting among the communist accused.'

Comrade Yusuf takes advantage of the Bengali traitor's dramatic pause to rise and give the most courtly bow I have ever seen outside accounts of travellers to the Mogul court. He and his comrades are quite recovered from their kicking. Iyer who had the worst of it has a look of hardened cement. Rain or shine, they're ready for battle. There's a hint of a smile on Yusuf's attractive face as he listens to the seditious call of a co-religionist made a few years ago.

'"Oh Mohammedans,"' the lawyer quotes, '"respond to Comrade Lenin. Be afraid instead of the sea wolves who live on pillage of the world."'

This dramatic pause is ruined by a tooting horn outside, while the Soviet-style muezzin's cry echoes bizarrely on the man's Harrow-Hooghly tongue. But the point he is making is that my stance on turbans makes me accessory to a crazy Mohammedan's treason. His diatribe and Nauzer's replies are typed out by the judge on his smart portable, read by the court reader, and by the time all the typing and reading are done the charge against me has rocketed from political to elemental and fundamental, from depriving the King Emperor of his sovereignty to uprooter of the social fabric.

'An aim we are familiar with, my lord. How different is he then – as his counsel's plea has sought to establish – from the communists in the dock?'

At this point the comrades and I exchange a tired gleam in place of the tart, leaping rejoinder they might have flung back eighteen months ago. We look at each other across Bhaiji, who has slumped low in his chair and isn't, we suddenly realize, sleeping. He has fainted. Proceedings are halted while the stretcher bearers take him back to the jail. Then Nauzer deals adroitly with the enemy.

'My client is an agnostic. But he has the utmost respect for Hinduism and Islam, and no wish to demolish the sacred beliefs of either. He is a poet and he may be forgiven his poet's vision of a realm where all gods are one. I would go further and say he dreams of a dawn when there will be no dividing characteristics of race, colour, feature, worship left on earth. These are his politics, my lord, this is his vision.'

The typewriter stops its agitated clanking. The judge looks up warily. His cheeks are pinker. He wants to know if I have any concrete plans for bringing about such a state of affairs. Satisfied I have none, the typewriter clacks on. Nauzer says he realizes visions don't count as evidence in a court of law, but since his client's character has been so wrongfully attacked, he wants to say no vision such as his client's can come to a man who is not motivated by the highest ideals.

'On one occasion, my lord, as that very seventeen-year-old we have heard so cruelly denigrated, he had an actual experience when – to use the language of your own religion, my lord – he felt he had been baptized by the Holy Ghost.'

'This is not the Middle Ages,' says the judge. 'It is not the accused's state of soul which is on trial.'

I feel it has gone rather well, but at the end of the day Nauzer is worried. They've shifted their attack. From a disreputable wastrel I've become a saboteur.

The jail infirmary doesn't know what ails Bhaiji. I'm not surprised. It consists of three beds, an enema can, malaria pills and carbolic acid. Bhaiji needs morphia. He is in pain. His cough stabs his chest and leaves him groaning. He shivers with fever. A tenant Munna dealt with too severely in the ribs got a condition somewhat like Bhaiji's and died in hospital of water in the lung. I ask him where his family is, but he is that museum specimen among Indians. He has no next of kin. His leader is his next of kin. But none of us has even a nodding acquaintance with Gandhi and can't drop him a postcard to his jail in Poona, letting him know an obscure khaddar worker in a God-forsaken jail seems to be petering out painfully for want of proper treatment. They might not release him if he asked, but he won't ask. Our helpless fury is about equally distributed between Bhaiji and the jail authorities. Being the chronic insomniac among us, I help him to sit up when he coughs at night. He leans against me and I joke with him about the Vedic lifespan. In the dark I sense his ghostly anguished grin. I hold him till he drowses off. The twins sleep like logs and when they're awake they blubber. One night Bhaiji remembers the yarn he and the twins have spun, and says I should request the jail super-intendent to send a message to his fallen sisters, who will come and collect it. He sleeps better when this is done.

Christmas comes and the judge takes a few days' holiday. When the court reopens he and the cross-examiner get back to me. It is mid-February 1931 when I survey a row of objects on a wooden tray held up to me, and irritably confirm these are the objects I surrendered to the jailer on the far-off day the sergeant brought me here. Whose, if not mine? They came out of my pockets, didn't they? But they want me to be certain, to identify each one. An initialled wallet of blue Roman leather I bought on the year before last's trip abroad. It had contained a few hundred rupees I've spent paying for my meals, cigarettes, warder's bribes and sweeper's tips etc. My gold Vacheron et Constantin. A flat gold cigarette case inscribed: 'Jumbo from Sylla – wishing him many loving returns of the battle for Afium Quarahisar.' My passport folder without the passport, which they must have kept. A thumbnail-size bronze Ganesh I travel with at Mother's insistence. A sharp, exquisitely wrought paper knife with a blade as fine as silk, unusual for its sword shape in a miniature silver scabbard. I had forgotten I was carrying it. It, too, had travelled with me over the years. On that last evening at the Taj I must have put it distractedly into my pocket, and not in the flap of my suitcase with other knicknacks. I doubt if I have ever examined an object so thoroughly from every angle to the court's satisfaction before I identify it as mine. A gift from the friend whose initials are embossed on it.

'Is this the friend?'

I recognize him immediately. He could be risen from the grave as he rises from his chair in the last row. Across the room he has the scarcely altered face of a cadaver whose furrowed greyness now fits it better. He is shown the wooden tray and says the paper knife is his.

'Did you make a gift of it to the accused?'

'I most emphatically did not.'

But he does remember the year, month and day to the hour – as he has this information in an old appointment diary – when it must have been stolen from his desk. No, he had not been aware of the theft at that precise moment. He would not have turned a blind eye to a criminal act if he had had the slightest suspicion. It was obviously pilfered when he was at the other end of the room on a step ladder hunting for a book with his back to his desk. Plenty of time for a dextrous sleight of hand. He had not missed it until he reached for it many days later to open an unusually thickly layered registered parcel. It was a favourite of his, the most efficient little paper knife he had, apart from its value in silver and as a collector's item of unique shape and carving. He had been very sorry to lose it. Frankly, it does not surprise him to learn who the thief is.

The judge tap-taps while he talks. I study the space where the tray was held up for my inspection and see an array of penknives and paper knives laid in a dusted, polished row beside two cut-glass inkpots in their silver salver.

'What can you tell us of the accused's character from what you know of him?'

The ex-Commissioner smiles thinly.

'I can tell you he was a born troublemaker. After the second riot his father had to send him away to keep him out of mischief, and others out of danger. All the way to America. I did not approve. Home is the place for discipline. His criminal instincts should have been taken in hand at home.'

Nauzer is up, visibly disturbed. Which of us, as boys, has not succumbed to a chance temptation, he pleads. Can this be called theft? Criminal? Delinquent? Once his client had impulsively picked up the paper knife and put it into his pocket, wouldn't it have been impossibly awkward for him to try and put it back? But leaving that aspect of it aside . . . And Nauzer leaves it aside to expound a lyrical psychology. He pleads with the rosy judge to understand the yearnings of a scion of a household of the martial caste that has been deprived of its traditional weapons. The sword-shaped paper knife becomes a yearning, not a theft. It becomes a symbol of the sword it resembles, of an ancestral right. It is an object to be cherished for the tradition it once represented. This act, says Nauzer, was a matter of face, honour, prestige. He draws once again on the judge's Bible.

'The Bible tells us man's first free act was one of disobedience, indeed of theft. It tells us we sin, and repent, and are forgiven.'

Nauzer has been magnificent, but on the lorry ride home to jail Comrade Yusuf remarks, 'Why did Mr Vacha make such a mountain out of a molehill?' Comrade Dey adds that capitalists have a weird sense of proportion. Hours can be spent in their courts of law attacking and defending a man who purloined a penknife. But sail out and loot a country, bash up the population and make a scavengers' feast of their remains, and you went down in history as Something the Great. They all laugh. I'm not in the mood. My thoughts are muddled and disconnected.

I wake quickly to help Bhaiji up. Sometimes I'm awake for the rest of the night, or in a light half-sleep. I rehearse past events, the first time I heard about the imbecile, for instance, by sheer accident. Suppose I hadn't walked into Mother's room at that very instant, would that instant left out of my life have altered its course? It is as useless to ask as where my beloved and I would have been today if she had not knelt down to pray just when she did. Then I keep wondering why, on that June night of my arrival in Bombay Sylla let me force her to stay for dinner, and let herself be practically dragged to bed before dinner came. Once there, she was more than willing, and she could, of course, have left whenever she liked, but why had she behaved so untypically, and why had I forced myself on her the first night we met after a long separation? No such boorish breach of manners had ever happened between us. Sylla is neither helpless nor coy, but she let me behave like a cad, and if she stayed for old times' sake, why didn't she see me alone after that, when I was prolonging my stay in Bombay at *her* request, to act in *her* play. No project had ever kept her that busy in the past. She could always find time. But there I was, at a loose end, roaming around the hotel, going up and down the lift with the Turkish children, chatting about the rain with the sheikh on the stairs, spending my time with total strangers.

I don't agree with my companions that Nauzer made too much of the paper-knife episode. I have had complete confidence in him since the day I spoke to him about my inner promptings. I remember how he took out his handkerchief and hurriedly touched the corners of his eyes with it, leaving them damp and bright as windowpanes after rain. He had a clean cologne smell and the labyrinths of law had not dimmed his sensitivity. That day, and from them on, I felt he was defending me, not a 'client'. He was taking my side not merely because he had been professionally engaged to do so, but because he personally cared about the outcome. I had touched a chord in him. Now I wish I had been less resistant to him in the beginning. Things I should have done or not done jostle claustrophobically in my brain. Events that do not seem to be, but must in some way be, connected with each other, come and go.

These two years we have wasted here, says Comrade Pillai, could be subtracted from our sentences if we're sentenced, or might wipe out our sentences altogether. There's something wrong with these men. They are forever divining and devising escape routes based on fantastic theses. Their optimism is absolutely unrelated to the world around them. Forget it, I say. You've been conked on the head with rifle butts. You've been thrown on the court floor and kicked in the testicles. One of you has vanished without a trace. Their eyes shine. Of such ordeals is the history of struggle. Victory is a scientific certainty. No sadhu of Mother's was madder. I can't be like them. Nor can I resign myself to come what may like Bhaiji and the twins. But I must make an effort to integrate these claustrophobic thoughts of mine before the trial ends and I have to start coping with the outside again.

Bhaiji is very ill. And now I drowse off myself while I sit on his cot holding him securely in my arms. I see Mother on her journey crossing endless rivers that flow down valleys to the sea. They roll up in vapour, unroll again as rain, and she keeps going. Now she comes to the hills, climbs higher, higher, past bare rock and gigantic boulders toward a hidden summit. A cold stiff breeze pulls her hair, tears at her sari. In the spectral light I realize with a shock her feet are bare. She looks up at the moon and draws her shawl tighter about her. If she is thinking, how freezing and desolate it is up here, she never once asks. 'Why am I going?' She seems to know. The stars are few and scattered. The sky is vast and naked as the last lap of her ascent has been of foliage. But now she rounds a rock and sees the summit. Her feet are so light, she could be floating. Dust turns to gold beneath her feet. Gold dust crowns her hair. The earth has never seen such radiant anticipation. She's there at last, at the mouth of the cave.

None of us went with her, Bittan always said when the tale was told and retold. We didn't have her stamina, and she insisted this part of the pilgrimage had to be suffered barefoot and alone. None of us could have done it. But she was alone and unafraid at the holy heights, with the lighted tents of Father's camp far, far below. Father drank, dined, played cards, made a musical night of it. We maidservants slept, said Bittan.

Before I lower Bhaiji to his pillow and go to my own cot I have a hopeless desire to see arms reach out to embrace her, a voice say, 'Beloved, I will love you all our lives,' and the light of a million suns transfigure them both for that one night.

Perhaps that is how it happened, my tireless pilgrim, my mother, or whoever you are, and Father's stray droplets had nothing to do with it.

# Chapter Fifteen

The Lahore Conspiracy Case is closed – with three hangings. The twins are back from the superintendent's office where their lawyer gave them the news. Bhagat Singh and his two close colleagues were executed in Lahore Jail yesterday, March 23, and surreptitiously cremated on the banks of the Sutlej river. The government rejected the public petition of mercy raised on their behalf. Gandhi is out of jail but he couldn't get the execution stayed. Bhaiji, rigid with anger, says from his cot, 'And this Viceroy calls himself a Christian. This is the Viceroy who a month ago said, "Goodnight, Mr Gandhi, my prayers go with you." A curse upon the Viceroy's prayers.'

The comrades say a lot more in floods of impassioned invective. In this ominous empire the thirst for freedom is a crime, so let there be more crime, if that's what they call it. A country under foreign bayonets is perpetually at war with the government. This government was not content with a twenty-year sentence and transportation for life for Bhagat Singh and his aides. They had to kill them.

No one sleeps, but no one except me is alive to a warning of individual deadly danger. The night divides into the groans and startled sleep cries of the men across the yard, and the warder's numerical count through a forest of regurgitated phlegm. The twins lie still as stones, and one by one the comrades succumb. I listen for Bhaiji's grinding cough. It doesn't come. A few quarter-hours of this and I am thoroughly awake, and uneasy. Then I know why he doesn't cough. He's dead. He must have died soon after pronouncing judgement on the Viceroy. I have no idea how long I sit on the edge of my cot, elbows on my knees, and my fingers pressed to my aching eyeballs, summoning the will to do whatever has to be done. The dark grows less dense. The sky below the roof begins to show. The gap Sen went through is getting paler. Bhaiji seems at rest. The shrivelled bag of bones his illness made of him has lengthened and smoothed. The relief on his face is a man's with no debts to repay. He paid as he went. For some reason I fumble for a final word or thought by way of farewell, but I'm not good at holy thoughts and the poetry I can think of would not appeal to Bhaiji. It's best to let him speak his own epitaph. His reedy voice dispersing Sanskrit wisdom and his own handspun handwoven gems comes to me. I pick out a Sanskrit saying. It goes something like this: When we are born, we cry and others laugh. Let's live so that when we die, others may cry, but we will laugh. If this is a true saying, Bhaiji, you must be laughing your head off, while I, in a sorrow that must be purely impersonal – for how long did I know you, and would we have ever met again after jail? – I will now give myself up to fulfilling the other half of it. Nearly morning now, I weep my last and wake the others, who stumble to their feet, still in a sleep stupor. We, his next of kin, have to reach a quick decision.

The jail authorities will never let us cremate him here, and we cannot surrender Bhaiji to a mass cremation ground where he will be thrown on a paupers' collective funeral pyre, short of wood and ceremony, and set insanitarily afloat half-roasted for crocodiles reclining down-river. Well might his body be his 'outer garment', thankfully cast off, but since his outer garment is all we have left of him, we are resolved it must be treated with respect. As a last resort I suggest the fallen sisters who took away the yarn. They are nearby and responded in a businesslike way before. The twins raise a ravaged howl of protest and say they will never consent to such an outrage. The comrades lash out at tradition and Pillai starts a lecture on the causes of prostitution. It becomes a fierce quarrel, badly shaken as we all are by death in our midst, the news from Lahore and a bad night. But sunrise and the remorseless logic of a dead body on a warm

March day don't leave much scope for argument. As light slips into the barrack we reach a consensus – the fallen sisters – but the jailer, who we thought would be anxious to have the body off the premises, sends us word that according to Rule 1032 of the jail manual: 'Nobody can lay claim to a corpse as it is not property.' This is based, he explains, on the Common Law of England. I send him a note reminding him we are not low-class persons, but respectable middle-class (though high and low in the middle) prisoners, and he has given us his word that the government knows the difference. The sun has risen higher by the time he relents. But now he sends a message on our behalf and arranges jail transport for the body's removal. Another hour, and the warder comes to tell us the woman is here, the same one who came for the yarn. One of us is to accompany him to the outer gate and give her instructions. My companions assume I am the man to deal with a fallen sister. The weeping twins start washing Bhaiji's body and preparing it as best they can.

The sister superior of the fallen stands at the gate, her open burka a formal concession to this outing, a big-bellied mountain of a woman with hennaed hair. She stares at me and before I can say a word she exclaims sharply, 'Ma sha' 'llah! Can it be you?' I'm at a loss. 'What in Almighty's name are *you* doing here?' She slaps her forehead and suddenly I recognize this middle-aged mountain as my teacher. She it was whose humorous generous ease initiated a sixteen-year-old into the rites he has been embroidering and improvising on ever since, she who laid the foundation of what might have become the backbone of a Hollywood fortune. Fancy meeting you here, we both say. A vivacious teacher, swift to praise, she'd once had a lovely smile. It's lost in folds of fat and she is as agitated as a mother at what boarding school has done to her child. I stem her torrent of questions by asking her about herself. That quietens her. She tells me she moved to this area years ago to set up a small select establishment of her own. The Nawab Sahib of Ramnagar helped her with money and recommendations until he died and now she has his son's patronage and is doing very comfortably thank you, teaching the gentry their ABC. It is such a pleasure not having coarse crude low types to deal with.

'These are all gentlemen and my girls are well looked after. But what have they done to you? Look how thin and dark you've become. I'll send you some good nourishing food. No problem. I've done the jailer several favours.'

She refuses to take money for Bhaiji's cremation. She has already sent a servant to a well-heeled Hindu client who has offered to pay for the ceremonies apart from arranging them, but she'll pay expenses herself. It's the least she can do for Bhaiji. A dear good man. Not a penny to his name but otherwise a perfect gentleman.

'How did you meet him?'

'He came to apologize to us for the lust of his fellow men. He said it made him hang his head in shame. He asked the girls if they would give up the life they were leading if they could earn their living doing something else. Of course they wouldn't. By then, you see, we were in clover. But he took it well. He said he appreciated their honesty and that their moral lot would improve as soon as they started spinning. Well, why not, we thought, and then we got involved in his other activities. We picketed the local liquor shop in our burkas – he's an awful scoundrel, that dealer, and I was delighted to do him down – and we promised Bhaiji we would boycott the Prince of Wales's minions if the prince came our way, but he didn't.'

Yusuf, Pillai and the twins carry Bhaiji's body out on a bier and place it in the ancient van. It's time to go. The driver cranks the engine and gets in. The van vibrates as its engine roars. My teacher lifts her hand in imitation of its once graceful salute to each of us in turn. What the gesture has lost in slenderness it retains in polish and *politesse*. A gracious lady who I am confident will deal graciously with Bhaiji's mortal remains. As the van roars off we rush to get ready for court.

On arrival, Comrade Pillai says he doesn't know the ins and outs of court procedure but he wishes to make a statement. The court has not yet settled down and the judge hasn't made up his mind how to respond when Pillai gets up from his chair, steps forward into the room and starts reading it: 'We are attending court today under the grim shadow of a dastardly execution, a most gruesome piece of imperial justice, a cowardly act of white terror. We honour these men as martyrs to the cause of national revolution in India.' The judge forbids him to go on. Pillai goes on. The judge gives notice he will punish defiance by adjourning the court. I protest as loudly as the others at this threat. Pillai sits down where he his, arms across his chest, and has to be bodily removed to his chair.

I am in a state of gibbering relief when Nauzer returns and I feel like hitting him when he says I have nothing to worry about. He'll be saying so when I'm swinging from the gallows. A respite in Bombay has restored Nauzer's nerves to normal. He says it's no wonder I am jittery. The atmosphere in court must be getting me down. The Lahore death sentences have taken the country by storm. Even the Parsee community is up in arms.

'Why did they hang those men?'

Nauzer gravely agrees the government has gone too far. Sylla's uncle, a member of the Viceroy's Council, has resigned in protest. Other prominent citizens whose loyalty to the government was never in doubt have openly condemned the executions. Nauzer admits the judgement may influence other conspiracy cases.

'And you're telling me I have nothing to worry about.'

'I know how you feel,' he sympathizes. 'It looks serious for the men with you. But don't be depressed. It will be over soon as far as you're concerned.'

We both know it's nearly two years since he first said so.

'Sylla sent her love. She's ashamed she hasn't written, but she never expected such a drawn-out trial. She's hoping for a face-to-face chat soon.'

Is she now? Does anyone wait two years for a chat? And is a chat what one has after two locked-up years? I feel ill and drained of hope. Next to Nauzer I look an evil mess.

'You're lying, Nauzer,' I snap, scraping back my chair.

'I wouldn't lie to you,' he replies with dignity. 'Calm down, my friend. A little more patience. We have a great deal to talk about once this is over.'

He goes off to Bombay again, leaving me to wrestle with my demons. I have a premonition of imminent disaster as Comrade Iyer, spokesman for his group, takes the stand and begins reading the tome they have prepared together. It opens with a sentence of vast incomparable idiocy. These demented optimists haven't yet grasped the danger they are in.

'In a conspiracy case,' reads Comrade Iyer, 'it is expected the accused will show whether or not they are communists. Therefore we wish to inform you at the outset that we are communists.'

He has said so in this room two years ago. Today it's not hilariously obvious. It is catastrophic. Bhaiji's approval of honesty is for fools. The prosecution parade laid snares for us and we have fallen in. But not content with the damage, these men are setting sail for the high seas in a boat they've taken care to punch holes in.

'We don't believe the English have the authority to arrest us, or any English court the authority to detain us in prison and pass sentence on us. We do not recognize this court You are not our judge. This is why we have no counsel to defend us.'

My head is bowed, supported by my hands. I sit as though at another deathbed. This is another death rattle, but merry and bright. It is a pearl out of the same illusory necklace we all wear that keeps us from believing what we see, what starkly stares us in the face. Comrade Iyer is in the dock, no two ways about it. Why doesn't he believe it? There was I, while the sadhu held his breath for a hundred and eight minutes and the fire walker's soles stayed cool and unscorched, but I didn't believe it. And Mother who knows marriage for the chamber of horrors it is, hunts for a modest curtained bride for me. Is there no limit to our pearly illusions?

'We do not accept the charge against us. We wish to rephrase it as follows: "The accused are pledged to deprive British financial capital of its sovereign right to exploit the Indian masses." We also stand accused of influencing the young.'

I will not be able to endure the strain and tedium of this next stretch of statement and cross-examination. The end of this trial is nowhere near and propaganda, whether it is Iyer's or the prosecution's, is dry dreary stuff.

But I'm wrong. This comrade has an ear for the march of words. His cadences grip my jaded attention. Nonsense you may be speaking, comrade, but how compellingly you speak it. Against my will I hear a fairy tale unfold. This world won't long remain a warring jungle where man eats man. A day will dawn when it will unite, take root – history has decreed it – in purified new foundations. Its people will be one. Its very streams and mountains will be new. Humanity is on its way to it. No terror can halt the caravans. On the appointed day – it is written – they shall arrive, enter the gates and be reborn, a truly human race no longer motivated by greed or grab, to live as equals, in peace for ever more amen.

I shiver and cover my eyes, and the music passes, leaving me, a bystander, on the roadside with its harmonies and their echoes sounding in my ears. To each his own paradise, Iyer. We've heard of other apocalyptic visions, why not this one? But though he moves on from revelation to industrial affairs, his prophecy continues to hang in the courtroom like a map of tomorrow.

Iyer upbraids the government for hiding its intentions behind the drama of national and international conspiracy, when the real issue is the pack animal we call the Indian working man. For asserting the rights of these, he and his comrades are facing trial for 'conspiracy'.

'We have never conspired,' he proudly declares. 'Our aims are open. If thousands have downed their tools it's not because we told them to, but because the human animal tires of his pack and crawling on all fours.'

He might as well be a town crier trumpeting 'Hear me! Hear me!' till he pierces the deafest ear-drum. But these are dull facts and statistics. The judge probably knows them and doesn't turn a hair. It is the shimmering domes and spires of Iyer's prophecy that will not go away. The judge is rigidly absorbed, not in workers' wages, but in this rival blueprint to his Christian heaven. It strikes me that those who have had military control of the world – the Muslims, the Christians – don't care for rival blueprints. Heaven had better be their heaven. Never say to one of these, 'All gods are one; men call them by different names.' They will impale you on their ignorant stares, snarl infidel, and attack. Winners can't live and let live. Their ongoing jihads, crusades and inquisitions are evidence of that. And history has few sights in its showcase as gory as jihad against crusade. It takes the wide philosophical gaze of the defeated to allow each man his own paradise. Let's drink to the losers, judge, and to the rainbow harvest of defeat.

'We've been deprived of rights every Englishman enjoys. Illegal imprisonment. Our third year of it. Don't hunt for evidence to accuse us. We accuse *you*! Of illegal occupation. Of conditions in this country. Of murder. Too many corpses lie between us and the British government. Most recently, three in Lahore, one this morning in our barrack, last year a boy who in two years' time would have completed the average lifespan in this country under the King Emperor, but you got him sooner.'

So Sen is dead. Comradely intuition, or literary flourish? Yet Sen, it is clear, is dead. And buried with the other two on the night of 'mutiny'. The Common Law of England decrees nobody can lay claim to a corpse as it is not property. The jail manual says so. And in his crescendo of mounting accusations Comrade Iyer seems to be proclaiming, 'Sen is dead. Long live the Sens.' I envy Iyer his fighting spirit. I just don't have it. I cannot think in terms of Sens. I add one more futile grief to the register. Shall I mourn this one, wiped out so very young? He will never be married or a clerk, nor ever scale another prison wall to stop another prisoner's flogging nightmare. The causes of grief and rejoicing are evenly balanced in Sen's case.

Nauzer is not here. The communist tome is lengthy – they're taking turns reading it – and Nauzer will be back from Bombay before it is over. But I've become dependent on his presence. The courtroom is a sea of sharks. Not one of us is safe and our solidarity has worn thin. Holding the floor has exhilarated the comrades. They discuss the day's testimony among themselves, bound and nurtured by its umbilical cord. The twins have withdrawn into their own despondencies. Our sole common bond is that there's no evidence against any of us. But with the town crier's hearty welcome the comrades keep extending to 'mass revolutionary violence', it won't matter that none of us has committed it.

Nauzer writes asking me to look ahead, beyond my acquittal. 'All this will soon be over.' I know I have a future but its exact shape eludes me. I'm out of touch – with Sylla, with Vijaygarh, with poetry – the triangle that does duty as my life. Of its three corners, Sylla is the link with reality, yet when I picture meeting her it's a decorous affair of tea and cakes at the Taj. The Taj, my last setting as a free man, looms large. I wander through its public rooms. Two Turkish children wait with bright eyes and bated breath for me to enter the lift and dash in after me before the door closes. Their father is mightily amused when I comment on their gentlemanly manners.

'Wait till their mother brings them back with their new shoes. They'll be making a racket showing them off all over the hotel. She has a weakness for new shoes too. They will all three be as excited and noisy as two-year-olds.'

I dream I have gone home to Vijaygarh. There is a hush as I walk in before delighted pandemonium breaks loose. I have to get past an obstacle race of five or six chattering women to reach Mother and hug her to me. We link arms and go into her rose garden where a table for two has been laid on a stone-paved platform off the grass. The garden is heavy with the scent of roses and a surrounding undefinable bouquet. Then in my dream I see summer and winter flowers blooming side by side, hosts of them. Mother doesn't share my drink but the unaccustomed whisky in my veins is mutually, deliciously relaxing. And there's food, as ever, to rub out misery. It's Father's favourite, rice cooked in the juice and rind of oranges, fragrant with saffron. She speaks gaily of Father, as if she's bouncing a ball and he's the ball. We hear the cry of a water-fowl from the riverbed, and a deer's broken whine.

'You and I are going on a holiday,' I say. 'You name the place.'

'Where it snows,' she replies. 'I've never seen snow falling, only lying cold and dead on the high mountains. Make it snow for me.'

I monkey my five-year-old self, inflate my chest, blow out my cheeks to make her laugh, flail my arms to make the snow come thick and fast till we two run for shelter. It's a game we've played, flying away together to other climes.

The comrades are jubilant. They've been discovered by the

Communist Party. Reams of material arrives in a lawyer's brief bag. The next day Yusuf holds up a poster in court: 'Rally to Trafalgar Square! On Sunday December 15 at 2.30 p.m. London workers! The Indian workers' fight is your fight!' The rally is over, a year and a half ago. So is the remaining material with him out of date, appealing to the Crown to call off its prosecutions against conspiracy prisoners. There's a letter to the newspapers from H. G. Wells and other signatories. It's dated December 8, 1929 and asks for amnesty or bail, or, if the trials must go on, trial by jury, and access to friends and advisers. There's a 1930 resolution passed by Glasgow workers demanding abandonment of the cases, and another by miners and their wives in Dysart who 'view with horror and indignation the treatment meted out to trade-union and working-class leaders imprisoned by the British Labour Government'. A council of workers in Birmingham sincerely deplores its government's actions in India. All it seems to prove is, as Yusuf happily sums up, 'There are two Englands and the England of labour is with us.'

Which proves what? It's another shimmering spire for the judge to behold up there on Iyer's map. The comradeship of Englishmen won't help the comrades' cause.

Nauzer has urged me to make plans but I tend to go backward. No one has exact recall, and by now I have gone over the scene so many times – my unannounced arrival in Mother's room when I heard, or misheard, about the imbecile's impending marriage – that the repeated mental exercise has robbed it of any fresh detail it might later have dredged up. I see Bittan near the dressing table, combing hairs out of Mother's silver brush. She shuts up as soon as I enter. I'm certain of it. She exchanges a look with Mother and Mother asks her to go on. But after all these years can I be sure exactly what she said? If I could, would it have changed anything? Whatever her actual words were, there was no mistaking the message I received. It affected me so violently, I had to get up and leave or be sick, or turn savage and unruly in Mother's room. If a message had this stunning, verifiable impact, so forceful that one must obey it, how can it have been wrong? Would there have been a Muslim empire from Spain to the borders of Mongolia within a hundred years of

Mohammed's death but for a message – that mystical sign from heaven – he was sure he had received? Or did Mohammed decode it wrong and set a roaring gale of conquest in motion by mistake? I would never have believed a message so clear could be misinterpreted but for an evening eleven years later at the Taj. It was Sylla's play's opening night. I was ready to leave for Lady Daruvala's private theatre. There were boisterous child voices in the corridor and my Turkish friend's above them. I couldn't understand the language but from its sprinkling of English words I gathered he and the boys were heading down-stairs for the lounge, leaving the mother to finish dressing in peace. I had time to spare. I watched the harbour lights, went over my lines, and wondered what I would do after the play if I didn't feel like joining Lady Daruvala's supper party. As I turned the key in my door I saw the door to the Turk's suite was open. The drawing room was empty and dark but for the diffuse glow of street lighting and a pencil of light showing under the bed-room door. A woman walked out of the bedroom into the glimmering darkness, switched on the light and went to the mirror under it to put on an ear-ring. The scene sprang into a cheerful family clutter, toys on the floor, newspapers on the sofa, a tea tray with remnants of buttered toast. The Turk's wife was leaning close to the mirror. She wore narrow high-heeled shoes. Her frock was of a fabric that had the delicate transparency of glass and swirled about her knees. I had expected a man as well dressed as my Turkish friend to have a stylish wife, but I had been unprepared for glamour, for a woman so altogether suited to adorn the court of Turkey's legendary leader. Seldom had I found a brief wait so pleasurable. I didn't think the lady would mind if, presuming on my acquaintance with her husband, I lingered to introduce myself after she finished putting on her ear-rings. She got them on, surveyed the effect and turned around. Under the electric light she had the shadowless brilliance of a creature reared in love, who has never known a day's re-jection. She gave a nervous start to find a stranger on her threshold, a stranger who stepped in, held out his hands and said in shaken wonder, 'So it's you.' The marvellous eyes opened wide as they had the evening she had sighted her hoary tongawallah. She came swiftly forward and put her hands in mine. I tried to speak, but she covered my stammering attempts with her own warm enquiries, quite accustomed to the spells she cast.

'How I wish I could ask you to stay but I have to go out. My husband is waiting downstairs.'

'And your children.'

'You've met them then.'

'And your shoes are new.'

'Yes, how did you know?' she laughed. 'You must have lunch with us tomorrow. Can you?'

I meant to keep that engagement. We went down in the lift together. I left her with her family and went to Lady Daruvala's. I saw myself through my lines and walked out of the theatre as soon as I could because opening night festivities would be too immense a task to measure up to. A man who sees a cyclone coming in all its fury takes shelter. I reached my hotel room in the nick of time and let it come. When it was spent and I could think again I decided to leave for Vijaygarh immediately. There were hours, before the Anglo-Indian sergeant arrested me, to come to terms with the fact that my search was over and nothing would ever need my whole soul's concentration again. A dread blankness assailed me. But probe it and it had a grinning underlayer, a good example of the Potter's brand of frolic. A monstrous trick of fate – or hearing – had sent me seeking where she never could be found. The joke was on me. I had gone in search of a victim and events had revealed a goddess of surpassing splendour. Even this I could have borne. My despair, my sense of inner death that night came of realizing that my life's most dedicated act had been useless, utterly worthless. I had well and truly been taken for a ride. The imbecile was just another bazaar imbecile. He was nothing to do with Razia. I need never have spared him a thought, wasted time tracking him down, or burned in hell because of him. I can see him now crumpled at my feet. I did not, or course, run off to the bazaar for ping-pong balls. What I did first was to lean hard against the wall, overcome by the enormous tremulous relief of accomplishment. I had to use main force to push myself away from the wall and start hunting for the paper knife, that stiletto-sharp miniature silver sword I had driven into his flesh with inspired accuracy or, if there is such a thing, hereditary aim, until it found its mark, and then cleanly withdrawn it. When I looked for the sword it had disappeared. In my staggering relief I had dropped it. I scrabbled in the dust for it, gave up and ran off to buy ping-pong balls. But I came back not much later, found it and went home, all fairly fast. And all for nothing. The imbecile was irrelevant, my torment more so.

It is three years to the day since my arrest.

# Chapter Sixteen

The case of the King Emperor versus us ends in July 1931 and the judge drives out of the steam heat in his Rolls to spend a few months in the Kumaon hills writing his judgement. The jail population is thinner, just criminals and ourselves now that Salt March prisoners are being released. The comrades are scathing about Gandhi's Round Table politics and bitter about his pact with the Christian Viceroy. Their mutual prayers didn't prevent the Lahore death sentences. They call Gandhi the stretcher bearer of imperialism. I don't think the comrades and I are living in the same space-time. According to them Mussolini is a feather and imperialism is a corpse. By October I have reread every book in the jail's meagre tattered library and pondered the amount of repetition in my life, tales retold at home, books reread in jail, my train journeys back and forth between Vijaygarh and Bombay, wheels endlessly revolving, the same acreage, the same people, my bicycle going round and round in older wheel tracks and now my thoughts. A yoked ox circumambulating a well. It is December when we appear again in court.

The magistrate's bungalow has armies camped around it. No vehicle, including our police lorry, is allowed within a hundred yards of the building. We have to trek to the courtroom through a police corridor. It is the day of judgement. Even the comrades are nervy. We walk in silence. If Nauzer is to be believed, an archangel will blow a trumpet and set me free.

Can this be the judge? The air of the hills has put roses back into his cheeks. But that's not all. He is rejuvenated, transformed. He steps up to the dais frisky as a Christmas fairy, frothy as eggnog. He's ready for peace on earth. His cheek muscles keep relaxing in benign involuntary smiles. It's a big change from his hostility to Comrade Iyer's map of tomorrow, his minuet, and his inscrutable tap-tap on his typewriter. All the tension is gone. Two enormous documents in front of him have the nobility of sheer weight. One hand rests on this edifice. But my own tension is so great I am hardly listening to the shorter version he is reading. Even this condensation takes a tedious time. We stand to hear him pronounce our sentences and now I listen appalled. We are all Guilty. The decision we have been kept waiting two and a half years for is briskly announced. It's over in a flash. And in a flash the judge minds his step, swishes his robe and is out of the room. He's taking no chances with the sullen temper toward judges trying conspiracy cases. We later wager he streaked like greased lightning to England in his Rolls, not risking getting out to board a steamer. We are marched out of the room weighed down with copies of his two-volume Christmas present to us, piled into the lorry and taken to another barrack in the jail. It is barer in the only way a barrack can be. It has no cots. We are issued with straw mats, shabby cotton blankets and jail clothes, shirtsleeves cut off at the elbows and pyjamas cut off mid-leg. The jailer is his old benevolent self. He explains that though we are educated and middle class, C-class treatment has been ordered for those who claim to represent peasants and workers. The comrades are taken unawares and have no retort and we are all too dazed to protest. The myth of my difference from the others, my privileged category and separate fate, is blown at last.

At night a rough blow on the head shocks me awake. It is the convict warder who bellows my number. I sit up cursing, hurl a mouthful of abuse at him, lunge at his leg and send him sprawling. He lets forth a yell. My companions jump up, help me to drag him out by the legs and dump him in the yard. He broadcasts his threat to take it up with the jailer, but it is one of those soundless winter nights when heads and ears are muffled, and bodies are curled embryos under whatever covering people have. Nothing stirs. He won't try that dodge again, at least with us. The next day a team of convicts brings us a load of hemp to twist into rope and gives us lessons in rope-making. We've been spared quarrying, carrying brickloads or pounding grain, thanks to the jailer's kind heart, or to the Lahore boy martyr who died to save us all from filth and hard labour. Our new life has begun. I sit on the ground, my legs stretched out, with a strand of tough grass between my toes and twist it in my hands. There are no separate fates, I am a rope-maker the same as the others. I will be one for six years, the twins for nine and the comrades for twelve.

The twins' party has taken charge of filing an appeal for them in the high court at Allahabad, the comrades are filing their own, and Nauzer is busy somewhere on my behalf while I twist hemp into rope. On New Year's Day 1932 he shows up, bluish with fatigue, to tell me about the appeal he, too, has filed at Allahabad.

'Happy New Year,' he greets, which would be sordid if he didn't look so worn out with his anxiety for my welfare.

He shakes my hand, more vigorously than usual as it's New Year's Day. He shakes hands at every meeting and parting, and once he jumped up and shook my hand like a Swiss who has scored a conversational point. His hand vigour is at odds with him today. Nauzer is full of remorse for lulling me into a false sense of security. He begs me to believe no one could have foretold the severity of my sentence. The Lahore judgement had been a pointer to the way trends were shaping – though only three out of the twenty-four were hanged – but by then it was far too late for him to change his tack.

'The fact is, these are unusual times. The government has understandably lost its nerve. It feels beleaguered and threatened. The crisis affects the entire gamut of law and order. Apart from Bolshevik conspiracy –'

I grab the table between us and rock it violently.

'Bugger the Bolsheviks!' I shout. 'You've got Bolsheviks on the brain. They were coming when I was in America. They've been coming here for three years. Whether they're coming or going, what in hell's thunder has it got to do with me?'

'Law and order is a large subject,' Nauzer flows smoothly on, waving his left hand reassuringly at the jail superintendent who is also on his feet. 'The Hindu–Muslim question is a live wire –'

'Don't give me that bullshit. People who've sat on the same soil together for close to a thousand years grow one fat arse in common and stay put on it. And they damned well learn to bugger along together if nobody meddles. Tell your government that.'

'Your idealism does you credit.'

'Bugger my idealism. When the hell are you getting me out of here?'

'Please don't shout. Now please sit down. There, that's better. If you will let me finish, you heard the prosecution say they didn't care whether or not any of you had committed an illegal act. You were guilty because your ultimate purpose was illegal. That, I believe, is what accounts for your sentence.'

'Look here, Nauzer, I don't care what accounts for the fucking sentence. The law and all the little maggots crawling around its loops and crevices are your affair. I don't give a fuck what goes on in the government's maggoty mind. It's your job to get me out of here. Now get me the hell out.'

'I'm coming to that. I just want you to know I have sat up nights discussing all the ramifications of the case with a senior colleague in Bombay who is as astounded as I am by the sentences. And I have filed an appeal – forgive me but I thought it best – on grounds of unstable temperament.'

'You are declaring me off my head?'

'Unsoundness of mind is a mitigating factor in certain situations. You are a poet, a dreamer. You have fantasies of wiping out the dividing lines between Hindus and Muslims. On the other hand you have no plot or plan to unite them, no strategy aimed at destroying government's policy or the status quo. A poet may dream.'

My laugh bulges out coarse and loutish. It goes with my cutoff clothes, my dishevelled hair, my skinned hands. He squeezes my arm to quiet me.

'There now, is that all right with you?' he asks.

I go into another whooping paroxysm.

'Why not? Tell them what you like. Tell them I collect scrambled eggs for a hobby and have a trunkful at home.'

Nauzer seats me. The jail superintendent's servant brings me a glass of water. I'm told the appeal will be heard in about three months. Nauzer estimates the hearing will take another couple of months. With only about five months to go, he urges the importance of making plans, an immediate programme if nothing longer-term. I must think ahead.

'Think about whether you want to go to Vijaygarh or Bombay when you leave here,' he suggests. 'Let me know what messages to send. I'll make all arrangements.'

The thinking portion of my brain is empty. But I'm open to impressions. I see the face of Nauzer Vacha. It is indelibly printed on my memory now and for ever more. What I will be doing five months from now I shall worry about in five months' time. He has landed me once too often with a future that didn't arrive.

'Never mind,' he soothes. 'We will discuss your plans in due course.'

I am quite relieved to be rid of his handshake and restored to rope-making. It is amazing what hemp goes through before it reaches us. It is grown, cut, broken, beaten, combed, cleaned, dried. At this stage I feel like hemp. I go to the library in my hemp-free periods but these visits, too, are connected with hemp. There is nothing left to reread, which is why I recall a book about rope-making. Rope-making has been around since the Stone Age, and Stone Agers must have made it the way we are making it in this jail. Other jails may have advanced as far as the ancient Egyptian or Red Indian method, or the Chinese method of 2800 BC which went on into Europe when Europeans finally caught up with the civilized world during their own dismal Middle Ages. This is how it went. The spinner wrapped a wad of combed fibres round his waist, attaching a few to a hook on a spinning wheel which was turned by a boy. (The spinner was apt to be the boy's father.) Then he walked backwards from the wheel, letting out the fibres from each hand as he walked, while the father–son relationship flourished. You cannot be walking backwards from a wheel all day without chatting with the fellow at the wheel or giving him a piece of your mind. Talk definitely went on. It is extraordinary that this advantage of rope-making has never been listed. The whole exercise was known as a ropewalk and would have been more fun than what we're having to do. Eventually ropewalks became long low buildings for the ropewalker to walk backwards in, with the spinner getting unwound and the wheel getting wound. By this time I suppose they weren't father and son any more, but still chaps together. Modern times have cut out the talk. Rope yarn is mounted on revolving discs. It goes through holes in a sheet of metal and then through a tube and when it comes out of the tube it's twisted into a strand. Three or four of these and you've got a rope. And the reason why it doesn't get untwisted again is that the fibres are always twisted in the opposite direction from the time before.

Bhaiji used to do a concentration exercise. After rope-making sessions I take a sheet of paper and write *rope* in the middle of it. I draw a circle around the word and arrows projecting from it. I close my eyes and think of rope. Then I jot down the thoughts that come into my mind, one for each arrow. For instance, 'tie knots', 'skip', 'vanish', 'climb a mountain', 'hang yourself', etc. Bhaiji called this exercise returning to the centre. When I can't think of any more arrow words I give up and fall asleep, and funnily enough I sleep. So it's a useful exercise. When I'm awake it stops my mind from wandering and keeps it riveted. I am knotted, bound and hung with rope. I am rope. I don't seem able to forget about rope as my companions do when it leaves their toes. They aren't thinking about it even while it's there. Optimism has caught up with the comrades again, and the twins, too, talk constantly about what they'll be doing when they're out. As for me, I graduate to ever subtler varieties of rope, a mark of successful concentration. I see long silken filaments, too transparent a tissue to be the product of human hands. These are laid out by ant larvae which my spidery tutor keeps in a glass box. It starts as a sticky fluid that hardens into delicate thread, grows into a skein of threads and they into a woven, nearly invisible sheet lining the box's interior. I can see it, just barely, only when I smash the glass.

I thought we were to leave by train for Allahabad but we are taken the one hundred and fifty bumpy miles by lorry. On this particular road, with two breakdowns, it takes the longest seven hours I have ever known. During the breakdowns we amble listlessly across the scrub that stretches to the horizon, relieving ourselves in the open, and amble back to the lorry like dogs when called. The second time I watch in mild surprise as my urine squirts riotously over a bristly red shrub. I've been so preoccupied with the overflow and holdback of my bowels that it's pleasing to see this forgotten appendage still has a life and will of its own.

Nauzer's estimate was three months, maybe two, but the appeal hearing finishes in fifteen days. An English and an Indian judge make short work of the district judge's two-volume masterpiece. Their verdict finds none of us guilty of conspiracy to unseat the King Emperor and they don't bother to take my mental instability into account. The twins and I are acquitted. The comrades' twelve-year sentences are reduced to one year, but as they have already served three, this is counted as having been served. We stand outside the Allahabad high court blinking in the noonday sun, dumbfounded at the ways of justice and providence. Comrade Dey shakes a clenched fist and vows to get even with the rosy judge, preferably by assassinating him when he returns by Rolls Royce from England. The comrades are ebullient in the bus as we are driven back to our temporary jail across the Jumna bridge to collect our belongings. They are cured of the folly of private enterprise in revolution. They are going to head straight for the nearest Communist Party office and start to organize! organize! organize! They are bubbling with resolve. The twins, it appears, have wives, children, aunts, uncles and neighbours, a network spanning generations, not to mention friends and a party gearing up for a massive offensive in the countryside. They can soon look forward to the honour of breaking laws and going to jail again, but first, as he has no parents, the dumpy twin is proceeding to his maternal uncle's village to get his blessing for his forthcoming ventures. We say prolonged and cordial goodbyes, ritually embracing but omitting to say 'till we meet again' as there is not the remotest chance we will.

Nauzer waits outside the prison gates in a car he has on loan. We've had a mutual hearty exchange of emotions complete with handshakes in court and now his mind is on lunch. He gives the driver instructions as I get in.

'This is a fair-sized city,' he observes, reeling off size, population and landmarks. 'It has a high court, a university, Alfred Park, the Ganges, the Jumna, and a non-existent river called the Saraswati, plus a galaxy of national leaders all the way from orthodox to liberal,' which since my jail education is a nose-to-mouth hop, 'but would you believe it, it has no restaurant. There's only one hotel, and that's where we have to eat, a gloomy place called the Alliance Hotel. I've discovered a Barnett's confectioners, but I don't fancy Viennese cream cakes and jam tarts for lunch, do you? You must be ready for a decent meal.'

He keeps up an amiable monologue.

'I'm told there was a Buncome and Co., Chemists and Druggists, an Anglo-Indian firm patronized by Europeans. The owner, Gregory, poor man, had five daughters. Well, one of the Miss Gregorys married this Mr Barnett and set up Barnetts. Their popular speciality is a cake with sponge wafers round it, fresh cream on top, and orange slices for decoration. I wonder why they don't open a lunch room. I suppose no one upcountry eats out.'

The driver takes us through Alfred Park. (Who was Alfred?) Apparently he is taking us sightseeing, past the bandstand and the matronly marble empress whose figure, though not her sternness, makes me nostalgic for my kindly teacher, Bhaiji's fallen sister.

'This is where a revolutionary was shot last year in February,' says Nauzer, and asks the driver to point out the spot.

The driver obliges. Azad, he tells us, was betrayed by a companion. When the police surrounded Alfred Park, Azad fought alone with a revolver in each hand. He killed several policemen, wounded the British police superintendent, and died fighting, riddled with bullets. Nauzer exclaims and replies. To me it has the sound of a lullaby. It was to these soporific strains of revolution that Sen's nineteen-year-old eyes closed in peaceful sleep. The grass has grown green over the bloodbath in Alfred Park. Nobody knows who Alfred is. But Nauzer, meticulous researcher that he is, will ferret out the information one of these days and then we shall know all there is to know about Alfred.

We are the only people in the small white-washed dining room of the Alliance Hotel. By jail standards the tablecloth and cutlery are clean. It is probably wise to pass through the Alliance Hotel preparatory to rejoining the world, where today the April temperature is touching 100°. The hundred-year-old menu in this purgatory arrives course by course from hot Scotch broth to vinegary curry to steamed pudding with treacle to tough cheese and tougher biscuits. I had imagined a menu-starved man would fall to and eat. I do the best I can and my burning tongue bears witness to the effort. Nauzer chews, swallows and talks with a pragmatic Parsee appreciation of whatever life has to offer.

'The English are a remarkable race,' he says, and I agree that the menu has confronted and overcome the weather and culture of a continent, but that's not what he means.

'I knew we could depend upon their law courts and justice. Didn't I tell you we weren't dealing with an oriental despot mentality?'

After lunch he shakes hands. 'As you're leaving for Vijaygarh this afternoon, I'll be getting back to Bombay. Whenabouts will you be coming?'

No dates yet but I will let him know.

Father's fossil meets my train. Vijaygarh has a small railway station and I see him as soon as the train pulls in, standing on the deserted platform with both hands on the knob of his cane. Behind him is the plaque with the names of tenants Father sent to their death in 1915. As I step down covered with dust, he lifts one hand with a flourish to salute me, totters, and quickly puts it back. Two liveried house servants and the chauffeur hasten forward with the station master to greet and garland me. They escort me with a subdued and pitiful pomp to the exit where an evergreen cattle-proof hedge planted in honour of Father's third wedding is kept trimmed to five feet. It is also white ant proof, says the station master. He bows me into Father's new Nash. I feel siphoned and dissolved into the scene, this being the difference between home and other cities.

In the car the fossil sits as he stands, with his cane between his feet and both hands on the knob. He tells me the Raja Sahib is in the south of France with the third ranee. He took the second ranee to the Norwegian fiords last summer. The Raja Sahib leads a quiet contented family life. He doesn't speak of Mother. Behind our car dust swallows the servants' tonga. The sun sulks behind a heavy haze and fades instead of setting. Homecoming weather.

On arrival the head gardener presents me with a nosegay. There is cool clear bath water in pails of gleaming brass and a new servant has laid out freshly ironed clothes. He waits in the bedroom, the test of a trained servant being one who can help his master in and out of his native or foreign trousers. My calves don't fill my pyjama legs as well as they used to and my *kurta* hangs absurdly loose. He squats to dry and powder my feet and place them in slippers. I notice an unopened bottle of whisky and a glass on a tray, and direct him to take it to Mother's apartment. Now I'm ready to meet her.

# Chapter Seventeen

She was in her room. In the deepening twilight she looked pale and preserved. If I had unwrapped and examined her I would have found her unaged by the cycle of night and day, waking and sleeping. The cycle went on without her. She had refused to take her turn in the south of France or at the fiords, this woman to whom I had become a distant event, another mystically tolled Armistice perhaps. She got up. Her hand groped over my face in blind fashion, tactically ensuring it was me before she accepted the evidence of her eyes. She said enigmatically, 'No, you are quite all right,' as if she had feared brain or soul damage.

Later when I was settled with a drink and there was a shadow of the old smiling bustle as lights were switched on and dinner ordered, she said in the mechanical way she now dealt with externals, 'Your bad stars are over. I have one or two girls in mind.'

Bittan was dead with all her secrets. I didn't know the current crop of geese. We were alone as we had never been.

'They'll keep,' I replied. 'I must go to Bombay. I have to see Sylla.'

'Sylla?' She had a puzzled frown. 'Oh, the Parsee. Why her? You were never love-mad for her.'

It was her dividing line between mere love and the desperate excess that was true love. And she was right. I was sane about Sylla.

'Love-mad you certainly were about that school inspector's chit of a girl when you were still a brat yourself.'

'What happened to her? Did you ever hear?'

'Your father did. The man was pathetically grateful to your father for getting him transferred from Vijaygarh. Within two years of the transfer the girl was off his hands. And entirely without arrangement. She had an incredible kismet. You may have heard the leader of Turkey sent an unofficial delegation to India after he came to power, to find out how Indian Muslims felt about the Khilafat – so that he could ignore their opinion, I suppose, since he abolished it. It was a member of this delegation who caught a glimpse of her at a gathering where she had boldly raised her veil over her head – quite the little firecracker – and had moved around talking to people like a man. Many purdah women were attending those Khilafat meetings but they kept their burkas on. After all that trouble here one would have expected the girl to behave herself. This man was so smitten he asked for her hand, stayed on and married her and took her away with him. Such things have been known to happen but few and far between. Who would have believed a disgraced girl would be so lucky?'

Another difference between home and other cities was that one need say nothing. After a subdued dinner I asked, 'Do you remember there used to be an imbecile in the bazaar?'

'Dear God, the bazaar is full of imbeciles, and the lame and the halt. Which one do you want me to remember? Go now, sleep soundly in your own comfortable bed. It's late.'

But I was too wound up to sleep. If we couldn't play carefree games, we could at least chit-chat, about the old days, the household, my new servant. She had had to replace my former personal servant because he hadn't been the same since a visit to his village when he caught his wife in the arms of his cousin–brother, chopped up both with an axe, and came back completely dotty. He had been clumsy and stupid before, he was useless now.

'Where is he?'

'Somewhere around. He's not too dotty to come and get his meals here.'

'And what is my spidery tutor up to these days?'

'That snoop. It was his job to follow you around but he couldn't help inventing yarns to make himself important. I dislike the man. He was the one who told your father you were taking the girl to the riverbed. There was no need for him to work your father up into a rage and get a search party sent there. All the nastiness could have been avoided if it had been handled discreetly. These things have happened before and will happen again. I sent for him and gave him a dressing down. He had the cheek to tell me he hadn't been spying on you, he'd been chasing some insect, as if it's natural for a grown man to be chasing insects. I said I'd have him dismissed but he gave me his word it wouldn't happen again, and he'd keep his mouth shut in future. Well what d'you suppose, the year before you went to America, he charged in here with a garbled story about your killing a man. He was so hysterical Bittan and I couldn't get him to tell it straight. He kept choking on the other side of the curtain, swearing he had bent over the body and it wasn't breathing. We gave him tea and aspirin and got rid of him.'

'What is he doing now?'

'He's got himself a teaching post in the new school. He came here for my blessing and took away a supply of quinine and iodine instead of books. Evidently books aren't important in a Basic School. The Congress fellow who hired him had come earlier to ask Father for a place to set it up and been given that rat-infested godown in the grain market where sacks used to be stored.'

Again she urged me to go to bed and this time I did. It was well and truly night. Compared with it jail nights had been safe and I had had the comfort of knowing what the next day would bring. No such comfort now. I could leave Vijaygarh once and for all, transport myself for life to the Riviera and never be seen again. But the prospect numbed me. There are no other lives, only this, the one I'm living. Another solution might be to confront this witness to my past. The mere sight of me coming towards him had been enough to devastate his composure in the past. Dealing with him should be fairly simple.

In the morning I went to the grain godown. It had a large new padlock on it. Holiday time. I wouldn't catch him till June when schools opened. The window panes had been soaped and left to dry in swirls against prying eyes. The cobbled strip outside was clean. It was swept clean every day.

'May is not a month to be careering around all day,' Mother warned. 'You'll be ill with heatstroke. Sit down.'

She offered me two pictures of little girls with smooth round faces and neatly braided hair.

'Here they are. What do you think? A sweet pair, isn't it?'

'But Mother, these are children!'

'They were when these were taken. This girl with the dimple was twelve and the serious one was thirteen, but that was eight years ago. I could send for more recent ones if you really want me to.'

I compared them. Dimple or no, I couldn't tell them apart.

'Which do you fancy?'

'Out of two peas in a pod, it's hard to say. Shall I toss up?'

She laughed. 'Leave it to me then. They're equally suitable.'

'Or why not both?' I bantered.

Her head went up with its old hint of endangered cobra poised to strike. Some things were better left unsaid even in the timeless zone she now inhabited. No twilight is as timeless as all that. I changed the subject.

'I told you, Mother, I have to meet Sylla.'

'Yes, yes, you keep saying so. We'll leave this decision for your return.'

But planning a trip was a tremendous exertion. Nightly I went to Bombay. Sylla and I married and lived a carefree modern life – one dream that was still within reach. Our travels took us westward. I never saw Vijaygarh, or my tutor, again. I had a nagging curiosity about him. I wanted to make certain if it was him. Mother's information was not necessarily the most recent or reliable these days.

It was four on the clockface above the grain godown when I made my way to the Basic School some weeks later. At that hour the children would have gone home but the teacher would still be there. The soap had been washed off the windows and I saw into the limewashed room. It had a blackboard against one wall and a homely improvised brick bookshelf against another. A poster of flower sections faced me and there was a spinning wheel in the corner. But, as I had suspected, my tutor was not the man in charge. An erect substantial figure dressed in coarse homespun sat on the floor at a low table, ticking off paragraphs on an exercise book before him with a firm unwavering pencil. His eyes met mine and they were the tutor's after all. The shock was all mine and I must have showed it as he opened the door.

'How you have changed!' he said pityingly. 'Come in, come in.' And he actually helped me in.

We were not the two men who had known each other. A convict who had served his sentence stood before the tutor, and there was nothing for me to deal with in this man, so clearly master of his fate.

The June heat was searing when I left for Bombay. I took a room at the Taj and went to Sylla's house, thankful that her father was a man who could say, 'Look who's here, long time no see,' when he knew I had been in jail for three years and was not at all sure what for. I stepped in among the carved black chairs without a trace of awkwardness. Sylla's mother came in, plump, damp and pleasantly perfumed. She welcomed me with an uncertain smile, not because of jail but my inexplicably unjelled relationship with Sylla. She sent for tea, and they sat on the boat-shaped sofa studying me with the friendly distrust parents have for daughters' suitors whom they can't fit into a niche. They told me the new Viceroy had been a former Governor of Bombay. We talked about bridge, mah-jong and the Ripon Club, and I heard about a new club, the Willingdon after the Viceroy. They described Bombay's new marvel, talking pictures. If I would forgive them, they had tickets to a talkie and would have to leave me alone. Didn't Sylla know I was coming? She knew roughly, I said, but I hadn't been able to give her an exact date. They smiled solicitously and instructed the bearer to look after me.

The drawing room had doors opening into other rooms and the front door gave on to a veranda that circled the house. It was a very public room where nothing private could ever have been said. I felt I was sitting in an elaborately carved black forest ringed by a highroad. It started to drizzle. The bearer came in to shut a window, switch on table lamps, and ask if I wanted a drink. He put one at my elbow though I declined. A little later a taxi drove into the portico, the bearer on hand to open its door. Sylla got out, her hair wet from swimming, in a cotton frock and old sandals I recognized. She paid the taxi driver, put the change into her purse and ran up the steps to the entrance.

'Jumbo! Oh my poor Jumbo!' Her whisper had the frenzy of a cry.

We sat down still clutching each other on the boat-shaped sofa. The angular black forest bloomed around us. We could not have chosen a more public thoroughfare for our reunion, but we had reached the stage when there's an actual craving to share the glory. No other room would have suited our passionate commitment. Why did lovers have to limp and stumble toward this revelation, nursing their broken bones along the way? Why wasn't love born full-blown from the start? Why hadn't we spared each other agonies of misunderstanding? Why had we thrown away so many years? Astonishing new questions I had not anticipated. The old unanswered ones had disappeared. At last we took our trembling hands from one another and drifted into calm, strong, permanent waters. Sylla's head was on my shoulder and I had never known such peace.

She spoke first, despairingly. 'You do see why we can't marry, don't you, Jumbo?'

A mind so long jail-tranquillized doesn't leap easily to new formulas. Only horses have instinctive warning of abysses at their feet. What kept me from going over the edge was the wracked forlornness of her tone. We were together on the edge. I argued with her. I bullied, I begged. Dear God, I went down on my knees to her, pressed my face to her legs, cravenly pleaded for a life for us. At last when I couldn't move her I cried, 'For God's sake, Sylla, have mercy on me.'

She shrank from me in fear.

'It's a word you keep using but you don't believe in any god or you'd have asked forgiveness, made amends, or something.'

So that was why. In two weeks Nauzer had discovered all there was to know about Allahabad. The Gregory girls, Mr Barnett, the confrontation in Alfred Park. A first-rate lawyer is a thorough man. It is his business to know what his clients don't tell him, and knowing the facts, to serve them faithfully regardless. I could find no fault with Nauzer. Or with Sylla. I had always known and dreaded her invincible kindness.

'I'm going to marry Nauzer,' she said quietly.

'Yes,' I agreed.

'And you, my Jumbo? What will you do?'

I, too, would be all right, I assured her. I got up to sit beside her. I kissed her gently on the forehead. I caressed her hair as a parent would, for in many ways she was my child. As the servant-lover I had also been, I bent again to pull her sandals out from under the sofa and kneeling, buckled her feet into them. I looked up at her for the last time. 'Goodbye, my love,' I said, got to my feet, and walked out of her house. So ended our story.

Outside Sylla's house car tyres slithered in the rain. Passing headlights gored me. The wet black road moved after them. I stood under a lamp-post in a puddle of sickly light. Outside Sylla's house there was Hindu–Muslim madness. It took myriad forms, fancying it saw divinity in all things, imagining under bush and briar the fire that wasn't there, hearing voices in the desert. And perfect love stayed out of reach. So men and women worshipped stones and clay instead, and others smashed these with as perfect love. Mohammed in the desert under a noonday sun. Mother locked into the path of fire and light along her spinal cord. I stood still, weary of all journeying, above all of this shuttle between Vijaygarh and Bombay, from one self to another. I would not come this way again.

# Chapter Eighteen

I've framed their pictures, the pretty little girls who were twelve and thirteen years old eight years ago, and I wander about the bazaar. It's a furnace. I feel there's a flaming bandage around my forehead. It's all I can do to prevent myself from hanging my tongue out and panting like a dog. The air has the static windless scorch of drought. We've had a succession of days when leaves have not rustled. Cattle droppings, petals off a passing bier, squashed tamarind pods shrivel and disintegrate where they fall. Spilled curd soaks into the ground but you can see caked white remains of it on scraps of broken earthenware. The mango did not blossom and has no fruit. Soon we'll see the ribcages beneath goat and buffalo hides and count the notches on the spines of their trotting skeletons.

I went to the imbecile's house today. The property is decaying. Every noxious parasite breeds on the premises. No one wants it – the evil eye, I suppose – and the municipal board doesn't seem to care if there's a cholera epidemic. No one goes near the place but today I saw a grey-ringleted vagabond sidestepping around the courtyard, his back scraping the wall. He wore someone's torn purple-striped pyjamas and someone else's dirty cast-off shirt. A typical old derelict but for the measured rhythm of his steps and his intricate gestures. Thumbs and forefingers joined, his hands could have been bird beaks plunging for seed, or plucking flowers out of the ether and threading them industriously into a garland. Whatever, he was rapt. When he reached the drain where the rodent long ago had delivered her vermin litter, he came away from the wall with flakes of its yellow plaster sticking to his shirt and swept all four limbs into a wild ecstatic dance to his own Divine Orchestra, no doubt. Crazy as they come. I lolled against that once impregnable door, chewing a neem twig, wondering if this then was the last dance, a dance I'd have to end up learning from this frowsy old crow. Rather different this from Willie-May's de-dum-dum bouncing Bunny Hug punctuated by soft happy gasps, or the Turk's command to 'Disperse through the ballroom! Dance!' I quaked with helpless laughter which he heard. His hands completed two crescent moons. His toes still pointed inward, he cocked me one of those shrewd fanatical grins I've seen around, and believe it or not, it was none other than my former servant. Exactly my age once. but he'd been catapulted into old age with a reckless speed that made me fear I wore an old man's mask myself. It would explain why Mother had finger-read my face before she greeted me and Sylla's whisper had pierced me like a scream.

'Hey, you witless wonder,' I called casually, in imitation of the old days. 'What are you up to, you bloody fool?'

He whirled dreamily, drowning deeper in trance. I went up to him, jerked him to a stop and thrust my face into his, but he ducked out of my grip with a glance of injured dignity.

I tried authority. 'See here, it's me, your master.'

He was beyond it all. He'd crossed the river and escaped, or wanted me to think he had. But I wasn't going to let him get away with playing the fool, pretending he didn't know me. I grabbed hold of him, repulsive though he was and forced him to look me full in the face. And then I thought I must be going mad myself for his eyes were eyes, his skin had the texture of skin beneath my palms. I could not tell where he left off and I began. The lunatic retreated in fright – my wails would have terrified a saner man – and I lay twitching on the ground, not knowing how I'd bear the pain of what I'd done.

For the time being Mother has stopped asking me which girl I prefer, especially as either will do. Everything is in abeyance. What manages to grow stays stunted and poky as porcupine. Indoors our house is cool, fanned, fragrant. Plants are kept watered in their pots. A marine light filters through green glass transoms. But I'm a natural wanderer and when I've done my rounds I generally wind up at the imbecile's house. It's a refuge of sorts from the barren countryside, a regular carnival you might say. Crows collect to forage for garbage thrown over the wall. Colonies of ants scurry up the stem of a tamarisk with straw, twigs and grass to build a nest. Cattle have been in and out because there's a tribe of scavenging beetles on a dungheap, furiously moulding it into little pellets and rolling them away to bury. The thorn shrubs against the front wall sprout a commune of spiders, forty or fifty fat ones, sucking the body juice out of trapped insects with cannibal speed and relish. All will be eaten except a heap of rusty nails. Termites can't yet demolish iron.

I chose a nail from the heap one day. It looked the right size. I was fiddling with the lock on one of the interior doors, trying to fit the nail into it when I heard a vaguely familiar voice behind me. It was Comrade Yusuf with a haversack over his shoulders, a traveller's dust-covered vision in stained and crumpled white. I couldn't believe it was him. I think I would have been as overjoyed to see the jailer, and Yusuf hailed me as joyfully.

'Why this haggard look?' he patted me on both cheeks. 'What have you been doing, apart from picking locks?'

'Nothing much,' I replied.

'True to your testimony in the magistrate's bungalow.'

'Oh that!'

God, it was wonderful to see him. I threw away the rusty nail. Yusuf had descended on me like a compass. I knew where north was again.

'You've had a dustbath, but you look marvellous,' I said.

'I feel it. It's a marvellous time.'

I had forgotten that drought and desolation would put a spring in his stride. All calamity was heaven-sent, grist to their mill, these political crazies. If they had a prayer it would be Hail crisis, full of grace, blessed is this chance to sway the people.

'I've been on the go,' he said, 'house-hunting in the district so we can set up a youth centre. This property is going a-begging, I'm told, dirt cheap. We can fix it up.' And, never forgetting his manners: 'I mean to call on your father.'

'Why don't you set up a centre in your own province?'

'We've done so. We're expanding, preparing a big offensive. This year should see more repression let loose by the Government than any other year.' He looked young and debonair in anticipation.

Father and the third ranee went from the Côte d'Azure to the Tyrolean Alps, so he called on Mother. After the stiff formalities were out of the way they talked through her curtain as if they had known each other all their lives.

'What a cultured man,' remarked Mother. 'He's delightful. He must stay with us while he's in Vijaygarh.'

'He's only staying the night, but he'll be back. He's buying a dilapidated property near the bazaar.'

'He can't leave tomorrow. What's his hurry? Tell him I insist he spend a few days with us, and longer when he returns. Who is he?'

I told her about Yusuf's family, and that his father, a devout Muslim, had wept when Soviet republics were established in Russian Turkistan.

'Did he indeed? Your friend shows that breeding. Tell him I'll get Father's office to see to the sale. It's years since I've enjoyed the company of anyone so refined.'

It would have been tactless to spoil her pleasure by telling her Yusuf's co-believers had bumped off the Tsar. And what if they had? Our lives had accommodated each other's murderers from Mohammed Ghori down to us more refined and graceful fiends. If Yusuf himself had shot the Tsar I wouldn't have mentioned it. Her fragile new animation could not have borne it.

The next few days were the most deliciously relaxed I had spent since my release. Yusuf went about his business during the day. After dinner he and I climbed to the roof terrace. The sky swarmed with stars. We sat under their dense dazzle while he outlined his campaign to open Profullo Sen Centres for the young all over the province.

'They killed him. We'll resurrect him a hundredfold.' It was a pledge.

He told me his party had joined forces with the nationalists as this was no time to go it alone. He brought me up to date with politics. The government had passed thirteen ordinances – more than at any time since the Mutiny – outlawing practically every activity – peasant groups, youth leagues, khaddar workers, strikes, nationalists and communists. About eighty thousand people were already in jail for defying the bans, and he had seen a confidential circular saying prisoners would be 'dealt with grimly'.

'So what's new!' he concluded with a satisfied sigh. 'We'll soon have some splendid agitation in Vijaygarh. What we need is songs. Why don't you write some for us?'

Yusuf might be an organizing genius and more refined than Chinese torture, but he didn't know the difference between a poem and a diesel engine. My words would be of no use to him, and in any case my well was dry. He spoke more soberly about events overseas.

'And you thought Mussolini would be blown away in a breeze,' I accused.

'Eventually, my dear boy,' Yusuf corrected, which on his time schedule could mean the century after next.

Meanwhile, he said, dictators had never had it so good, though they were as bankrupt as ever of ideas. Odd that men in a hurry should adopt the old Prussian style of march past. The thigh was elevated to a right angle with the body at every step as they marched. Yusuf demonstrated. He had forgotten what the arms did but the whole thing put a definite damper on speed.

After he had gone I continued to relax on the roof terrace. Night after night I lay in an armchair under the sky's upheaval. Constellations collided and broke apart into towering formations. So it happened that one night I sat staring up at my handwriting in the sky as a poem dropped on to the dark page in my lap.

Yusuf is back and Sen's resurrection is under way. The imbecile's house has been scraped inside and out and is being painted. The courtyard has been cleared and Yusuf's hopeful helpers are digging flowerbeds. The biggest waste of energy I ever saw. What was the point of planting when there had been no rain? Yusuf says the Basic School children fetch river water from a mile away. I know how they fetch it. I've seen them skipping back, sloshing it from paraffin cans hung from poles across their shoulders. Precious little reaches the flowerbeds. But there's one thing to be said for Yusuf's project. It has made this the liveliest drought in our annals. Everyone employed in it is working at top speed. As I look on the imbecile's house disappears and the monument to Sen rises. In there they'll be subverting the young, holding banned meetings, discussing defiance, chalking out plans to bring repression to Vijaygarh and Vijaygarh abreast with the rest of the country. Yes, modern times are coming to Vijaygarh. I can picture the turmoil in the streets when the procession goes out from here. My no longer spidery tutor and Yusuf's men will be in the lead. My lunatic servant will stay on the sidelines as I've seen lunatics do at wedding and Dussehra processions. The singing and drumming will activate his limbs. He'll thrill and prance to it. Some sixth sense will warn him off the road as if the tar is boiling. Once or twice he'll succumb but pull his scalded toes out again. I'm certain his wits will alert him to run for shelter when the lathis swing.

'Your father has sent word asking if we need furniture or other equipment for the centre,' said Yusuf.

'Good Lord, really?'

'You see, I called on him the day he returned from Europe and we had a pleasant chat. Besides,' Yusuf's eyes twinkled, 'the sovereign power has changed so often on this plain. Another decade, and who knows who'll be in power? Maybe a deaf and dumb peasant has tipped the Raja Sahib a prophecy! Think he'll join our procession?'

That he wouldn't. Nor would I. But I would watch it from a balcony in the bazaar.

I had pictured the procession accurately. I'd had plenty of practice. The three hundred prosecution witnesses at our trial had left out no detail of atmosphere or artistic description. But their processions had not included women so the small group carrying flags and babies came as a surprise. They had their saris pulled so low over their faces, they couldn't have seen anything but their feet, but their voices gathered volume as they went. A few hadn't covered their heads or their faces. One of these looked up at my balcony, a glance I didn't register because I had heard hooves on the cobbled strip at the grain market and seen what she couldn't see, the whole procession securely herded into the congested bazaar alley by mounted police armed with truncheons and batons, awaiting the signal to strike. Terror of a sort I had never felt, for people I didn't know, engulfed me. In minutes the horses rode through, truncheons hit heads and those who risked squeezing through the solid mass to the shops for shelter were crushed and flattened. And in minutes it was over, leaving trampled and suffocated bodies, some with bleeding skulls, in the alley. My lunatic servant didn't survive his split skull. Another shortfall in my calculations. I had pictured a tarred city road, not an alley with no way out. It took all day to send his body for cremation, and for others I recognized to be treated in hospital. I could not visit the Profullo Sen Centre until evening to get Yusuf's news. The place was packed. Yusuf had his arm about the girl who had looked up at my balcony before hell broke loose. She had hers in splints. Yusuf sounded badly shaken as he said, 'Meet my daughter.'

Many married years later whenever she and I went back to our beginning to discover what it was that had attracted us to each other, we got it all wrong. My wife insisted she saw political commitment writ large on my face. I, on my part, said I'd never been able to resist a woman's beauty or the culture of Islam. The truth is, her heart went out to a frightened poet, and mine was bewitched by a sign of the times. No banner blazing in the heavens, this sign came out of the hell under my nose. She stood her ground so heroically, I had no way of knowing she had a fractured arm, brutally broken in the bazaar of Vijaygarh, my birthplace, our home.

I'm a quiet, home-loving man. I'm at home writing for hours every day, and she has all of Vijaygarh to organize. We are addicted to our piece of earth, unlike our meteoric parents. And this is where Mother's story begins. Early one morning she left the family mansion. I saw her hesitate for a second at the entrance and hold her breath before she walked out to star in the most sensational scandal of the generation. Society has not forgiven this liaison between an illiterate ranee and her communist lover, and the shameless public exhibition they make of it. But Mother and Yusuf are so love-mad, they haven't noticed their notoriety. I can't say any of it surprises me as far as Mother is concerned. As I said, this is the Ganges heartland where we breathe the air of miracles. Besides, I've known this woman since she was twenty-two, and sentenced to that greenish light of unfulfilled desire. I couldn't have guessed she'd escape it, but before long I was sure no sun would have the nerve to melt her if she did. It is Yusuf whose capacities I never suspected. He's like a modern artist with a mania for the angles and contours of a woman's body, and paints her naked, dressed, asleep, awake, front and behind, right side up and upside down, curled up, stretched out, with one colossus of a breast or three little pointed ones in a row. Yusuf is that being, lost, found, surrounded and submerged. Great love is a serious, whole-time business. He won't go high in the party hierarchy now. He'll stay where he is, at the middle rungs. And Mother won't care. With money, manners, and lineage, who needs a job? Mother is extremely vague about his job. She knows nothing about communism but she knows a man when she embraces one. This winter they'll be in Leningrad where she'll see falling snow.

# *Glossary*

**achkan** – long, closed-collar coat
**Allahu Akbar** – Allah is Great
**anna** – one-sixteenth of a rupee in the British era
**Baba** – old man
**Bande Mataram** – Hail Motherland
**bhakt** – devotee
**bhang** – opium
**burka** – enveloping outer garment worn by Muslim women
**chawl** – tenement
**cheetal** – deer
**chota peg** – a small whisky
**dhansak** – Parsee dish of meat and lentils
**dhoti** – length of cloth tied around waist and draped between legs
**Dussehra** – autumn festival to mark the victory of Rama over the demon Ravan
**fez** – tasselled headgear, shaped like an inverted flowerpot
**Ganesh** – elephant god
**gharara** – full divided skirt worn by Muslim women
**Gujerati** – a language of western India
**Hanuman** – monkey god
**Hari Om** – a sacred invocation for Hindus
**Hindoo** – old British spelling of Hindu
**Hooghly** – a river in Bengal
**Inquilab Zindabad** – Long live revolution
**jihad** – holy war
**kajal** – kohl
**khaddar** – handspun cloth
**Khalifa** – the Ottoman Caliph
**Khilafat** – the Caliphate

**kisan** – peasant

**Koi hai?** – Who's there? (to summon a servant)

**kotha** – upper storey, also where a brothel is often located

**kurta** – long loose shirt

**lathi** – rod (steel-tipped when used by the police)

**lungi** – 'length of cloth wrapped around waist, reaching to ankles

**machan** – high platform in jungle where hunter waits for his quarry to appear

**Magh Mela** – an annual religious fair

**Mahatma Gandhi ki jai** – Victory to Mahatma Gandhi

**Ma sha 'llah!** – By Allah!

**mofussil** – countryside

**mohalla** – neighbourhood

**Mohammedan, Moslem** (old British spelling), **Mussalman** (Indian word) – synonyms for Muslim

**namaz** – Muslim prayer

**Om** – sacred syllable for Hindus

**pandit** – Hindu scholar

**Parsee** – follower of Zoroaster

**puja** – worship

**purdah** – segregation of women

**Rajput** – member of the martial caste

**Ram Ram** – both a prayer and a greeting for Hindus

**ranee** – wife of raja

**satyagrahi** – non-violent freedom fighter

**shalwar** – baggy trousers

**shikaree** – hunter

**sola topi** – sun hat (worn by British sahibs)

**tabla** – a type of drum

**takli** – used for hand-spinning

**taluk** – an agglomeration of villages connected with a revenue-paying authority

**talukdar** – rent-receiving landlord who was intermediary between the *taluk* and the raj. After 1860 the term applied to the great landlords who were given rent-collecting authority by the British

**tantric** – occult

**tonga** – horse carriage used in provincial towns

**tongawallah** – its driver

**ulema** – Muslim scholar

**Wah!** – exclamation of admiration, approval

**zenana** – women's section of the house